I0653680

HANNAH

Jane Lightbourne

First published in 2024 in Great Britain by Nevada Street Press.
www.janelightbourne.co.uk

Print ISBN: 978-1-83821-689-4

PRAISE FOR HANNAH

PROLOGUE
London, 2018

Twilight, and ochre-coloured rays filtered through storm clouds, glazing the streets with a tobacco-tinted haze. Shops spilled light the colour of butter onto gleaming pavements. Buses emerged from the gloom like roses in bloom. A dog strained at its lead, eyes bulging, barking frantically at a girl as she rushed past. The girl looked to be around fourteen – long-limbed, with a head of dark, unruly curls, and eyes a startling green. She seemed half-formed, her development arrested mid-breath, at that point at which she was almost, but not quite, a woman. The girl was a fast runner, just like her mother. And she was running away *from* her mother.

A voice cut through the semi-darkness, calling out, "Ella! Ella!"

The girl, startled, looked back over her shoulder at the encroaching shadows. "Fuck!" she muttered. She picked up her pace.

As Ella ran, images of the house she had just left flashed through her mind: cluttered, claustrophobic, its pressure insidious, relentless, like that of virulent ivy. Once the trouble had started at school, her longing to leave home had become impossible to ignore. So here she was, running at speed through familiar streets, desperate to just *disappear*. Why couldn't her parents just let her go? But no: Ella had to fight for everything she wanted – cash, piercings, tattoos, booze, and above all, freedom – when all they wanted was to strip it all from her. Well, they wouldn't succeed, she thought, as she pounded the streets, ignoring the buzzing of her phone in her pocket. Not this time.

Only that morning, just as she'd left the house, she had heard her father pleading: "Stop going at her, Hannah."

But her mother just couldn't help herself.

Well, Ella would make them both sorry.

Just as she passed Clapton Station, Ella lost her footing. She stumbled to the ground, slamming onto both hands, grazing the heels of her palms. The pain cut through her. She put one hand to her mouth, tasting the bitter tang of blood.

She heard a voice call out, "You okay, love?" Its owner appeared out of nowhere. Her face was haggard; filled with concern. She was Ella's mother's age.

"Fine," the girl gasped. She stood up, leaning against the wall of the station, head against the brick. She reached in her pocket for her vape; cursed when she realised she'd left it at home. Then she started moving again, more slowly this time, towards a bus stop further down the street.

At the stop, she looked back. A man was running down the street in her direction; his hair was greying, plastered against his temples, and yet he seemed fit, untroubled by the run. The man stopped dead when he saw Ella; raised his hand.

Ella turned away. A bus pulled up at the stop and she boarded it just as the doors were about to close, without looking at its destination. She didn't look back.

She stood among pale, rain-soaked commuters, glued to their mobile phones, and closed her eyes. It might not be that far to the end of the route, but to her it was as far as the ends of the earth. As the engine purred beneath her, she imagined standing on the edge of the world: a dark, limitless void before her, stars in the palms of her hands.

PART 1
HANNAH

Chapter 1
London, 1977

It all started when Hannah was seven. That was the first time she ended up doing something she just knew was wrong.

She was in Mrs K's Sweet Store at the time; a little innocent, just staring at the sweets: Flying Saucers, Pop Rocks, Dip Dabs, Space Dust, Drumsticks – you name them; they were in Mrs K's shop. Hannah's young eyes widened with wonder as she gazed at this earthly paradise; this multicoloured Garden of Eden. If she'd had enough money, she'd have bought up the whole shop. She brought her thumb slowly to her mouth and sucked, eyes on the rainbowed array in front of her.

Mrs K, who must have been around eighty if she was a day, shifted her thick, black-rimmed glasses and asked, in a cracked voice, "Hello, Hannah. Not at school today?"

Hannah's eyes followed the swirl of the sweets, like one in a trance. "We finished early, Mrs K," she lied. In fact she had ducked out of school before the final bell, complaining of a toothache.

It was a Monday, and the shop was quiet. On Saturdays it was full of drooling kids, fighting and joking, grabbing up fistfuls of sweets, squandering pocket money all in one go. But Hannah and her sister Sal hadn't visited last Saturday, or the one before, because their brother Michael had got them into trouble with their father, as usual.

Michael was thirteen and a big bully. His arms already had thick dark hairs on them, and his voice was breaking so it was low and growly one minute and silly and squeaky the next. Hannah *hated* her brother. She wouldn't care if he dropped down dead, she liked to tell Sal. Look at the great pleasure he took in spinning the hamster wheel so fast that the hamster became a blur, working at breakneck speed, or the joy with which he taunted his sisters, grabbing the biggest portions of food or controlling the remote so that they could never watch anything they wanted on TV. In short, he was a far uglier, far viler version of their father, without any of Jake's redeeming qualities.

When Michael had come up to Hannah and Sal that day with a bored, mean look on his greasy face, they'd known it meant trouble. They watched him hover for a bit. Suddenly, he took hold of Sal's arm.

"Ow! Let go!"

"Ask me nicely."

Michael twisted, Sal yelled, and Hannah sat there, thumb in her mouth, shivering a shiver of pure hatred.

"Got to beg for it, Sal!" Michael told Sal.

"*Please!*"

But he just twisted harder, laughing like some dark demon.

Finally, Hannah took her thumb out of her mouth. "Stop it, Michael."

He went for her, then, as she'd known he would. He grabbed a fistful of her long dark hair and yanked. Hannah told herself she wouldn't cry like Sal, the big, blubbering baby; she wouldn't let him know that she was scared. Michael's pasty face moved closer, his teeth yellow and snappy, his dirty breath all over her.

When she kicked him, he took his hand from her hair and scooped her up, squeezing her like a giant python. The floor moved away from her, and the stairs loomed; that long bank of stairs that seemed to go on forever. So she started praying, over and over, *Please, God, make him let go. Please, God; please, God…*

Just at that moment, their father stormed in, bringing with him the acidic reek of chemicals and the burn of smoke. He'd been paint-stripping, and his overalls were ripped and filthy. His large form darkened the doorway like an avenging angel's. Then he started moving up the stairs towards Michael.

It was the first time in Hannah's short life that she'd been pleased to see her father.

Jake came to a stop half way up the stairs. "What's going on?"

His voice was dead quiet. You'd have to know him as well as they did to know how mad he was. "Put her down, Michael."

Michael couldn't let go fast enough then, dropping his sister onto the floor like a piece of rubbish.

Hannah screwed her eyes tight, heart beating like a rabbit's in a trap. She knew her brother wasn't going to get in trouble – it was mostly Sal and Hannah Jake had it in for.

This time, though, he had just looked in disgust at the lot of them, stabbing the air with one meaty finger. "No sweets for a month. Understood? Or there'll be far worse to come."

They'd stayed as silent as dumb animals, fearing those massive hands of his: nails bitten and filthy; veins protruding like bunched ropes.

Hannah contemplated all of this as she stared at the sweets, desperate to cram her mouth full, to taste their sour sweetness on her tongue. She glanced furtively at Mrs K. She was busy with someone else's sweets now, and she was half blind anyhow.

Hannah extended one sweaty, tentative hand towards a jar of Flying Saucers. She unscrewed the jar, grabbed a handful, and stuffed them in her pocket. Then she snatched some fruit gums and two gobstoppers. Her heart banged like a drum. Her stomach clenched. If Mrs K looked up now, she'd had it.

She moved towards the exit. Only three steps to go. One, two… three. She turned to wave at Mrs K, while her other hand caressed the sweets in her pocket. Mrs K looked at her with vague, myopic eyes and smiled. There was a black gap in her mouth where one of her front teeth should have been. She hadn't seen a thing.

Outside, Hannah leaned against a wall, shaking. She'd hide the sweets under her pillow, she told herself. She'd be sleeping on a sticky paradise that night. They'd be a little uncomfortable, but she was sure her dreams would be all the colours of the rainbow.

She moved to the opposite side of the street, crossing back only when she was outside Mrs K's limited line of vision. To the right of the shop was a blue door. Its paint was peeling, and the wall to one side was covered in graffiti. Hannah took out a key, opened the door and slammed it behind her. She was in the hallway, at the far end of which was a back door that led to a small backyard. Both the yard and the hallway were shared with Mrs K. Stairs led up to the maisonette above the shop that Hannah and her family occupied: a property spread over two floors. Quickly, Hannah ran up the stairs to her home.

Hannah continued to steal from Mrs K's sweet shop as frequently as she dared. She told herself she'd be damned for it, but that she didn't care. This was better than waiting for the tooth fairy, whom the other kids boasted about but who never came to their place – no, not ever. Sal approved. After all, she would argue, it was their parents' fault. What did they expect when they took their kids to live above a sweet shop? They'd have to be angels to ignore that kind of temptation. And God knows, they were very far from that.

Chapter 2

Hannah liked to squeeze herself into small, dark spaces and hide, just as a cat does. There, she felt safe and so free to fire up her imagination and take herself somewhere else entirely, therefore succeeding by these means in leaving her difficult existence without moving anywhere at all.

Hannah would dream that her real dad would rescue her one day; that he'd turn up on her doorstep and walk right in, ignoring Sal, Michael, their mother; even Jake with his hard hands and his hard voice and his name that never came out soft. Jake would try to stare him down, clenching and unclenching his fists, but he'd be helpless in the face of Hannah's real dad; not because he was weaker, but because her real dad actually loved her – loved her enough to take her away in his gleaming, fancy car filled with shiny new toys.

Or she'd dream of her guardian angel: gorgeous, graceful as a swan, her voice low and shot through with music, who would lead Hannah to a room with walls soft enough to sleep on, lit by a thousand pieces of glowing glass, filling the space with rotating circles of light. There would be music, and Hannah would bend her body, curving into it. After that would come the applause: thunderous, rapt, like rain beating the ground. But eventually the music and the applause would fade, and Hannah would find herself back in the claustrophobic space she'd squeezed into, her limbs cramped and aching.

Once she must have managed to daydream at the dinner table, because when the dreams died she found herself staring at her mother's cooking set down in front of her.

"Hannah, take that vacant look off your face," Jake told her.

Michael pinched Hannah's arm hard, while she just twisted her fork around, head bent low, as if to hide the dreams inside it.

Just occasionally – but only if she'd really lost them; if she'd really managed to escape – she would feel music rise through her again – a single chord – only to move back down and die, its sweetness forgotten.

These were golden fantasies, whose nectar she allowed to nurture her through her darkest hours at home. But there were other visions that came unwilled, uninvited, and only at night. Sometimes an unknown figure – silent, hooded – would come at her through the darkness, arms outstretched. The scariest thing about this person was that he or she had *no face*. At other times Hannah would find herself in an enclosed underground space, cold and lightless, crouching on the floor, listening to a banging at the door, the hollow sound reverberating through the gloomy room. A voice would call out to her, an unfamiliar voice, but

Hannah was too scared to stand, to answer the door, to do anything at all. And then the walls of the space would start to curve towards her; the ceiling to descend towards her head. She would wake, gasping, while her sister slept on in the room they shared, then leap out of bed, open her bedroom window as far as she could, and lean out, taking in gulps of cool night air.

Hannah had first had the basement dream when she was eight, after her parents' terrifying fight by candlelight, as she and Sal called it. It was their mother's fault, that row, just like Jake told them it was. He said she was talking too much. Hannah had wanted her to stop, she'd *willed* her to stop, but she wouldn't; she *couldn't*. That night, whenever her mother leaned over a lit match to light a cigarette, the flame softened her features, making her look beautiful. And she seemed happy – happier than she'd been for an age. All the while she was talking, Jake was watching her, and Hannah was watching him, holding her breath, waiting. At last a softness blurred his features too, and Hannah told herself it would be okay because it must have been tenderness; it was only later that she realised that it had been desire. But when her mother started talking about her talents – her *wasted* talents – Jake's expression changed and his face twisted up, the scar across his right cheekbone becoming red and angry.

Hannah began banging against the table leg with one knee: softly at first, then harder.

"Cut it out," she heard Jake say.

But she couldn't.

"Hannah!" he yelled.

She covered her ears.

Jake caught her mother's hand and held it down on the table. Her fingers were pinioned, like trapped birds; fingers that a short while ago had been fluttering freely around her throat. Her voice trailed off and a cloud covered her eyes. Sal, Hannah, Michael – they all sat there, unable to move or to do anything at all. Hannah couldn't stop staring at her mother's fingers. And then blind rage took hold of her, scarlet swirled in front of her eyes, and she cried out.

Jake let go of her mother's hand and slammed both palms down on the table. Hannah jumped back. The others just stayed there, glued to their seats.

Her mother drew into a corner of the kitchen, turned her back on them all and ran the tap.

Hannah ran from the room. She heard Michael offering to go after her, their mother crying at Jake not to let him, and their father barking, "Leave her be!" like he was suddenly exhausted. Then… nothing.

Upstairs, Hannah threw herself down on her bed and stuffed her fingers in her ears, holding her breath. Downstairs, she could hear screaming and then, finally, footsteps coming up the stairs, as she'd known they would, steady and heavy. She started counting down from ten, whispering into her pillow. "Ten, nine, eight…"

Closer and closer the steps came.

"...seven, six, five..."

Suddenly another set of footsteps could be heard running up the stairs – lighter and quicker, these ones – and Hannah heard Sal's voice, breathless and high-pitched. "Sorry – got to pee bad. Got to get to the room—"

"...four, three, two..."

"Sal!" Jake thundered.

"...one."

Hannah breathed out in relief when she heard the door to the bedroom slam shut and looked up to see Sal's face grinning back at her.

Later that night, when she was unable to sleep, Hannah heard strange noises coming from her parents' room. Silently, she left her room, crept along the hallway, and pushed the door open a crack.

Light from the street flooded through a gap in the curtains. On the bed Hannah could see flesh: blue where the shadows smothered it and orange where the street light hit it. At first she couldn't separate the mound of flesh, until at last she made out Jake on top of her mother, pressing down on her, arms and legs all over her, squashing, squeezing, suffocating...

It was her mother who was making the strange, high-pitched sounds. Finally, her head fell back, her mouth opened in a dark 'o', and a gurgling noise came from her throat, like her breath was locked inside and couldn't get out.

Hannah fled.

The following morning, when she approached the room again, her mother was lying alone, her pale head disappearing into the folds of the sheet, her eyes dull and vacant. The space looked different in the daylight. But Hannah could never forget what she'd seen, even after Sal had told her that, no, Jake wasn't killing their mum; not that time, at least. And she had smirked at Hannah, and Hannah had felt that she was missing out on something; that they were all in on some big secret, and she was left with nothing – nothing but the nightmares, and nothing she could do could make them stop.

Chapter 3

"Menangitis is what did it," Michael told them.

They had all witnessed the big drama the night before: heard the slam of the front door, watched their parents leave, Jake striding ahead across pavements lit an eerie blue with flashing lights, their mother carrying a bundle towards the screaming ambulance.

They had got back hours later, very early in the morning, without the baby. Their mother hadn't left her room since.

"What's that?" Sal asked Michael now.

"A deadly disease. It killed the baby, apparently."

"How do you know?"

"Mum told me."

"Don't believe it." Sal pouted.

"You calling me a liar?" Their brother smirked. "Cheer up, girls. You were constantly whining about that baby. Now you got your wish."

He had a point. They'd been jealous of the little creature that, like a sponge, had soaked up any leftover love their mother might have had for them. But now, just as they'd begun to be charmed by its gummy smile; tiny, crumpled face; and helpless pink fists, it had gone. Instead of feeling relieved that they need never joke about its bald head or complain about its loud, lusty crying again, they felt bad, as if their continual sniping had suddenly done it in. Sal scuffed the top stair with her heel, the corners of her mouth turning down.

"Do you think he's sad about it?" Hannah asked her, after Michael had gone.

"Who?"

"Jake, of course. One less to feed, and all that." Hannah could just imagine him saying that.

"He's not a monster, you know."

"No?"

"So take it back, what you said."

"Seriously, Sal, do you think he did the baby in?"

"Take that back, Hannah, or I'll pummel you flat as a pancake, I swear I will."

Hannah leapt up then and ran to their room, and Sal ran after her. They started fighting, and the only thing that made them stop was the sound of crying.

"You go," Sal said, and she pushed Hannah towards the crying.

Hannah stood, faltering, at the door to her parents' bedroom. Her mother was lying down, clutching a handkerchief, winding it over and around her fingers until the material was wrecked and torn and hopeless looking. Hannah held her breath, as if by doing so she could stop the crying. Her mother paused then, but as soon as Hannah released her breath, the crying started again, and she could have kicked herself. Finally, all she could hear was the sound of breathing and an occasional hiccup.

Slowly Hannah moved towards her mother. On the

mantelpiece sat a photograph of the baby, its pale face rising from a black background, as the belly of a fish rises from the dark water behind it. Hannah reached up and turned the photograph to the wall. Then she pressed her face against the bed frame so hard that the bars made marks on her face.

Her mother's eyes, milky and obscure, turned to her. They seemed to see right through her. Her white throat moved up to capture a sob, gulping it down. "It's all my fault," she whispered.

"No, Mum. Michael said men… men…"

Her mother started sobbing again, violently, twisting the handkerchief so tight the ends of her fingers grew pale and bloodless.

"Shall I get Jake?" Hannah asked in a panic. She regretted it the moment she said it.

"Fat lot of use he'd be." Her mother took a cigarette from a packet by the bed, lit up and inhaled. Then she appeared to notice her daughter for the first time. "I'm sorry, love. Come here."

It was almost painful to submit to her mother's embrace. The smoke from her cigarette curled into Hannah's nose, making her sneeze.

Her mother buried her head in Hannah's hair and breathed her in, as if drawing all of her daughter's life into her. When at last she did speak, it was in a whisper, and the words were slow and secretive. "There is a bigger, better life than this. *There is.*"

Hannah knew then that she was being let in on a very big secret; a better one than that Sal had hinted at after Hannah had seen her parents in their room the night following their fight. She'd never forget her mother's words, she told herself, not for the rest of her life. There were better lives in the world; brighter ones, with more than mere promise in them. All she, Hannah, had to do was find one. This was her chance; the chance her mother had had and lost. And Hannah was certain that things would work out for her. Her good dreams were a prequel to a golden future, and at nine years old there was no doubt in her mind that that future was hers for the taking. Absolutely no doubt at all.

Chapter 4

"He's not a monster, you know," Sal had told Hannah when she had felt that their father was under attack.

Sal often defended Jake when Hannah criticised him. He was just as mean to her as he was to Hannah, so Hannah wasn't sure why that was, but she suspected it stemmed from her sister's almost primitive sense of loyalty.

Hannah did concede that their father had attractive qualities that coated his surface as gilt might iron. He was blessed with striking good looks: he was fair-skinned, with green-grey eyes and wild dark hair. Strangers fell for him; people stared at him in the street – men with envy; women with longing. And he was charming. When he walked into a room, his presence was tangible. If he chose to focus on a particular person, he or she would be made to feel special. In addition (Hannah had to admit this), he made the family laugh, though admittedly not as often as he made them cry. He could be generous too, sporadically, and never in a way that any of them could predict. But beneath all of that was an almost fanatical desire to control. They were like insects stuck in aspic, unable to move or breathe, when he was around. Any attempt to escape his grip was quashed. Any show of spirit or creativity he hated. He was jealous of what he couldn't understand, and when he was jealous, he got angry, and when he got angry, he got cruel. He was like a charioteer who uses fear and cruelty to control his horses, keeping such a tight rein on them that, strain and choke as they might, they have no choice but to obey.

Though Jake had been raised a Catholic, he seldom went to church. And yet, after he had been particularly horrible to one of his family, Hannah might hear an occasional remorseful prayer, a plea to God for forgiveness. Even so, he was usually in a remarkably good mood at breakfast, despite having said or done something truly terrible the night before. After each such extreme incident, things would go quiet for a while; not because he felt bad about what he'd done, but because he'd proved – to himself and to all of them – that he was in complete control.

Hannah's tendency to dream, her heightened sensitivity, her imagination may have given her the ability to escape at times (if not literally), but it also made her a target; a canvas on which others could spill their cruelties and aggression like paint, each word or act leaving its own indelible mark. Yet, in time, she (like Sal and Michael before her) learned to exercise a form of primitive cunning to outwit their father and so survive. She would hide any show of strength or spirit from him and disguise any fear or unhappiness, because although Jake demanded total submission, he despised what he perceived to be weakness. But this was difficult – almost impossible at times – and sometimes

Hannah was punished anyway, for no reason that she could think of.

Underneath it all, she soaked up the terror in the household like a sponge.

Of course, it wasn't Jake's mania for control, but his good looks and charm that had attracted Hannah's mother to him in the first place; that and a certain wildness about him; something rebellious and uncontrollable coursing through him that fascinated her.

Hannah's mother's name was Madeleine, but no one in the family used it any more – it was another thing about her that her marriage had removed; her own identity gradually eroded by those of household and husband.

Madeleine had had little contact with men in her early life; her father was something of a disciplinarian and her upbringing had been strict and sheltered. Her imagination was so powerful that the contrast between what went on in her head and the tedium of her reality was the source of the utmost frustration to her. Having attended the Catholic girls' school chosen for her by her father, the passionate, guilt-soaked nature of that religion continued to fascinate her. She'd spent a significant amount of time in confession, fingering the softness of the curtains in the box and speaking of impossible acts of which she imagined she was guilty. Being acutely aware of life's romantic possibilities and having a susceptible nature, yet too passive to change her own circumstances, it was only a matter of time before someone came along who would be the embodiment of all the excitement that had so far been denied to her.

By the time she met Jake, Madeleine was nineteen and waiting for life as she thought she wanted it to begin. With him, she stopped waiting and started living. She married him three months later, in what was to be her first and last rebellious act. From that time onwards, her own development was frozen. She submitted to him without question, without thought, unconditionally. She was in love.

Jake started up a business buying and selling antiques in London, and they lived in a small, scruffy flat near Bermondsey market. There wasn't much money. There was never going to be much money. What there was came from Hannah's maternal grandparents and, as they were comfortable, the couple just managed to stay afloat. Occasionally business would pick up and then there would be some spare cash, and then there would be a slump and no one would buy anything, and Jake would rant and rail against the trade and take up another job, only to then go back to the antiques. After Hannah came along they moved to the place above the sweet shop in a street off the Edgware Road because it was near to another antiques market, and it was cheap.

Shortly after Madeleine had ceased to read (her husband thought books a waste of space), it occurred to her that being in love was not the pleasant state the novels portrayed. They mostly talked about falling in love anyway, less frequently its consummation, and never, *ever* what happened after that. Physically, she was still drawn to Jake, but his cruelties, his moods and his jealous temper conspired to wear her down so that sometimes the very thought of him made her tired. In time she became aware that the jolt in her stomach whenever her husband came close to her was caused more by nervous apprehension than by excitement. She would still say without hesitation that she loved Jake, and yet she knew that loving him had destroyed a part of her. Just occasionally, she would be sad for days and mourn its passing.

Over time, she seemed to fade even further. She'd sit on a chair in the kitchen (the one that Jake had managed to break in two places and then reconstruct, badly), her eyes on some distant point, lids drawing down over them like blinds closing.

But when Jake was around, Hannah's mother became at times quite lively, and Hannah, knowing what her father would do then, prayed that her mother would have the sense to stay silent and hold herself back, as her children had learned to do. But she couldn't, and Hannah had to admit that even if she had, any harm he inflicted would likely have happened anyway. Afterwards, Hannah would see Jake move towards her mother with a strange light in his eyes, mumbling tender apologies. On the rare occasions when her mother didn't push him away immediately, it was as if all he'd done had been forgiven already, even forgotten, and they were right back where they'd started.

It was this that shocked Hannah; this that she could never understand. She wanted to feel sorry for her mother, but sometimes her pity was submerged beneath a sort of shame, mixed with rage. She hated herself for that, but she couldn't make the feelings disappear. While she stayed in that house, around her parents, the shame never really left – it buried itself deep inside her, and all the time it made her ill.

Chapter 5

On the morning of Sal's first day at the local secondary school that Michael already attended (when he could be bothered), their mother cooked a special breakfast – strips of salty bacon and eggs with yolks like shining suns – and Sal was allowed two eggs and Michael none because he'd started teasing Sal about school.

After a couple of weeks, a strange girl with green hair would wait for Sal outside the sweet shop in the mornings. The girl chewed gum and wore thick black eyeliner and heavy Doc Martens. She looked around thirty. Her name was Maeve. She'd stand there, blowing big, gummy bubbles, and then the two girls would walk along to school as if moving to music, all swaying hips and messy hair and attitude.

Sal fitted into her new school as a hermit crab fits into its shell. People always said that she had the looks in the family (which wasn't surprising, with Hannah's big nose and Michael looking like a dirty monkey), and now she blossomed further. She was like a ripening peach; Lolitaesque. She'd spend an age in front of the mirror, separating mascaraed eyelashes, plucking her eyebrows, or fanning out her fair hair over her shoulders. And Hannah would watch her, sucking her thumb, rolling it round and round in her mouth, striving to appear unimpressed, when really she thought that Sal was the most beautiful thing she'd ever seen. Michael loved to call Sal a dumb blonde – and certainly she wasn't academic, but she was getting ahead at school. She was popular, charming, and outwardly obedient. Her teachers loved her. Her friends might get into trouble, but not Sal. And yet, although she did not have the imagination to instigate outrageous incidents, she always offered encouragement from behind the scenes, as she did with the theft of Mrs K's sweets. In short, school for Sal was a glorious change from her turbulent home life; a welcome imposition of order on chaos.

It was a tough act for Hannah to follow.

When the time came for Hannah to start at the same school, she woke to a distant murmur of thunder that matched the uneasy stirring of her stomach.

On the journey to school that first day Hannah felt like a small goblin next to her willowy sister. Occasionally, she slipped on the wet leaves plastering the shining pavements. She stood deliberately on all the cracks in the paving stones, ignoring the small, superstitious voice inside her.

The school was in one of those old-fashioned, red-brick Victorian buildings, with very high ceilings and huge cast iron radiators. With a bright wave, Sal left Hannah standing at one end of a long, linoleum-covered corridor, while older pupils, like great, gabbling beasts, passed her, moving in packs. Eventually, she was taken to a colourless classroom and told to stand in a line behind a door with a window of wire-mesh-covered glass in it. A bell clanged, and the corridors heaved with children, Hannah among them, crowding into a room with high windows to listen to a man talk about God while rain beat against the glass. An elderly teacher barked instructions at them: stand, sing, sit, pray, up, down, and then out.

It was only at break time that Hannah found herself free of the perpetual and seemingly futile routines, walking within the confines of a concrete playground encircled by tall walls topped by pieces of coloured glass. She went over to a quiet corner, drew her knees up to her chin and brought her head down, her mind an unhappy blank.

Suddenly, there was a sharp jab between her shoulder blades, and she was looking up at a girl, who was leering at her. The girl had a large gap between her two front teeth.

"Hey, Kate!" the gap-toothed girl called, gesturing to a girl wearing a skirt that barely covered her thighs and fishnet tights. The pair looked down at Hannah as if she were an exhibit in a freak show. "What you doing? Why ain't you with other kids?" The gap-toothed girl brought her leg forward and nudged Hannah's shin tentatively, as if unsure if she would bite. "Why ain't you joinin' in, I said?"

"Aw, leave her alone, Lise," the girl with fishnets told her. She bent down so that her eyes were level with

Hannah's. "Get up."

Hannah said nothing.

"Reckon she's dumb," Kate said at last. She stood, put one hand on her hip, and flipped her hair back. She tilted her chin and looked down on Hannah, as if from a great height. "She's ugly as well."

"What's up? Cat got your tongue, Witchy?" Lise got hold of a fistful of Hannah's hair and pulled.

Her face came at Hannah, and Hannah could see the dark, puffy bits beneath her eyes and the red veins running through their whites. A wave of nausea moved up through her, like the tide rising. She felt saliva building up in her mouth, and when she could hold it in no longer she spat it out. A great big gob of spit flew through the air, narrowly missing Lise's shoulder.

"You bitch." Lise let go of Hannah's hair. "Kate, help!"

Together, the girls dragged Hannah to her feet. She struggled, but they held on to her wrists, fingers pressing into her skin.

"What now?" Kate was panting. She was a thin girl, frail-looking. Hannah couldn't believe the tightness of her grip.

Lise gestured to the outside loos; their crumbling walls covered in graffiti. "In there."

The loos were damp inside, lit only by dim daylight from a grime-encrusted window above the tin sinks. They smelled of damp and urine. On the floor, an oily liquid oozed, a translucent sheen on its surface. The air was stale and stank of smoke.

"Shall we leave her here?" Kate asked Lise.

Lise suddenly looked bored and tired. "Yeah, I saw a bolt on the outside. Let's lock her in." She sniffed and pushed her face into Hannah's. "She can rot in this stinking hole like the toad she is." She laughed and poked Hannah, this time in the ribs. That jab was even more painful, as if her finger had gone right through Hannah's skin.

Hannah heard the bolt being drawn, and then she was left alone in that dark, festering space. She heard a single drop of water hit the floor. She turned into one of the cubicles and vomited.

A boy was watching Lise and Kate as they walked away from the loos, sniggering. His hair was fair, and it grew long over his eyes and then rested on cheekbones which were also long and high, making his features appear refined. His eyes were a tawny gold; the colour of brick baked by the sun. His mouth was firm; his chin set. He looked from the girls to the door of the loos and then back, and stood up, pushing his hair back from his face. It was only then that you realised how tall he was, and how long his limbs. He called after the girls.

"It's Robert," Kate whispered to her friend.

"Who?"

"You know," Kate hissed. "The tall boy Spence tried to beat up. He gave Spence a black eye, remember?"

Lise spun round and eyed Robert malevolently. "What you want?"

Robert towered over her. She carried on chewing her gum. She looked nervous, though; eyes flicking from Kate to Robert and back again. Her chewing got louder still.

"Why did you hassle that girl?"

"What's it to you?"

"Like it's any of your business," Kate added.

Lise put one hand on her hip. Kate did the same.

"You going to let her out?"

Lise raised her chin. "She deserves to be locked up. Snotty little bitch," she added under her breath.

Robert took her by the arm.

"Piss off!" she screamed. "Let go of me!"

By now a few other kids were watching the scene, fascinated. They jeered at Lise. Robert tightened his grip.

"Oi! Let go!" Lise protested.

Robert pushed her back towards the loos and stood her in front of the door. They could hear a steady kicking sound coming from the other side of it. He placed both hands on Lise's shoulders. "Open the door."

"I'm not opening it, you sadistic pig," she hissed.

"Do it."

"Fuck off."

"Lise, I won't let you go till you open the door. I'll wait all day if I have to." Robert spoke almost pleasantly this time. And then he grinned at her and yawned.

"Go on, Lise," said Kate.

"Yeah, go on!" some of the other kids called out.

Meanwhile, the banging on the other side of the door had stopped.

"Get your hands off me and I'll open it," Lise hissed. She slithered out of Robert's grasp and slowly drew back the bolt.

Hannah emerged, looking rather dishevelled. The boy standing in front of her – her rescuer, she assumed – was tall, with hair the colour of flax. He was smiling at her – a curious kind of half-smile that lit up his face – and as she looked at him he pushed back his hair and his eyes shone.

To one side of him stood Lise, glowering. Then she turned away. "C'mon, Kate!" she called out. Her friend joined her, and they ran off. Once at a safe distance, Lise yelled back, "You're in for it, you hear me? You got it coming!"

Hannah looked at the boy.

"Don't worry about it." He smiled. "I'm Robert, by the way."

Hannah was too unhappy about her plight, too acutely conscious of her snot-covered face and her dirty clothing, to do more than grimace back. "I'm Hannah," she mumbled, flushing. "Thank you," she added hurriedly under her breath. Then she rushed past him and into the school building.

The first teacher she met took one look at her dirty,

blotchy face and demanded an explanation. Hannah had a choice: she could either tell on Lise and Kate and get it in the neck, or she could keep quiet and get it anyway. She chose to speak out. And from then on, it was war.

Chapter 6

Lise was clever: after that, she only instigated an attack when Robert wasn't around. Three days later, she pushed Hannah over for the third time – this time onto the gravel by the water fountain, scraping the skin on her knee. The first time, Hannah had tried to push back and failed. The second, she'd got in there first, but Lise's hand had shot up as quick as lightning and she'd dragged Hannah down with her. This time, Lise came at her from behind, and before Hannah knew it, she was falling. She spread out her hands but still didn't manage to save her knee. In the moment of falling she closed her eyes. When at last she opened them all she could see was Lise looming above her with an evil grin on her face, pointing at her. Some of the other kids came and pointed too.

Afterwards, as Hannah was busy with her bleeding knee, picking dark bits of gravel from it and flicking them away, she felt a shadow fall across her. It was a sunny day, and the shadow blocked out the sun so that Hannah suddenly felt cold. She looked up. A girl was looking down at her – or, rather, she wasn't looking at Hannah, but at her knee. There was the most peculiar look on the girl's face: a look part way between fascination and horror, with something else in the mix – a sort of wistfulness. The girl was like a blonde doll, with an exquisitely formed nose and teeth straight out of a toothpaste ad. She was rosy-cheeked, (unlike Hannah, who at times looked rather pallid), and her hair was like spun silken thread. Two plastic daisy clips held it back, and she was wearing a daisy-chain necklace.

A pang in Hannah's chest matched the pain in her knee. This girl was perfect. She had the kind of pristine prettiness Hannah had always coveted. She made Sal look like an oversized pavlova.

"Here, take this." The girl held out a handkerchief: white, lace-trimmed. Still staring at the blood, she gulped. Her placid, rather expressionless eyes clouded over with sympathy. "You okay?"

Hannah nodded.

"Who did it?"

"Lise. I *hate* her." Hannah spat the words at the sky.

"I do too." The girl was calm, matter-of-fact.

Touched by her solidarity, Hannah grinned. "You do?"

"Oh, yes." The girl looked down at the ground and hesitated. Hannah thought she was going to brush the dirt away before she sat down. But she carefully lowered herself so that she was sitting alongside Hannah. "I'm Diana," she said.

"Hannah."

The two girls looked at each other for a bit in silence.

Hannah was the first to speak. "Our names rhyme," she said.

Diana thought for a bit. Hannah waited, half-expecting her to come up with something spectacular. But she just said, "What does your dad do?"

Hannah frowned, puzzled.

"I mean, what does he do for a living?" (Diana tended to pursue a point with dogged persistence until she got a satisfactory answer. Hannah would, in time, come to realise this.)

"He's an antiques dealer."

Diana's eyes widened. "Does he enjoy it?"

Hannah shrugged her shoulders. Diana did ask some odd questions, she thought. "It's his job, I guess. He complains about it. But he complains about everything."

"My dad's a bank manager at a branch in Edgware. Or, rather, he was," Diana corrected. She adjusted one hair clip slightly and sighed. "If I tell you a secret, will you promise not to tell anyone?"

Hannah nodded, wide-eyed.

"He was made redundant two weeks ago. So now Mummy says there's much less money. She says it in many ways, but mostly she's angry when she says it. That's why I have to go to school here."

"Do you like it here?"

"It's okay, I suppose." Diana spoke clearly and evenly, giving each word almost equal emphasis. "I don't suppose I'll stay long. Things are bound to change soon. That's what Mummy says. She says Daddy's mother is going to die soon and give us all her money. Or, rather," she frowned, struggling to be accurate, "she says she *hopes* she dies soon and gives us all her money. She tells me not to breathe a word to Daddy; else he'll kill her. Mummy, that is. But that's what she says."

Hannah thought of her own parents. "He'll kill her?"

"No, not *actually*, silly. But they'll have another row about it."

Hannah digested this. "Do *you* hope she dies soon?"

"Who?"

"Your grandmother."

"Not really." Diana didn't seem too emphatic about it. "I hope Daddy gets another job soon, though. I don't want to be poor."

"Me neither." Hannah was shocked by the force with which she spoke. It was the first time she had acknowledged her secret conviction that if, as she suspected, there was a bigger, brighter world out there (and it certainly wasn't school, whatever Sal told her), then money must surely line the path up to it.

The two girls continued talking until the bell rang. By the time they got up and Diana had smoothed imaginary creases from her neatly ironed skirt, and Hannah had shaken her leg several times to get rid of any cramp, they were the best of friends, as only two schoolgirls who have known each other for just one hour can be.

Chapter 7

Hannah was lying on Sal's bed, watching Sal take off her make-up. Since becoming friends with Diana, Hannah didn't think Sal looked too pretty after all, particularly without make-up.

"Why do you wear so much of that stuff?"

"I'm practising."

"For what?"

Sal pouted at her reflection in the mirror. "To be a beautician."

"You sure you're pretty enough?"

Sal turned on her. "Take that back, you little cow."

"I just don't want you to get vain, that's all."

Sal sniffed, slightly mollified. "I'm better-looking than you, anyhow. Cowpat-Nose."

Hannah raised herself up on one elbow and looked at her. "I made a new friend at school."

Sal threw her a bored look. "Who?"

"Diana."

"That blonde in your class? The new girl? Dolly-Features?" Sal sighed. "Some friend she'll turn out to be. She's stuck-up."

"She's not."

"Is so."

"Her dad got made redundant, so she's struggling like the rest of us." Hannah felt only a momentary pang of guilt at the breach of confidence. The words had been spoken in her new friend's defence, after all.

"Hmm." Sal sounded unconvinced, but no longer interested. "What do I care, anyhow? She's your friend. You going to bring her home to visit? See if Michael likes her?"

Hannah stared at the cracked paint on their bedroom walls, and the unwashed windows. "I don't think so."

Sal sniggered. "Don't blame you. What 'bout your other friend?"

"Don't have any others."

"Your knight in shining armour… whatshisname… Robert. The one who rescued you from the loos."

"How do you know about that?"

"Everyone knows. Big drama, that was."

Hannah watched Sal rub moisturiser into her left cheek. The cream made her smell of babies.

"Robert's a weirdo, Maeve says. Always off on his own, doing strange things."

"Like what?"

Sal shrugged her shoulders. "Reading."

"That's not strange."

"It is to me. And he looks strange, too. Fancy having yellow eyes."

"They're not yellow."

"They are too." Sal turned her attention to the other cheek. "And he broke another kid's nose, Maeve said."

"Whose nose?"

"Spence's nose."

"He did not!"

"Maeve said Spence said he was minding his own business when Robert comes up and – bam! – his nose is all over the place."

"That's a lie. From what I hear about Spence, I'm sure he started it." Spence was an evil, scruffy boy, always courting trouble.

"Believe that, you'll believe anything." Sal paused. "And then there's Robert's mum…"

"What about her?"

Sal sucked in both cheeks and tilted her head sideways. "People say she's even stranger than he is. Apparently she's always ill."

"What with?"

"Nothing. It's all in her head, Maeve says. And she lets Robert stay off school for days on end, and no one bollocks him 'cause he comes top of the class anyway. *And* his dad ran off and left them."

"So?"

"So nothing. I'm just telling you what I know. I wouldn't bother, 'cept you're pestering me with questions. Make friends with whoever you like, Hannah. See if I care. But don't say I didn't warn you, that's all."

Sal closed the moisturiser pot with a snap, signalling an end to the conversation. Then she went over to the cassette player and put 'Tainted Love' on loud, until Jake's voice could be heard above the track, yelling at them to "Turn that *fucking* music down."

Chapter 8

Hannah first visited Diana's house on a close, windless day in June, for a party to celebrate her friend's twelfth birthday. It was a baking hot day, the air slowly sucking all energy from all living things, so that people could do nothing but sit and sweat and the dust-coated leaves on the thirsty trees wilted and died. Hannah's house was stifling; she felt as if she were living in a pressure cooker and she and her family were about to explode any minute. She was glad to escape, and arrived at Diana's place an hour before the party was due to begin, as her friend had requested. She had to take the District Line from Edgware Road to the end of the line to get there.

Diana's house was semi-detached, standing in a street of identical 1920s houses with windows made up of little diamond panes and broad beams of stained timber running over the outside walls. Hannah rang the doorbell and listened to its three separate rising notes, until Diana answered the door with a look on her face that would have been smug if shyness hadn't disguised it.

In the kitchen a fridge spewed out ice, and the gleaming surfaces looked as if you could eat off them. Hannah thought of her chaotic kitchen at home with its sticky surfaces and lingering smell of steamed vegetables. She turned, wide-eyed, to Diana. "Does anyone actually cook in here?"

She followed her friend into a living room that was large and cool with a cream carpet; its pile thick and luxuriant, like the fur of a long-haired cat. The wallpaper was as soft as silk. A glossy black piano stood alone in one corner; rows of photographs arranged neatly on it. Outside, the patio was neatly paved, with immaculate hedging and, beyond it, a lawn that was impossibly green.

Hannah sat awkwardly on the edge of a beige sofa, long legs dangling down, examining the living-room carpet, looking for a speck of dirt somewhere – anywhere. "How do you get things so *clean*?" she asked her friend.

Diana looked surprised. "We have a cleaner, of course."

Diana's mother appeared a few minutes later, her movements languid as a cat's drugged by the sun. The skin beneath her eyes was puffy and her cheeks seemed to sag slightly, though her jawline was stretched and tight. Even the brightness of her red lipstick and her glossy nail polish couldn't hide the weariness on her face. Hannah wondered what could possibly be making her so tired. She tried to imagine her own mother, made up and wrinkle-free, in Diana's mother's polished surroundings instead of the squalor of her own.

"I'm Cheryl," Diana's mother told her. "Hannah, right? Didn't your father collect you from school once?

I see the resemblance."

Hannah nodded. Jake, curious to check out where she and her sister spent most of their time, had picked them up the one time. He hadn't been back since.

"I was sitting in my car, waiting for Diana…" Cheryl paused and then continued, in an almost dreamlike state. "He was very tall and dark and angry-looking. Powerful…" Her voice trailed off.

Hannah thought of her father's rough, hard hands. She winced. "Yes, he's quite strong."

Cheryl's eyes gleamed. She glanced at the mantelpiece. There was a photograph of a man there: small and podgy, with a face like that of a pug. Her smile was strained. "Well, wouldn't that be nice? It would be so much more… he would be so much more… *useful.*" She stared at the photograph for a bit, and then blinked not once but twice, slowly, dreamily. "Tell him I said hello."

Hannah kicked nervously at the sofa, trying to reassure herself with the rhythm, half-hoping that her foot would leave a mark on the soft fabric.

Hours later, Diana's father could be seen wandering around the garden with a pallid, anguished face, trying and failing to tidy up. Cheryl barked instructions at him, while passing around "my delicious butterfly cupcakes, home baked," leaving Hannah astonished at the blatancy of the lie: she'd seen the boxes out of which the cakes had appeared. Kids crammed their mouths full, and Diana's father scuttled around with tissues. Laughter rose from the manicured lawn to the pale sky. At one point, a girl let go of a single helium balloon, which drifted skywards, getting smaller and smaller until finally it disappeared.

Towards the end of the afternoon, Cheryl suggested they all play Dead Lions. Her parents had actively encouraged this game when she was growing up, she told them. The participants had to lie down and remain totally still for as long as possible. The children, glad of an excuse to rest, threw themselves onto the grass, playing dead, while Cheryl, with a weariness born of relief, retreated to her bedroom with a headache, leaving her perspiring husband in charge.

Diana won the game three times. On the last occasion, the others crowded around her inert body. One boy prodded her, trying in vain to stir her; another girl thought she had died, and burst into tears. No one else could even get close to achieving that perfect stillness.

After that, parents arrived in swift succession to collect their exhausted children. Cheryl reappeared to see them off and hand out party bags. Soon, Hannah was the only child left.

"Isn't anyone going to come and pick you up?" Cheryl asked her.

"I can get the Tube."

Cheryl raised two perfectly shaped eyebrows in surprise. "I'll drop you back."

"It's okay," Hannah said hurriedly.

"I insist."

Cheryl's car was shiny and silver with cream upholstery. Its insides smelled of money. Before they set off, Cheryl paused to reapply her lipstick while gazing in the car mirror, adjusting the tinted glasses she was wearing, even though she had to peer through them to see anything at all. Outside Hannah's place, Cheryl pulled off her glasses and followed Hannah to the sweet shop, and to the door of her home next to it.

"I'm fine really," Hannah told her.

"It's no trouble. We must see you home safely."

Hannah's mother came to the door. Her hair was dirty, and the smell of cooking hung about her. She gave the smartly dressed lady on her doorstep a curt nod, and then quickly closed the door in her face. "Life's difficult enough without making time for types like that," she said to her daughter, and, without another word, she pushed her inside.

Chapter 9

One bright afternoon, Hannah and Diana were sitting on the tin roof of the wooden shed in one corner of the playground. A tall rowan tree on the other side of the school wall grew over its roof, its leaves forming a hot but private space for them to sit in. Diana sat very still, her back to the wall that flanked the shed. Hannah was lying down. She was full of nervous energy, banging one leg against the roof, making the air reverberate with the hollow sound. The sunlight filtering through the rowan leaves formed patterns on her face and made her green eyes glow. She fanned her face with a folded piece of paper. Below her, she could see Robert sitting in a patch of sunlight, his head bent over a book. The sun made his hair shine so that he looked as if he were wearing a halo.

She was just about to point him out to her friend when Diana leaned forwards and whispered, "If I tell you something, promise you won't tell anyone?"

Hannah propped herself up on one elbow and nodded very solemnly.

"Cross your heart and hope to die?"

"Cross my heart."

"Stick a needle—?"

"Yeah, and all that."

Diana studied her knees. "I'm engaged."

Hannah tried to imagine her friend walking down the aisle, looking like the Snow Queen, except that her face was still that of a twelve-year-old, and that of her future husband was a blur. "Who to?"

Diana hesitated.

"Tell me," Hannah insisted. Her eyes were limpid pools that contained all the cool promise of the afternoon. "Don't you trust me?"

"John."

John was a boy in their class who seemed inoffensive if a bit dim.

"You're joking, right?"

Diana shook her head.

"But isn't he a teeny bit... *dull?*"

Diana shrugged her shoulders. She dealt in certainties, and Hannah was sure that she would do exactly as she said. She knew her own mind and seemed to have the self-belief to obtain from life what she wanted. Which wasn't much, in Hannah's opinion.

"And after you get married, then what?"

"After the wedding and the honeymoon? And the nice house and the car? Well, there'll be a baby—"

"Just one?"

"One is too few and three is too many, so two, I suppose. After that we'll need a bigger house and an even bigger car. And then..." Diana's words tailed off.

"Then nothing? That's it?"

"Well, what will *you* do?"

Her friend had a habit of doing that: turning

Hannah's questions back on her when she, Diana, had reached a dead end. Hannah had great aspirations, but still no direction for the wild desires that surged within her. Her ambition had not yet fixed upon the real; it merely made buoyant the rich fantasies that swirled around her head. Now she traced an intricate pattern on her pale leg with one hand while with the other she reached up and made a wide sweeping gesture in the air, higher and higher until she could go no further, and so she stopped. "Oh, I expect I shall do something very glamorous indeed. I'll be an actress, probably, or a singer, and everyone will adore me, and I'll make a ton of cash."

"What will you spend it on?"

"The usual. Designer clothes. Bags. Jewellery. I'll *drip* with diamonds."

Diana looked a little wistful. "I hope John will give me diamonds," she said.

Hannah sat up. "Diana, you do know that *what you do* when you're married, or before, can sometimes be quite *painful?*"

Diana shifted, blushed, and nodded slowly.

And then Hannah told her about her parents in their bedroom on the night of the fight by candlelight. "I thought he was killing her at first. Like, suffocating her. She was *crying*, as if she were in pain, but then... maybe she wasn't." She frowned.

Diana's doll eyes became cloudy with disgust. She seemed to have lost her habitual certainty. "I'm sure my parents don't do that," she said finally.

"How do you know?"

"I just know."

"And would you want to make a vow at your wedding to obey your husband?"

Diana looked as if she'd swallowed something disagreeable.

"Maybe you won't be in such a big rush, then?"

"Maybe."

Hannah shrugged her shoulders. What did it matter to her? She didn't have to live her friend's life for her, thank God. She'd have a difficult enough time living her own. She yawned. Below her, she could see Sal walk past arm in arm with Maeve, both swinging their hips. Robert was nowhere to be seen now. "I'm sure being with lots of different men would be more exciting, Diana. You can't sit and stare at one man forever."

"Why not?"

Hannah thought of her parents. "Because you end up hating each other, that's why."

"Maybe so, but you've got to try."

"No, you don't."

"Yes, you do."

"*Why?*"

Diana was lost for words only for a moment. "You have to, otherwise there's no point to anything."

She seemed upset, and Hannah immediately felt guilty. She had pushed the point, as usual, and now she had upset her friend. It was Diana's life, after all. She could do what she wished with it. Hannah reached into the pocket of her skirt and found a barley sugar left over from her latest swoop on Mrs K's Sweet Store. It was only slightly sticky. She passed it to her friend. "Here. Have this."

"Thanks."

As Diana munched contentedly, Hannah lay back. She noticed with relief that all the upset had vanished. Life was simple for Diana, she thought. Sweet as a sugared sweet. Hannah wished that she too could be turned around so easily, but she had the feeling that things would always be more difficult for her, as they had been so far. More difficult and a whole lot more complicated. She sighed. And then she reached up with one hand and once again, but more slowly this time, traced a wide arc through the sky – up, up, ever higher, and then down again, right down, as if she were following the blazing trail of a shooting star.

Chapter 10

The next time Hannah saw Robert in the playground, he was sitting, scrutinising the ground; a look of intense concentration on his face. She would have walked straight past him, but she wanted to know what he was doing. She told herself that she didn't care to know, but she did. Curious, she drew close to him, but as she did so, she felt self-conscious and shy.

"What you up to?"

He looked up at her, shading his eyes. Sunlight filtered through his hand, making it glow red and his eyes shine with flecks of light. "I'm studying the ants."

"What?"

"Look."

She bent over. "Can't see anything."

Robert pointed out a long line of tiny ants that were making their way from a hole in one corner of the playground wall and then up the wall. Their movement was laborious, even tortured; some of them laden like packhorses, carrying twice, even three times their weight.

Hannah sat down beside Robert, drawn for a while into the ants' miniature world, until she realised what she was doing. "Waste of time, watching ants," she sniffed, preparing to stand up.

"But look how industrious they are. They're always

working."

"They're stupid, then, aren't they? Who'd work if you didn't have to?"

"I would. I'd go mad otherwise."

"Hmm. My friend Diana just wants to sit around and be rich."

Robert grinned at her. "Won't she be bored?"

Hannah thought of Diana's mother and hesitated. "Doubt it," she told him. "I might try it too."

"You'd certainly be bored."

"It would take a long time for the novelty to wear off."

Robert laughed. "How's Lise?"

"Easing off a little."

"Good. Let me know if she causes any more trouble." He frowned then, and Hannah decided that he could look quite frightening at times.

"Did you really break Spence's nose once?" she blurted out.

"No. I hit him in the eye, but he kicked me first."

"Where did he kick you?"

"You wouldn't like to know." He flushed. "But it hurt like hell. I wouldn't have hit him except he kicked me first. I don't like hitting people."

"My brother hits me."

"Does he?"

"My father does, too."

Robert's face clouded over with sympathy. "Guess it's tricky for you to defend yourself if they're much bigger than you."

"I do okay."

"Call on me next time your father does it."

Hannah assessed Robert. He was tall, but he was still half the size of Jake. "I don't think you'd stand a chance," she said frankly.

"You never know."

They sat in silence until Hannah started to squirm. She hated silences. She wondered if Robert wanted her to leave. If so, she'd go, but she didn't know how to do so without seeming rude.

"You can go if you like," he told her.

"Do you want me to?"

"Only if you want to."

"I don't."

"Okay, then."

"Have you met Diana?" Hannah asked after a while.

"Your friend? The pretty one?"

Hannah sighed. "Yes."

Robert smiled. "You're pretty too."

"My sister says I've got a nose like a cowpat."

"I wouldn't say that. Anyhow, my nose is offensive too, so that makes two of us."

Hannah looked, rather critically, at Robert's nose. It was large and a bit crooked. "It's okay."

"Thanks."

"Did you just move here? Is that why you came to this school?"

"No – my mother wanted me to go here."

"Where were you before?"

"I wasn't. My mother was teaching me."

"You mean you weren't at school?"

"My mother didn't believe in it."

"Wow." Hannah studied him enviously.

Robert laughed again. He usually looked quite serious, but when he laughed, she liked it. His laugh sounded like it was coming from somewhere deep inside him. "You jealous? You wouldn't be if you had my mother as a teacher. She's a slave driver. She only stopped teaching me because she couldn't do it any more."

"Why not?"

"She was diagnosed with MS a while back. She gets very tired."

"Oh, I see." Hannah nodded wisely. "What about your father?"

"He… he's dead. He was hit by a car when I was five."

Shocked, Hannah blurted out, "I wish mine was. Dead, I mean." As she spoke the words, she felt as if she were hurtling through space at a great speed. She shook her head, as if to rid herself of the feeling. "I'm sorry. About your dad, I mean."

Robert's face crumpled, and that made her feel guilty about what she had said. "What about your father?" he asked gently.

"I live with Jake. But he's not my real dad. My real dad is coming to take me away. I'm not sure exactly when, but he's coming." She looked earnestly at Robert. It was suddenly of the utmost importance that he believed her.

"What's Jake like, then?"

"He's a monster."

"You shouldn't say that."

"Why not? You don't live with him."

"But don't say it."

Hannah flushed and looked down.

Robert looked at the ants. "Do you think that one's going to make it?" he said at last, pointing at an ant that was almost keeling over sideways, struggling with its load.

Hannah didn't answer. She couldn't have cared less about the ant. With one fingernail she flicked the insect over. It landed on its back, waving its tiny legs in the air frantically. "It's only an ant," she said, when she saw Robert's face. But, carefully, she flicked it back again. Now she felt guilty about the ant too. "I'll leave you to it." But when she stood, she felt sick and dizzy. She turned and started walking away.

She didn't turn back when Robert called, "Goodbye, Hannah!"

She could see some of the kids stop and stare, and she felt embarrassed about ignoring him. When she felt she couldn't do so any longer, she turned back and waved. He looked so friendly and smiling, then, that she couldn't understand why he'd upset her so. She was still puzzling about it after she'd left.

Chapter 11

For days after seeing Robert, Hannah was in a state of confusion, which only lessened slightly when she vowed to seek him out and make an apology for leaving so abruptly the last time. When she came across him again, he was sitting on the roof of the same shed where she had sat with Diana a while back. Hannah clambered onto the low wall at the side of the shed, reluctantly allowing Robert to take her arms and help her climb the rest of the way. Once on the roof, she smiled at him nervously, looking down to check that there were no teachers about. Teachers were always shouting at kids to get off the roof.

There was a pause, until Hannah took a deep breath and blurted out, "I'm sorry. You know… about leaving so quickly last time."

Robert shrugged his shoulders. "Don't worry about it." He smiled.

Hannah smiled too, glad to see that what had seemed to her like rudeness on her part was forgotten on his. He wasn't blaming her at all. That made a change. She was used to incessant blame and recrimination.

"I'm always saying what I think," he told her. "And it always gets me into trouble. I get that from my mother. She does the same thing. People don't like it, she says. They like to be flattered."

"*I* don't," Hannah protested.

"You sure?"

She flushed. "But I never have been so far – flattered, I mean – so it's difficult to tell, isn't it?"

"Well, most people like it." He laughed. "I guess that's why I'm not so popular here. Not that I care much about that."

Hannah hesitated. "I don't care either," she told him.

Robert looked at her then, and she felt as if he were looking right through her.

"Well… maybe a little," she admitted. She hated herself for it, but she did care. She cared *terribly*. She longed to be in the group of pretty, jaunty girls to whom everything came so easily. "Everyone wants to be popular at school, don't they?"

"Not me. To be popular you've got to please everyone all the time. And I just don't have the time. I've got too many other things to do."

"Like what?"

"Reading, for a start. And studying, and looking after my mum, even though my auntie helps with that. And other things. I go exploring sometimes." He hesitated. "Mostly on my own," he added. "But I'll take you with me one time if you like."

"When?"

"Whenever you like."

The thought of leaving home and school and going somewhere else entirely appealed to Hannah very much. Her face glowed.

"I tell you what. What are you doing next Sunday? It's my birthday. Why don't you come over and help me celebrate it? Bring anyone you like."

"Where do you live?"

"Just off the Edgware Road."

"So do I. Do you know Mrs K's Sweet Store? Well, I live above that."

"You live above a sweet shop? Wow. Surprised you've got any teeth left." As Robert spoke, the school bell rang. He scrambled off the roof, and then helped Hannah down. "I'll give you the address later. And, like I said, bring anyone you like. Even your sister if you want."

"I'm not sure she would come," Hannah told him.

Robert? That crackpot? I'm not wasting my Sunday on him."

"Fine." Hannah didn't care anyway. But just for good measure she added, "He isn't a crackpot, anyhow."

"He is. And he looks at you like some lovesick poet." Sal rolled her eyes in her head until the whites showed, and then writhed on the bed. "'Oh, Hannah, I love you. I love you so much I think I can't take it any more—'"

"Shut it, Sal."

"'Put me out of my misery, Hannah!'"

Hannah got up and punched her sister. Sal was laughing so much her mascara was running down her cheeks. She couldn't retaliate.

Afterwards, Hannah thought about what Sal had said. Maybe Robert did like her in that way? The thought made her so embarrassed that she began to dread Sunday.

On Sunday, Diana and Cheryl drove round to Hannah's house to pick up Hannah and take her to Robert's. Hannah was waiting outside when the car drew up.

Cheryl poked her head out of the window and waved – or, rather, raised her hand, as the Queen would do. "Well, hello." She blinked, not once but twice. She looked a little less tired than she had before, but the whole of the lower part of her face seemed to be under even more strain.

Hannah settled down on the soft leather upholstery of the car.

Cheryl redid her lipstick in the car mirror. "How's your father? Shouldn't I tell him I've taken his daughter off?" She smiled at Hannah, showing off brilliantly white teeth.

"I've already told him."

"Another time, maybe." Cheryl peered at the rubbish left over from the market, and at the graffiti on the shutters of the sweet shop. "Do you know the way to Robert's place? I'm a bit out of my depth here."

Hannah relayed the directions Robert had given her until they turned into a road where the cars were small and rusty and the houses dilapidated. They drew up in front of a tower block, alongside an abandoned vehicle with flat tyres and broken windows, and got out. The girls stared at the trashed car, at the bins overflowing with rubbish, and finally at the block. The flats inside seemed so tiny that they couldn't believe they housed people.

"It's like he lives in the sky," Hannah breathed.

The lift to Robert's flat was a small metal box with dents in the sides. The light in the lift made Cheryl's skin look pale and lined.

Hannah was expecting Robert's place to look as shabby as her own. But the walls of the living room had been painted a rich ochre colour. Bookshelves were everywhere, with more books packed along the floor underneath the lowest shelves and crammed beneath the ceiling at the top. The kitchen was small, but tidy and ordered. The air smelled of baking. If you looked out, you could see the whole of the city, stretching into the distance. When Hannah entered the room, she went straight up to the window and pressed her face against the glass. She didn't notice Robert come to stand by her side.

"Like the view?"

"I love it," she whispered.

"I'll show you something else in a bit."

"What is it?"

He grinned at her. "It's a surprise."

Hannah loved surprises. "Go on, then."

"Come and meet my mother first."

A woman was coming into the room. Her hair was the colour of an autumn leaf; her clothes elegant – too much so for her surroundings, as though they and she belonged to a different place entirely. She walked with a stick, but she seemed to be carrying the stick rather than the stick carrying her. Robert very gently drew her closer to Hannah, and the woman took her stick off the floor completely as she took hold of Hannah's hand.

"Hannah, this is my mother, Grace."

"Hello, Hannah." Grace's voice was soft but sad; too sad for its softness to be pleasing.

Hannah smiled, and Grace smiled back at her. Her face lightened and brightened with her smile, and her eyes, the same colour as her son's, shone.

"My son has told me about you. You live nearby, above Mrs K's Sweet Store, right?" Grace turned away from Hannah and stared out of the window at some distant spot on the horizon. "We didn't always live here. We used to have a place in Greece once. High up amongst the pine trees. That's where I first met Robert's father. We were happy there, weren't we, love?" She turned to her son. "But when his father died, I got lonely, and we came back here." She sighed. "Have you been to Greece, Hannah? No? You've never seen the Parthenon? You've never been to Delphi? To Corinth? To Ithaca?"

Again, Hannah shook her head.

"Maybe Robert will take you there, when you're older." Grace leaned closer to Hannah and whispered, "If you ever do make it to the Parthenon, go high up, as high as you can. Look up and turn your head right round to one side," she demonstrated, "and then all the way to the other side and carry on looking up… and do you know what you'll see?"

Hannah shook her head. A small part of her was starting to think that Sal had been right about Robert's mother, and she didn't want her to be.

"*Sky.* A giant stretch of it. Nothing else." Grace's eyes glazed over and darkened. "But we left, and it can't be helped. Do go some day, Hannah. It's beautiful…" Her eyes, filled with this far-off place, fixed on the glass of the window without looking through it. For a moment, she reminded Hannah of her own mother.

Grace didn't say much for the rest of the party; she just sat, looking out of the window, fingering the scarf around her throat with one shaking hand, while with the other she made a continual circular movement with her stick.

A few others arrived, and after they'd eaten Hannah left the group to go to the window again and watch the edges of the sky fill with red and gold.

Robert came up to her. "Come with me," he whispered. "Quick – before the others notice."

They left the flat, moving down the hallway until they came to a staircase at the end. The walls of the staircase were dark and cracked; the paint flaking. Robert started to climb, and Hannah followed. Soon they came to a metal door with a bar across it. The paint on the door was scratched and chipped. Robert pressed the bar to open the door. Hannah winced, expecting an alarm to sound, but Robert shook his head.

"It hasn't worked for ages," he whispered.

Beyond him, Hannah could see a square of sky lit by the dying sun.

Robert beckoned. "Follow me."

Hannah was too scared to move. She couldn't look down and she couldn't climb up either.

Robert took her arm and helped her up the stairs. "Don't look down. Don't. Just one step... That's it. We've done it."

And they were on the roof. Robert walked to the centre of the space and stood there, his eyes shining. Hannah made her way over to him. As she stood by his side, she felt safe to turn and look out, far out, over the jumble of roofs and the chimney pots that threw up dirty smoke into the air; far over the distant houses and the streets like winding rivers and the cars that looked like toys, until she could see the edges of the city where the trees and open fields began, all misty and hazy in the evening sun. Over her head stretched the great vault of the sky that seemed to go on without limits – beyond the city, beyond the country, right out to the ends of the earth.

"You like it?" Robert asked, his face glowing as if it were on fire.

Hannah turned to him. "Oh, I love it! Thanks so much for showing me. I'll never forget it."

"I come up here on my own sometimes. My mother trusts me, but she won't let me go up in the dark. She used to come with me – she'd say the air was fresher here – but she can't climb up the stairs now. She says that's the worst thing about being ill: not being able to climb." Robert looked out over the city again and then back at Hannah. "You're shivering."

"No, really – I'm fine." She didn't want to go downstairs. Downstairs meant going back to the real world. She wanted to stay on the roof forever.

"We'd better go back."

She followed him down from the roof. The corridor now seemed darker and damper than ever.

"Where've you been?" asked Diana once they were back in the flat.

Hannah said nothing. She concentrated on the first stars glimmering in the darkening sky outside.

She was surprised when Cheryl turned up to take them home. She hadn't realised it was time to go already. She didn't want to leave. Diana got up at once, carefully dusting down her skirt.

Before they left, both girls went over to Robert's mother to say goodbye. Grace was sitting on the same chair, completely still, apart from the hand that still moved her stick in circles and the one eye she opened when they came up. "How did you like the roof?" she asked Hannah.

Diana turned to her friend; eyes wide with disbelief. "You went on the *roof*? Isn't that *dangerous*?"

"Dangerous?" Grace echoed. "But the view there is stunning – you can see the entire sky. You can never usually see the sky in this city. It's so cramped. And there's no air; that's the main problem. Maybe I'll go up there again one day, when I'm feeling better. Meanwhile, I've got Robert to tell me about it..." She gripped Hannah's hand. "Good to see you, Hannah. Come again. Whenever you like."

Hannah followed Diana to the door.

Cheryl peered at the girls through her sunglasses. "All ready? You got your party bags?"

Diana turned expectantly to Robert.

"Where are they, then?" asked Cheryl.

"Did you forget them?" Diana asked sweetly.

"There aren't any." Robert didn't seem embarrassed. Hannah was embarrassed for him, though. She flushed and kept her eyes on the floor.

"Oh," said Diana. "I see." But she didn't.

Hannah said nothing.

Diana was still confused about the bags. "Maybe he forgot them," she told Hannah once they'd left.

How dumb Diana could be sometimes, thought Hannah. "Of course there weren't going to be any bags, Diana."

"Why not?"

"Because they can't afford them, that's why."

"Oh." Diana didn't say anything for a bit. Then, when they got into the car, she said, "They can't even afford *party bags*." Her eyes were wide with shame. She sat stunned for a few seconds, and then she went on, magnanimously, "It doesn't matter. Really, it doesn't, does it, Mummy?" She turned to Hannah. "And you like him, don't you, Hannah? He's very nice. He *is*."

Hannah's cheeks flamed. With one thumb she traced a round face in the condensation on the car window, and then she scrubbed it out. She couldn't help sticking her thumb in her mouth after that, though she was trying not to suck it; she was too old for all that now. Her thumb was all wet and cold where it had touched the window, so it was like sucking a slug.

When Cheryl drew up outside the sweet shop, Hannah was out of the car before it had even stopped moving. She was furious with Diana, with Cheryl, with everyone; even Robert. And she wasn't going to let Cheryl follow her to her home this time, she thought. Oh, no. She ran to the front door and let herself in, slamming the door behind her with all the force she could muster.

Chapter 12

To Hannah's great irritation and upset, Cheryl did finally get to meet Jake. And all because Hannah's mother had a migraine. If it hadn't been for that, Hannah found herself thinking, they never would have met. But then, Sal told her, Cheryl would have found a way.

It was Hannah's parents' evening at school and her mother couldn't go. She'd been lying in bed for twenty-four hours now, pale and washed-up; Sal and Hannah moving past her room on tiptoe, like a pair of ballerinas. She had wanted Jake to go instead, but Hannah thought that unlikely, if the argument they had had a few nights before was anything to go by.

"I wouldn't care if they came to mine or not," Sal told her sister.

"Why not?"

"I'm leaving school anyway."

"When?"

"When I'm sixteen."

"That's still over a year away."

"So? Less time than you. You've got ages yet."

"What you going to do instead?"

"Train as a beautician."

"You told Jake that?"

Sal was mutinous. "I couldn't care less if he finds out."

When Hannah got into school that day, Diana asked her which of her parents was coming to the parents' evening.

"Neither," she replied.

"Aren't they interested?"

"No."

But later that day, Hannah amazed when her father caught up with her at the school gates, just as she was about to go home. He seemed uncomfortable; no doubt because he was wearing a tie. His shirt was creased and dirty around the collar and he hadn't shaved for several days, and yet Hannah couldn't help feeling a sort of secret pride when they walked into the school hall. He was far more handsome than any of the other dads.

Hannah's English teacher, Mrs Beeker, who wore thick glasses and her hair in a tight bun, seemed more animated than usual when Hannah and Jake came up to her. "Hannah has a marvellous imagination," she told them.

"Fat lot of use that is to anyone," was all Jake said to that.

Hannah shrank back, embarrassed, but still, it could have been worse. At least Mrs Beeker had been nice about her.

Mr Klark, who taught mathematics, a scrawny fellow with a tight-lipped, agonised expression, and flaps of loose skin beneath his chin, didn't look anything like his nickname, which was, of course, 'Superman'. When he saw Jake, he screwed up his lips tightly and leafed through his notes. "Hannah has a certain numerical ability, but her concentration is poor," he said severely. "She needs to apply herself to achieve results."

"She applies herself when she wants to," Jake told him.

Hannah didn't know with whom Jake was angrier – her or Mr Klark – but that was when she started to get worried.

Miss Mostel, a young woman who taught history, and whom the kids called 'Miss Moustache' because she had a dark line of down on her upper lip, avoided eye contact with Jake. "Hannah is a bright girl, but she has absolutely no interest in Henry VIII whatsoever," she told him. "I can't get her to do her homework and she can be disruptive in class."

As they left Miss Mostel, Hannah steeled herself for Jake's assault. She waited, eyes squeezed shut, holding her breath. But oddly, her father didn't say a word. When Hannah opened her eyes, she realised why.

Diana's mother was coming towards them, her daughter trotting behind her like an obedient dog. Cheryl's lipstick was scarlet, and diamonds glittered in her ears. She was wearing crushed-velvet trousers, the colour of red wine, and her hair – which was blonde, very blonde – was piled up on top of her head. She moved with feline stealth and assurance. When she drew close to Hannah and her father, she removed her sunglasses. "Hannah!" She opened her arms; an extravagant gesture that didn't suit her at all.

Hannah didn't move. She could smell Cheryl's perfume, like the smell of overblown roses. It made her feel ungainly, awkward and ugly. Cheryl paused dramatically, waiting.

Hannah turned to her father. "This is Diana's mother, Cheryl."

"Jake." He held out his hand.

Hannah looked from one adult to the other. She knew that Cheryl was wishing she would disappear, but she wasn't going to. Oh, no. With one shoe she scraped the parquet floor, and then she kept on scraping.

"How's Hannah doing at school, then?" Cheryl asked Jake, with a smile that showed off her perfect teeth.

"Not too well, if you listen to them. But then again, they all said I was no good, and look what happened," Jake added. And then he returned her smile. He had a charming smile: it seemed to start in the centre of his mouth and move slowly outwards, its warmth steadily spreading and strengthening, like that of the sun. At its peak, it dazzled onlookers. Hannah didn't see that smile very often these days, but she remembered it well. Jake always used it if he wanted something.

Cheryl laughed. "Well, Diana's doing splendidly. But I'm sure you'll catch up soon enough, won't you, Hannah?"

Hannah just carried on scraping the floor.

In the car on the way back, Jake didn't berate Hannah about her performance at school, as she'd feared he would. Instead, he started up about Cheryl. He talked about her so much, Hannah could feel her sitting in the car between them.

"Do you like her?" she asked finally.

"She's all right."

That meant he liked her. Jake never said anything positive about anyone. Hannah gave the underbelly of the car a swift, vicious kick. Her home, miserable as it was, was under attack. And it was all Cheryl's fault. Hannah hated her. She hated her more than she hated Michael. And that meant she hated her more than anything.

Chapter 13

When Diana told Hannah she wanted to hold a party at her house to celebrate Hannah becoming a teenager, Hannah momentarily forgot how much she hated her friend's mother. Jake not only allowed Hannah to hold the party at Diana's house, but said he'd pick her up at the end of it, as it wasn't safe for her to be roaming the streets at night.

By the time Hannah reached Diana's house on the day of her party the sky had deepened to a dark cornflower blue, and it was filled with stars. The air was crisp and cold, like mountain air. At the far end of the garden, a fire was burning. Flames made a cracking, whooshing sound as they devoured wood and sent spirals of smoke up into the sky. A few teenagers were already dancing around the fire, holding sparklers, which they were waving around like weapons.

Inside the house candles glowed in the windows, and flames flickered and spat. Boys and girls flitted past Hannah, carrying drinks, their shadows sliding alongside them across the walls.

After a while, Hannah had to admit that she wasn't enjoying her own party. She stood on her own in a corner, shivering and sucking at her lips, biting off her lip gloss. She'd borrowed (or, rather, stolen) a pair of Guess jeans and a lime-green off-the-shoulder sweatshirt from Sal. The jeans were not too comfortable, and the lime green of the top seemed to accentuate the ghostly white of Hannah's skin. She had tried to curl her hair like her sister did, but it had snarled up, so that it now looked like a bird's nest. It was almost nine o'clock; the fun, such as it was, was over, the food had been eaten, and Hannah wanted to go home. She wondered when Jake would come and collect her.

Suddenly she felt a hand on her arm and Robert appeared by her side. He wasn't dressed like the other kids: he was wearing a V-necked sweater and a tartan scarf. That made Hannah warm to him – he looked like a misfit, and she felt like one.

"You just got here?"

"I was busy with Mum."

"I'm about to leave. I'm waiting for Jake to pick me up."

"Don't you want to see the fireworks?"

Hannah hesitated. She'd forgotten that Diana's dad was going to set off some fireworks. She didn't like to admit to Robert how much she had been looking forward to them earlier. He might think her childish, still loving fireworks. She shrugged her shoulders.

Robert smiled. "Let's go outside." He took off his jumper. "And put this on. You'll feel warmer."

The lawn nearer the house was a warm yellow with the light from the windows. They moved to the end of the garden and waited there for the display to begin. In between bursts of music and laughter, they could hear the rushing sound of burning wood. For a while neither of them said a word.

"Feel any different now you're thirteen?" Robert asked at last.

"No – it's just as shit."

"Come on, you're a teenager now. Before too long you'll be drinking legally. And soon you can leave school, like you always said you would."

"Hmm." Hannah adjusted her jeans. Like Sal, she knew she didn't want to stay at school, but unlike her sister, she didn't know if she wanted what came afterwards, either.

"You could stay; go to uni. You're certainly bright enough."

Hannah smiled. No one had ever called her bright before, apart from Miss Mostel, and that didn't count. "That where you're going?"

"Eventually, yes."

"What about your mother?"

"She wants me to go. Says she couldn't possibly stop me."

"But who'll look after her?"

"My aunt."

Hannah couldn't come up with any more objections. And now that she thought about it, it made perfect sense. Robert was always studying. She didn't know much about college, but if it were a continuation of the study, he would be just fine.

They continued standing in the darkness until

Hannah grew tired of waiting. "When are they going to start?" she demanded, as if Robert knew something she didn't.

Just as she spoke, a rocket exploded in the black void above their heads, filling it with plumes of scarlet. And then another burst into a million tiny flecks of gold, which drifted down the sky and died. With each explosion, the sky blossomed with light, and their faces glowed with this sudden flowering. Then, as abruptly as it began, the display ended and there was nothing in front of them; only the dark sky and the blinking of the stars through the ink.

For a while Hannah didn't move or speak. The fireworks had made the sky look like a carpet of flowers. Now the display was over, she felt almost sick with disappointment. She turned to Robert. He was still staring at the stars.

"Wonder where my father is?"

"Shall I take you home?"

"You don't mind?"

"'Course not. I'll go get our coats."

Robert was gone a while. Eventually, bored of waiting, Hannah turned and made her way back to the house to find him. She started walking up the stairs, her feet making no sound on the thick carpet. When she got to the landing on the second floor, she saw Robert standing in the hallway above her, his back to an open doorway, shock and disbelief on his face. Before she could call to him, he came down to her, one finger to his lips.

"Let's go downstairs," he whispered. She had never heard him speak with such urgency before. "C'mon."

"But we have to get our coats."

"No, Hannah!" He was gripping her arm now and pushing her down the soft-carpeted stairs.

Hannah hissed, "What's in the room, Robert? Let me go!" She pulled her arm from his grasp and ran up the stairs. Drawing close to the doorway where he had been standing, she held her breath and peered into the room.

A couple were standing by the window. They were lit by a lamp to one side of the bed, on which was a mountain of coats. The man was very tall, and the woman was pushed up against him, her breasts flattened against his chest. Their mouths were pressed together; their arms entwined, and they were squeezing each other tightly. At first, Hannah wasn't sure who they were, so bleary-eyed was she from being so long in the dark. But then she took a step closer, and she knew.

She felt Robert come up behind her. She was half relieved, half angry when he pulled her downstairs.

"Who is he with, your father?" he whispered. "Isn't that Diana's mother?"

Hannah stared at him, her eyes dark and wide. Finally, she nodded. A single sob dislodged itself from her throat. "Will you take me home, Robert?"

"Shouldn't I tell your dad we're going?"

"No. I don't care about him. Please."

She waited while Robert told Diana he was taking

her home. Diana smiled and nodded. She looked so carefree, so innocent, that Hannah felt a sudden stab of pain watching her.

On the walk to the Underground, Hannah tried to block out what she'd seen. But her imagination took her back inside the bedroom, and so to the locking together of flesh, and the sounds similar to those her parents had made in their bedroom that night, except that at least that was her parents, while *this* was something else entirely. She closed her eyes. She tried to close her mind tight as a trap, to shut the sickening images inside it.

"I hate my father," she told Robert as they sat on the District Line, the overhead strip lighting making her eyes smart.

"Don't say that."

"Don't tell me what to say!" she shouted. "You don't know the first thing about him! How do you think it feels, seeing him like that? It's all right for you!"

"At least you've got a dad." Robert's voice was very small.

As quickly as it had come, the rage left Hannah and a sick sadness took its place, welling up from somewhere deep inside her. "It doesn't work like that." She wiped her eyes with her arm. Sal's mascara she had applied earlier left a black trail on her sleeve.

He put his hand on her arm. "Hannah, I'm sorry. I shouldn't have said that."

"I'm sorry too." She stood up. "It's our stop."

When they reached her home, Hannah looked up to

see a light on in her mother's bedroom, while the rest of the place was in darkness. She sighed. The sickness in her stomach had intensified.

"You can come back to mine, if you like," Robert told her.

Hannah shook her head. "I can't," she told him. "Jake will kill me if I'm not at home when he gets back. But thank you." And she left him and let herself in.

Chapter 14

"It hurts!" Hannah wailed.

Sal squatted in front of her on the bathroom floor and started wiping up the bright spots of blood that had fallen there. For once, she was almost sympathetic: she didn't shout at her sister for stealing her clothes and offered her a sanitary towel as if it were a bandage. "Take this." She slipped a white pill into Hannah's hand. "And this."

"What is it?" Hannah asked suspiciously. She was never quite sure with Sal.

"Paracetamol, moron. What do you think I'm trying to do? Drug you up to the eyeballs?"

Hannah swallowed the pill. Despite Sal's efforts, there was still a trail of crimson spots on the bathroom floor in front of her. Hannah would never have believed the blood was a part of her if it weren't for the pain. Great birthday. First Jake at the party, then this. "Shall I tell Mum?" she whispered.

"Are you a complete idiot? Shut your mouth, Hannah, you hear me? Don't say a word. If I hear you've told her, I'll go mad. I'll set Michael on you; I swear I will."

"But how will we make them stop?" Hannah sobbed.

Sal looked at her as she would a piece of dirt on the ground. "Hannah, they're grown-ups. They can do what they like. And if you didn't know that by now, you're even stupider than I thought." And she flounced out of the bathroom, leaving Hannah to sort out the mess on the floor, to stagger to bed, and to cry herself very quietly to sleep.

The following day, when Hannah returned from school, she found her mother sitting in the kitchen, cradling her face with the palm of one hand. The bowl in front of her was brimming with cigarette ends. She looked up when she heard her daughter come in. Her eyes were the colour of ash; her face motionless.

Hannah's heart stopped when she saw her. *She knows*, she thought. "What's up?" she asked faintly.

She was almost relieved when her mother said, "It's Sal. She left earlier, to live with Maeve. She's refusing to finish school. Wants to start training as a beautician straight away, she says." She sighed. "Jake's going now to get her back."

Sal must have been more bothered about the business with Cheryl than she'd made out. But Hannah didn't have time to consider how much more bothered, because just at that moment, Jake came into the room. She felt him come in before she saw him.

"Hannah!" he yelled. "You come with me. Now!"

Jake's car jerked and choked under his angry hands. A few minutes later, they drew up outside a decaying Victorian house. Outside lay an abandoned mattress, its insides spilling over the pavement like rotting entrails. All around, bags of rubbish had been dumped. Something had chewed them open and their contents were falling out too. Jake looked at his surroundings in disgust. Hannah couldn't understand why he was so displeased; it wasn't as if their street was any better. He strode up to the door of the house and banged on it with his fist. No one answered, and he banged again.

"Awright!" they heard a voice yell from inside the house. Maeve opened the door. Her hair was now a shocking pink. She stood, arms folded, chewing gum. "What you want?"

"Where's Sal?"

"She don't want to see you."

Jake pushed past her and through into the back of the house. Hannah followed. The kitchen was squalid, its surfaces covered in discarded food and piles of filthy plates. On the floor, a grey cat sat beside various dishes that looked like they had at one time contained milk or meat. Sal was sitting at the table.

Jake went to stand in front of her, his hands gripping a chair between them. The knuckles showed white. "Come home now!" he yelled.

Sal's eyes widened. She shifted on her seat. "Why would I want to live with you? We've seen what you get up to!"

Jake's face paled. "What the fuck do you mean?"

"What do you think?"

Hannah caught her breath. It was the first time in ages that one of them had stood up to Jake. It terrified her. She stared at him, shaking.

Jake leaned towards Sal, speaking more slowly. "I'm giving you ten seconds to shift your butt from that chair and come with me. Starting now."

Sal's forehead was shiny beneath her make-up.

"Ten, nine, eight…"

The cat mewed. Maeve watched the scene intently, chewing loudly.

"…seven, six, five…" Jake's hands still gripped the chair. "…four, three, two…"

Suddenly he threw the chair away from him; it slammed against a kitchen cupboard with a loud crack. He drew closer to Sal. Sal got up from the table and backed away from him into a corner of the room. She put her hands up to her face.

"Sal!" Hannah cried. "Come with us!"

Suddenly, Maeve stepped in front of Sal, arms crossed. "She don't want to come with you. You leave her be."

Hannah winced and shut her eyes. But when she opened them, to her surprise, Jake hadn't moved. He'd just come to a halt a couple of feet away from Maeve. It was like something out of a horror film – as if some terrifying machine had been about to crush Sal, and then had suddenly, miraculously stopped.

"Sal, come home, please." Hannah's voice broke. "*Please.*"

No one spoke. Jake didn't move.

Finally, Sal spoke. Her voice was quiet but very firm. "No. I'll continue at school, but I'm not going back home. I'm *never* going back."

Jake moved past Maeve towards Sal. Hannah shut her eyes. It was her turn to start counting to ten, rapidly, in her head. She breathed out a quick prayer. When she got to ten and nothing happened, she opened her eyes again. Jake had his hand on Sal's arm, but his touch was so light, it was almost a caress.

Still Sal didn't move. "I'm not going," she said again.

Sal got her way. Jake left the house without her, in the foulest temper imaginable.

Hannah lingered. "I'd better go," she told Sal. A thick gloom had settled on her.

Sal said nothing.

Hannah heard her father's voice calling her again. She looked at her sister, hating her, admiring her, wanting to be her, even loving her, then hating her all over again. Above all, she wondered why yet again Sal seemed to get away with everything while she, Hannah, never got away with anything. Her eyes filled with tears. "I'll see you around." She started to back away. "I... I don't suppose... Can I come live here with you too?"

Sal blinked. "Aw, Hannah, you're still little."

"Anyhow, there ain't no room," Maeve added helpfully. "There's five of us here: me, Sal, me nan, Matt and Ant, and 'e's on the sofa and all."

When Jake and Hannah got back home, Hannah's mother ran to the door. She saw that Sal wasn't with them, drew Hannah to her and wrapped her arms around her, squeezing her close. Then she rocked her like a baby.

It was poor consolation for Hannah.

Hannah missed Sal. The atmosphere at home grew steadily worse, becoming increasingly strained as winter set in. Jake spent a couple of evenings a week away from home – in the company of Cheryl, Hannah suspected. At other times, Hannah thought she recognised Cheryl's perfume lingering in the kitchen, or in the bathroom after Jake had used it. Perhaps her mother smelled it too, though she wouldn't necessarily have linked the scent to Cheryl.

Hannah didn't dare confront her father over the affair. Whenever he came close to her, she turned her face, her whole body, away from him. The very sight of him repulsed her. And yet by the spring she found herself hoping that if her mother didn't already know about Cheryl, she would find out. Hannah wanted her to, for the affair was a secret she struggled to keep; an intolerable burden she longed to shake from her shoulders as soon as possible. But though she wanted to free herself of its weight, she would never have confessed to her mother what was going on, for that would inflict a degree of pain that would have been impossible for even Hannah to imagine.

Chapter 15

It was a fine autumn day, the clouds only occasionally hiding the sun. The air was still warm, and still. Hannah had left her room as soon as she'd heard her parents arguing, before she could even make out what the row was about, and was wandering outside around her home, restless, unsure where to go next.

When she first heard Michael's voice call out her name, she ignored him at first. But finally she spun round to see brother leering at her from the opening of an overgrown alleyway which ran down the side of one of the houses near the sweet shop. He gestured behind him with one thumb. Hannah could make out dark shapes in the gloom at his back.

Suddenly she heard him call out, "Darren!" and another boy – big-boned, with a shock of carrot-coloured hair – came running towards her.

Hannah turned and ran across the road, dodging a car whose horn blared at her. But the boys were too quick for her. They caught up with her in the sunlight on the opposite side of the street. She felt them right behind her, and the shock as each grabbed one of her arms. She struggled and kicked but couldn't break free.

"We've got a treat for you," Michael told her, grinning. "We think you'll like it." And he pushed her head down so that she was looking at nothing but his filthy rubber trainers, breathing in the dust they raised with each step.

When they reached the alleyway, the air smelled sweet and fungal. Hannah tried to raise her head, but her brother pushed it down again. After a couple of turns, the boys stopped. Hannah's arms were aching and so were her feet, directed by the boys' will, just like the poor paws of the family hamster, working its wheel in a frantic circle all those years ago. She looked around her. She was in an open space that had once been cultivated as a garden. There were shrubs growing and a few small fruit trees, but the ground had for a long time been a home to young, hungry weeds that flourished in the cracks between the paving stones and choked plants that tried to stand in their way.

Michael pushed Hannah towards the centre of the space, where there was an ornamental pond, its stone sides covered in lichen and its water in a kind of cress which was an acidic green. Another boy, Dave, was standing in front of the pond, grinning at her. She often saw him with her brother. He had curly brown hair, a chipped front tooth, and eyes so dark you couldn't see any expression in them. Dave and Michael were full of malevolent plans, the most recent being to terrorise kids into giving up their Sony Walkmans. They'd made quite a bit of cash that way, passing on the stolen Walkmans to dodgy outlets on the Edgware Road, no questions asked. They each had a fancy cassette player too.

Dave flashed his in Hannah's face now. "Like it?"

"Is that what you've brought me here to show me? Stolen goods?"

Michael sniggered. "Nah, sis. He's got other, much fancier goods to show you."

He and Darren burst into coarse laughter.

"Give us a kiss, Hannah," Dave wheedled.

"Go on," Michael told her. "You might like it. Won't know unless you try." He pushed her towards his friend.

Dave grabbed her. His breath smelled ripe and rotten, and his tongue was like a giant worm pushing into her mouth. Hannah shoved him away. This only inflamed him further, and he reached out again, laughing.

The sudden scream of a police siren in a nearby street cut through the air. The boys, shocked and guilty, looked towards it. Hannah seized her chance and ran. When she got to the end of the alleyway, instead of running towards her front door, she ran until she could hear nothing but the beat of blood in her ears; across the Edgware Road, until she got to Robert's block of flats, and she didn't stop there. She ran into the lift, and she would have run right into Robert's flat if the door hadn't been in the way. But it was shut, and so she had to stop. She banged at the door, listened, could hear nothing but her own breathing. She sank down against the door, leaning her whole weight into it, and so to the ground.

Chapter 16

"What's up?" Robert asked, when he came home a short while later and found Hannah slumped against his front door.

She just shook her head.

He scanned her face. "Do you want to come in?" he asked gently.

Inside, Robert handed her a plate of flapjacks. "Mum made these." He disappeared and reappeared, whispering, "That's why she didn't let you in. She's in a deep sleep."

Hannah savoured the comforting taste of sugared oats on her tongue. "Can I stay here awhile?" she asked. "With you?"

"Don't you want to go home?"

"I ran away."

"You'll be missed."

"Not yet."

"I was going to go to the lido. Want to come?"

"I… I didn't bring my costume with me."

Robert disappeared again, came back, and handed her a costume. "Here, take this. It's one of Mum's. And let's go."

The lido building was like a concrete bunker from the outside, but when they stepped through its murky entrance, the pool suddenly appeared in front of them, enclosed in its vast courtyard, gleaming like a giant sapphire in the sunlight. They stared at the water, mesmerised by the dance of the sun upon it.

Hannah headed to the changing cubicles and then came to stand by Robert's side at the water's edge; half naked, shivering slightly, feeling conscious of her nipples, swollen against the thin fabric of the costume, and her hips, the bones jutting out like half-moons. She followed Robert into the pool, shrieking as she hit the water, swam a couple of circles, and then lay on her back, floating, feeling the sun on her face, slowly spinning around. Just at that moment, floating in that shimmering pool, basking in the sunlight, she felt that she was exactly where she wanted to be.

Robert swam up and down in straight lines. Then he went down to the deep end, to the darker water which the sun didn't touch, and climbed up to the diving board. Nervously, Hannah watched him – his small silhouette against the bright, vast sky. Finally he hurtled down, his pale body throwing up bubbles as he cut through to the bottom of the pool. He sprang up again, gleaming like a seal, shaking droplets of water as he moved towards her.

After that, they sat on the side of the pool, dangling their legs in the water, laughing at how it distorted their shapes. Hannah was so close to Robert now; she could feel the hairs on his arm brush against hers. Acutely conscious of her own body and of his, she held her breath. A small fist of fear hovered somewhere on the edge of her subconscious, like a tiny cloud in a flawless sky. Robert touched her hand with his fingers, and points of pleasure fanned out across her skin. Then he leaned towards her and brushed his mouth against hers. Her lips burned where he'd touched them, and she felt her body move towards his just as her face pulled away. He didn't move towards her again, and they continued to sit side by side as if nothing had happened. And then, out of nowhere, a cloud hid the sun, and Hannah shivered. Robert jumped up and held her hand as he led her towards the changing cubicles. He took her hand again as they left the building, hair dripping, teeth chattering, and sat on the steps outside, letting the sun warm them through.

In the days after that, whenever Hannah was troubled by memories of Dave's leering face and his tongue in her mouth by that scummy pond, she'd screw her eyes still tighter, until at last that pool came back to her, the surface of the water glittering as if it were covered in gems, and then that other kiss, Robert's kiss, and the burning it had left on her lips and inside her. Whenever she remembered that, her head filled with a sense of liberation, light overwhelmed her, and finally, happiness came to her: fleeting, transient, but in that moment golden, glorious, and completely her own.

PART 2
KARL

Chapter 17

Sal pouted at her reflection in the mirror. Without turning her head, she picked up a cotton bud from a box on her left and dipped it into a bottle of surgical spirit on her right. Then she brought the bud up and delicately prodded a fresh piercing far up her left ear.

The sweet smell of the surgical spirit, like medicated perfume, drifted over Hannah as she lay on Sal's bed, watching her. Sal was getting ready to go to a club. Another one. She was seventeen, and ever since she'd left home, life had begun for her. Hannah, by contrast, was only fifteen, and still stuck with her parents. But she got the feeling that things were just about to change. In fact, if she could only persuade Sal to let her go to this club, tonight might well be the tipping point.

"Sal?"

"Hmm?" Sal had finished bathing her other ear in spirit while 'Take on Me' played on the cassette player. Now she moved even closer to her mirror and started applying lipstick, coats of it; a glorious, sticky red. Her eyes flicked to her younger sister and then back again. "What, Hannah?"

"You look nice."

"Thanks."

"Anyone in particular?" Hannah asked sweetly.

Sal shrugged her shoulders. "There's this one bloke.

He's okay."

"What's his name?"

"Karl." Sal eyed her sister suspiciously. "What's it to you, anyway? Aren't you too busy with Lover Boy to care?"

"Robert? He's just a friend. Honestly, Sal, I wouldn't want to go out with him. I don't fancy him, not at all."

"Methinks you protest too much, Hannah."

Hannah flushed scarlet. She hadn't kissed Robert again since that afternoon by the pool. He had seemed busy and preoccupied and would spend days at a time away from school. Occasionally he'd ask Hannah if she wanted to hang out, and she'd find some excuse, all the while feeling herself blushing. "Where are you going tonight?" she asked Sal now.

"The Cross."

"Can I go?"

"No." Sal pouted.

"Why not?"

"Too young."

"*Please?*" It was far too early in the conversation to be begging, and Hannah knew it, but she couldn't help it. If she could just get her pig of a sister to change that narrow mind of hers, she was sure a whole host of exciting things would happen to her that night.

Sal fished a tissue from another box on her left, still staring straight ahead, and blotted her lipstick firmly. "Stop hassling me, Hannah. There's no way Jake will let you go prancing around King's Cross at night. Go home. Play with Diana. Or listen to 'Like a Virgin' or something, I dunno." She grinned, untied her hair and shook it free. Finally, she turned to Hannah. "How do I look?" Hannah assessed her sister. Her hair was streaked yellow with Sun-In, and she was wearing tight, ripped yellow jeans, and a black cropped top fringed with lace.

"Like a wasp."

Sal sniffed. "Well, you look like a witch. And I know which I'd rather look like, Witchy." She laughed and flounced out of her room, leaving the sickly smell of cheap scent behind her.

Hannah lay on Sal's bed, covered her ears, and closed her eyes. Spots of colour swirled inside her lids. She imagined herself at the club, glowing and gorgeous, shifting through crowds of people who had crossed the room to talk to her. A good-looking stranger took hold of her. They moved past Sal in time to the music pumping around them, their bodies swaying to its beat. Hannah bent her head so that it touched the boy's shoulder. He told her he loved her hair; how soft it was, and shiny, and not like a witch's at all; oh, no.

Hannah sighed and opened her eyes. She could hear Bryan Adams thumping from the room next door. The walls of Maeve's house were even thinner than those in Hannah's own. She left Sal's room, went to the phone downstairs, and dialled a number. "Can you get out tonight?"

"Give me ten minutes," Diana said.

An hour later, the two girls were walking towards the station. Hannah had smeared Sal's eyeshadow – rather messily – over her eyelids. Diana was hastily removing butterfly clips from her hair, on her friend's advice. In front of them bands of cloud lined the sky, set alight by the setting sun, so that they glowed like bars of gold.

By the time the girls emerged at King's Cross, the sky was heavy with rain, and filled with purple clouds that piled up in huge banks and then shifted and thinned out again. Pavements shone and car exhausts smoked through the wet. The girls passed groups of clubbers, pasty-faced, huddled together. A car pulled up alongside a scantily clad girl. She leaned into its open window and then moved to get in the passenger side. A man stood in a doorway, pulling on a cigarette; his feet wrapped in newspaper. Vast, derelict, industrial warehouses formed the backdrop to the scene.

As they approached the pub, they could hear the party inside it; feel the street vibrating with the beat of music. Blue light filtered out onto the pavement. And it seemed to Hannah as if all of life, and all fun within it, was contained in that one place.

Inside, throbbing music assaulted their ears. Clothes steamed in the sudden heat. Faces were distorted and shiny with sweat. Everywhere bodies heaved, churned, twisting around and into each other so that flesh formed one vast, indistinguishable mass. Hannah and Diana weaved through the crowd until they spotted Sal, dancing with a tall man with dark hair. The light made the metal on his belt glimmer softly. Hannah approached her sister and pulled at her arm.

Sal's face was deathly pale in the blue light, the whites of her eyes shifting. "Hannah, what you doing here?" she sighed. She didn't introduce her sister to the man with the belt, who in any case started talking to a friend, before the crowd swallowed them up. Sal turned to Diana. "How did *you* get away?" she scoffed.

After that Hannah and her friend moved to a room away from the dancing where they could sit down. Smoke crept towards the ceiling, curling above their heads.

A boy with cropped hair offered Hannah a cigarette and a shot. "Vodka. Take it." Then he handed her another shot – tequila, he told her.

After that, the room swam slightly, as smoke filled Hannah's insides. The boy sat next to her and moved his face close to hers. She sensed her eyes glaze over; a torpor moving over her limbs. The boy pressed his lips to her neck; stale breath fanning her skin. She could just make out Diana's voice. All sound was muffled, as if she were underwater. Hannah nodded as her friend backed out of the room; then she tried to stand but couldn't, as the boy pulled her back towards him.

Finally, she staggered to her feet. "I've got to find Diana."

"I'll help," the boy told her. He took her hand. "This way."

But he led her to an even quieter room. Large cushions

were scattered on the floor, and the easiest thing to do was to lie down on one of them. Hannah did, and the ceiling moved towards her. She closed her eyes. She was aware of movement to her left; the sound of a belt buckle being undone. And then the boy pressed his face, its skin slightly damp, against hers in the darkness. Hannah tried to get up, but it was like trying to move a weight twice her own. She twisted away, but the boy pulled her towards him again, pushing her top down over her shoulders. She felt hot breath fan her breasts, as a wave of nausea moved through her.

"Open your mouth," the boy whispered urgently.

Hannah shook her head, tried to push back, tried to scream, but she couldn't get the scream out – it was just a strangled noise that stuck in her throat.

Suddenly the room was flooded with overhead light. "Fuck," a voice said. "Sorry – thought this was the loos."

The boy was shocked momentarily – enough to stop what he was doing, as he looked up towards the owner of the voice. It was the man Hannah had seen with Sal earlier; the one with the metal-trimmed belt. Seizing her chance, she gave the boy a forceful shove and hastily rearranged her clothing.

"He bothering you?" the man with the belt asked.

Hannah nodded.

The man reached the boy in two steps, yanked him up, and then punched him in the nose. The boy collapsed, blood streaming from one nostril.

The man came over to Hannah. "I'm Karl, by the

way. I know your sister. Get up," he told her, pulling her to her feet. "I'll take you home. Sal already left. Couldn't find you, she said."

Hannah stared shocked at the prostrate figure of the boy and then back at the man in front of her, into his heavy-lidded eyes. "Is he dead?" she whispered.

Karl struck the boy with his foot. "He'll live. Though he doesn't deserve to."

Hannah's throat was throbbing. She stumbled from the room and emerged, blinking, into the main room. She scanned the room. She couldn't see Diana, but it was almost too dark to see anyone.

Karl led Hannah home, all the way to her front door. "I'd best leave you here," he said. "Otherwise your dad will kill me." He smiled. Somehow it didn't seem like a proper smile: only one corner of his mouth turned up; the other was twisted with scar tissue. He leaned into Hannah, his mouth moving near to hers. "Tell you what," he whispered. "You need a proper kiss. Badly." He moved back. "But now's not the time. Go clean yourself up." He raised one hand and backed away into the night. "And next time I see you, I promise I'll give you that kiss."

It was half midnight by the time Hannah let herself in.

Jake was waiting for her in the kitchen. "Where the fuck have you been?"

"Nowhere."

"*Nowhere?* You little…"

She felt his hand come towards her, and winced.

"Your mother's been worried sick. Sneaking out like that. Tarting yourself around."

Hannah's mother appeared behind Jake, worry lining her face. "Go easy on her," she said.

Jake dragged Hannah to the bathroom, and to the mirror above the sink. "Look at you!" he hissed.

Hannah looked at her reflection in the bathroom light. She looked exhausted – her eyes like huge holes in her face, her cheeks hollow, her lips a bloodless crack.

Jake loosened his hold on her, as if he couldn't bear to touch her. "What are you like? Take a wash," he told her in a tired, disgusted voice.

Hannah's eyes filled with tears. Jake wouldn't let her out of his sight after this. Tears spilled from her eyes and down her cheeks. She removed her make-up, and then stood under the shower for some time. Finally, she drifted off to sleep, with the taste of tar in her mouth and the dark-haired man in her head, his belt glowing very faintly in the light, his hand hard on her arm as he helped her home.

Chapter 18

Diana leaned back against the wall.

"Careful," Hannah warned her.

In her upset, Diana had momentarily allowed her fair hair to rest against the brick; something she never normally did. Quickly, she moved her shining head and carefully smoothed any dirt out of her hair. "I'm sorry, Hannah. I thought you were okay; that's why I left. I got a cab home."

Hannah was sitting in front of her friend, her knees exposed to the bright sunlight. Now she bent her head so that her long dark hair brushed against them; a gesture she found soothing, both because she could hide and because the touch of her hair on her skin felt like silk. "I think that boy must have slipped something into my drink," she told her friend.

"Do you know who he is?" Diana asked her. Her round eyes, which had grown even more rotund when Hannah had told her her news, had now reverted to their usual shape.

"Who? Karl?"

"Not the man who rescued you. The other one."

"No. Do you?"

"Yes."

Hannah looked up in surprise.

"He's called Matt."

"How do you know?"

"Lise told me."

"How does Lise know?"

"He's a friend of her brother's. And her brother was at the club."

"Was he... was he hurt much?"

"Lise said he's shaken but fine."

Hannah sighed.

Diana leaned over and put a hand on her arm. "Don't worry about it, Hannah. And anyway, he didn't really do much, did he?"

"Feels like he did." Hannah shivered.

"Well, it could have happened to anyone."

"It didn't happen to *you*."

The two girls fell silent after that. And it was as if something had changed for them irrevocably; as if between them there was now a gulf so vast, neither one of them could ever cross it.

"What happened, Hannah?" Sal asked her sister after school. "Matt... didn't...?" Her eyes, full of concern, laden with mascara, assessed her sister.

"No... but he did enough." Hannah paused. "That was Karl you were dancing with before, with the metal belt, wasn't it?"

Sal smiled. "Yes."

"Do you like him?"

Sal had a faraway look on her face. "Maybe," she said. She flicked her hair over and then back. "Do I need to dye my hair again, Hannah? More Sun-In, perhaps?"

"Sal, can I ask you a question?"

"Of course."

"You've actually done it, right?"

"Yeah, I told you I did. Last year."

"Do you feel different?"

"I feel… well… more grown-up. As if I know what life's about." Sal smirked, as if she were privy to secrets that Hannah would never be a party to and Hannah should be envious of her good fortune. "It's your turn next. I'm sure Robert would be happy to oblige," she sniggered.

Hannah paled and shut her eyes, remembering the boy at the party. "I think I'll leave it, thanks." She spoke as if she were refusing a type of food that wasn't to her taste.

"For how long?"

"A while."

"You might be missing out."

"I don't think so."

"Seriously, why don't you try with Robert? Better with someone you know. And he fancies you."

"How do you know? He hasn't even asked me out."

"You haven't encouraged him enough, then."

"Don't do it with anyone; not even Robert," Diana told Hannah, when Hannah passed on what Sal had said.

"I wasn't about to," Hannah protested.

"My mother says wait until you know the man is dead keen. Until he's almost falling over himself to marry you. That's the most important thing, she says."

"What is?"

"Marriage. She says the sex thing is entirely secondary."

Hannah thought about the way Cheryl acted around Jake. She wasn't so sure.

Hannah and Diana were sitting outside a fast-food place on the Edgware Road. At that moment, Lise walked past them. She was wearing a pair of tights with diamond cut-outs all over them. Underneath the diamonds, the waxy white of her legs showed. On one thigh a large purple bruise showed through her tights. She'd lined her small, squinty eyes with black eyeliner, so they looked even smaller, like black slits in her face. "Spaz," she hissed at Hannah as she walked past.

"Go fuck yourself," Hannah retorted.

Lise turned and grinned at her. "Better than fucking some I could mention."

Hannah's eyes smarted. She turned to her friend. "God – what did he tell people, Diana?"

"He's an idiot." Diana took her arm. "It'll all blow over soon, really it will."

The following day was one of the rare occasions when Robert was at school. As a result of Grace's failing health, Hannah had heard rumours that she and her son now had even less money, so that Robert was always going hungry and so on. Certainly his clothes, which had never been smart, were scruffier than ever. His poverty, which Hannah's imagination magnified, embarrassed her, and in and around the embarrassment lurked something like disgust. She was ashamed of her feelings; they made her hate herself and hate Robert too. She didn't miss him, she thought, now that he wasn't at school so much, and in any case, even if she *did* miss him just a little, she was too busy with her attempts at creating a social life to think about him. But now, when he came up to her and put his hand on her arm – his touch gentle, his eyes concerned – she did feel a pang of guilt. His kindness made the guilt worse. It made her remember all the other times he had been kind to her when she felt she didn't deserve it.

"Everything all right, Hannah?"

"Fine."

Her face must have told him otherwise, but Robert didn't say anything. Maybe he hadn't found out yet about what had happened at The Cross. But Hannah was convinced that by now the news of her encounter with Matt had spread through the school like some virulent disease. She took a deep breath. "Have you heard anything about me recently, Robert?" she asked.

He wouldn't look her in the eye. *He knows*, she thought.

"I heard about… the pub…" he said eventually.

"What did you hear?"

"That you and Matt… you know. And that's fine,

Hannah. Whatever makes you happy. As long as it does. Make you happy, I mean." He seemed really embarrassed, as if it hurt him to speak; even to look at her.

Hannah was suddenly, inexplicably furious. Two spots of colour appeared on her cheeks. "You know what, Robert? Things would be a lot better if you minded your own business. You and the rest of the world."

His face reddened. "I was only checking you were okay. But if that's how you feel…" His mouth set in a thin line.

"It *is* how I feel."

"Right, then."

Hannah felt something detach from her insides and rise through her, like the tide. Robert was angry now – she'd never seen him so angry – and, more than that, he seemed disgusted. How *dare* he be disgusted with her?! "And you know what, Robert? Since you *do* make it your business, it was amazing, so there."

He looked as if he'd been punched in the stomach, but all he said was, "I'll see you later, then."

"Aren't you glad?"

"About what?"

"That it was good?"

"Like I said, whatever makes you happy, Hannah."

He walked away and left her standing there, and she felt as if he'd taken a fist and broken her into a million tiny bits, even though he hadn't laid a finger on her and she knew he never would. But what did she care, she told herself? She didn't need him any longer. She just needed every chance she could get to grab whatever experience came her way; to gain entry to that bigger, better life. So what if the entry fee was high? If she made a few mistakes on the way up? At least she was trying. At least she was *living*. Which was more than she could say for some, she thought.

Chapter 19

Hannah was right about Jake. As she'd suspected, he seldom let her out of his sight now, and on the rare occasion he did, Sal wouldn't let her come out with her. She would boast about the club nights she'd been to, the different types of alcohol she'd consumed, and, of course, the men she'd met. But Hannah didn't go anywhere. She was as trapped as a canary in a cage.

As it happened, just for one evening, Jake and Sal relented at the same time, and Hannah was allowed to accompany Sal to the funfair on Hampstead Heath. This was on condition that she wouldn't hassle Sal in future and would make herself scarce when she was asked to do so.

As she crossed East Heath Road and trudged up the hill behind Sal and Maeve, Hannah kept a fair distance between herself and her sister, as Sal had asked her to do, so that she and her friend could carry on with their private chat without being disturbed by Sal's hopelessly uncool younger sister. But Hannah longed to know what they were talking about. She could see Sal's head bent towards Maeve's; their cigarette ends burning in unison. The sun was setting in front of them, its dying rays making the girls' outlines glow. A feeble moon waited among the clouds to their left; a pale disc growing brighter as the sun sank. As they walked, darkness set in, until they could barely see the ground underfoot. In front of them, the white bulbs on the Big Wheel blinked against the sky. Behind them the Small Wheel flashed blue and silver. The Rotor Wheel spun in a rush of red to their right.

Suddenly the chaos of the funfair enveloped them: the flashing lights and blaring music and smell of candyfloss and cigarettes. Sal and Maeve made for the coconut shy. Sal tried to dislodge a coconut and failed. The stallholder gave her a small teddy bear anyway. She threw it to Hannah and Hannah caught it and held it gingerly with one hand. It was the ugliest thing she'd ever seen. She wanted to take a match to it. Sal and Maeve lounged against the stall, pulling on their cigarettes.

"How long they going to be?" Sal asked Maeve.

Maeve shrugged. "Anybody's guess."

The two girls continued to try to look relaxed.

"There they are!" Sal said finally. "Hannah," she hissed. "Do me a favour, will you? Get lost. Take yourself on some rides, why don't you?" She handed Hannah a tenner.

"On my own?"

But two boys had already come up to them. "All right, girls?" one of them – the taller, darker one – said. He looked at Hannah and smiled.

She remembered his face from the club. The colour of his eyes matched the metal on his belt. A pale scar ran from his left cheek down towards his mouth and across its left side, twisting it up and making his smile lopsided. Hannah felt herself blush.

"Hello, little sis," Karl said. "Remember me?"

Sal's eyes narrowed. "You already met?"

"The club night at The Cross, remember? You were so out of it, you probably forgot."

Karl took hold of Hannah's hand as he spoke, crushing her fingers. He pulled her close and then let go quickly, so that she felt as if she were falling backwards into space. She recovered, but she dropped the teddy bear on the muddy ground.

Karl gestured at his friend. "This is Jason, girls."

The shorter, fairer boy came forward. His features were squashed together, and he had slightly protuberant eyes.

Karl approached the shy, picked up a ball almost nonchalantly, as if he could barely be bothered with it, and drew his arm right back and over and forward, sending the ball hurtling into space, then bringing the arm back around in a full circle. He threw over and over again, glorying in his own strength. The coconuts cracked like eggs. Hannah watched Karl from the shadows. She watched the veins on his right arm rise as he bent it back. At the top of his arm was a tattoo of a cobra – Hannah watched its tight coils bend and flex with Karl's straining muscles, how his dark hair fell over his face as he threw, and the way his eyes lit up whenever he smashed a coconut off its stand.

When he'd stopped, Karl turned to the others. The

girls stood open-mouthed.

"Who wants this?" He gestured to the prize – a toy dog – in his hands. And then he threw it over to Hannah. "Bigger than the one you dropped," he said.

Hannah caught the prize. "Thanks." It was the first word she'd spoken for a while, and her mouth was cracked and dry.

"Where we going next?" Karl asked.

Without waiting for an answer, he led them to the Waltzer. They crowded into one of the cars, pressing up against each other. Karl leaned against Hannah, his arm resting along the back of the car behind her. When the car moved, he pressed down on her shoulder. The car picked up speed and then swung round in a half-circle. A boy leapt onto it and spun it faster and faster. The lights blurred before Hannah's eyes. The car kept spinning, as if it wanted to detach itself from the ride altogether and fly off into the sky. Whenever Karl was flung against Hannah, he pressed his whole weight upon her, his arm squeezing hers, his leg right up against hers. Each time, she felt the metal on his belt dig into her side and his breath hard against her cheek. Eventually, the movement slowed, the music faded, and the lights flickered off and then on again. Breathless, Hannah leaned back against the leather of the car, her head spinning. To her right, Sal was still screaming.

They left the Waltzer and headed towards the Dodgems, Sal in front, talking to Karl. Each time he put his hand on her sister's arm, Hannah's insides twisted up. Sal and Karl and Maeve and Jason got into two cars. The music started up, and Karl sent his car careering around the small patch of metal, aggressively bludgeoning every car in his way, making the brakes squeal. He sent two boys reeling against one side of the space, then rapidly removed his car from their line of fire and, sparks flying from its wheels, hurtled around in the opposite direction.

"Wanker!" one of the boys called after him.

The music stopped and Sal left the car, rubbing her arm. "I'm bruised all over," she yelled at Karl.

He followed her, laughing. "Sal! Come back! Don't get upset!"

They'd only walked a short way when Hannah heard footsteps running up behind them. "Oi, you!"

They all turned around.

"You!" The boy shouting at them was thickset, with short, spiky hair. He pointed one finger at Karl.

Karl smiled. "Who, me?"

"What's your problem? Why drive like a fuckin' maniac?"

"I thought that was the idea, mate." Karl's mouth was still smiling but his eyes were alert; his whole sensory system trained upon the boy in front of him.

The boy charged up to him. Swiftly, Karl moved to one side. The boy charged again. Again, Karl sidestepped him. Then Karl and Jason approached the boy. Karl grabbed his left wrist; Jason his right.

"Take him over there!" Karl shouted. He gestured to

his left, and they dragged the boy away from the girls, into the darkness in front of one of the white fairground vans. They heard Karl shouting, "Hold him!" and then saw the boy's shape struggling and squirming against the white of the van. There was a thud, and then a crack, and the shadow jerked and bent over.

"Stop it! Stop!" Hannah screamed. She didn't know if they'd heard her, but there was no sound after that.

When Karl staggered back to them, the gleam of the fight had left his eyes, and they were dull; the dull grey of gunmetal. "He asked for it," he told them. "Well, didn't he?"

"Is he okay?" Sal demanded.

"Yeah. We just shook him up a bit. He could walk away from us, anyway."

"Let's go," Sal said quickly. "Maeve; Hannah…"

Maeve went and stood by Sal.

"Hannah!"

Hannah was still staring at Karl. She watched him flip up the lid of a silver lighter and light a cigarette. He flipped the lid back again and the lighter shut with a crack. She could barely see his face; all she could see was the glow of his cigarette.

"Hannah!"

Hannah moved over to Sal.

"See you around," Karl said to the girls.

Sal didn't reply. Hannah followed her and Maeve out of the fairground.

"It was horrible, the way he did that. I won't be able

to sleep tonight," Sal was saying to her friend. "What a prick!"

Hannah said nothing. She was trembling. For a while as she walked, she thought about the anonymous boy, his face creased with pain. And then, as she moved further away from the noise and light of the fairground and the quiet darkness settled upon her, she thought about Karl. Once she'd started thinking about him, she couldn't stop. And when she thought of him, her stomach leapt like a fish into her chest and her heart banged against her ribs, beating so hard against them that she hurt.

Chapter 20

Hannah didn't see Karl again for a while. And then, as she was walking to school one day, she spotted him outside a café near the station, leaning against a street lamp, smoking. She walked straight past him.

"Hey, Hannah!" he called out.

She turned. He dropped his cigarette and came after her. She watched the cigarette roll across the pavement, still lit. Then she carried on walking.

He caught up with her and pulled on her arm, half angry, half amused. The material of her cardigan stretched tight with his grip. "What about that kiss we talked about?"

She pulled her arm away. "Get off me."

"What's your problem?" He was laughing, his eyes lit up.

"Don't laugh at me."

"Stop being so unfriendly, then." He threw his arm over her shoulders.

Hannah shrugged it off and carried on walking.

"Hey." He was frowning now, the lines on his forehead deeper and darker. "What's up with you?"

Hannah stopped. She moved one hand over the other and back again. Then she put both hands behind her back.

Karl grabbed her wrist and forced her hand forward.

"Your palms are sweating," he said. He kept one finger on her hand and then moved it round in circles on her palm. "Do I make you nervous?" He grinned. "Expecting that kiss I promised? I'll bet you can't wait."

Hannah slid her hand from his. "I'm in a hurry, Karl."

"Where you going?"

"School."

"*Still?* Waste of time." He moved closer to her. "Come play with me instead," he breathed. His smell, sweet and alien, washed over her.

Hannah drew herself up, took a deep breath and looked him in the eye. "Yeah, and we all know what kind of playing that is," she said. Then she walked off.

"You know what?" he called after her. "Playing hard to get won't do you any favours! We all know what you need. Don't come begging for it any time soon!"

Hannah started running. By the time she reached school, her insides were twisted up and her brain was fizzing. And she was scared. She'd made Karl mad. What if he came after her and punished her for walking off? What if he came to find her at home and Jake met him? What then?

She was unable to concentrate in Mr Klark's maths lesson after that. She leafed through the pages of a textbook, the print swimming before her eyes. Mr Klark, having written out a series of sums on the board, left the room briefly. Hannah breathed in air laced with stale teenage sweat, while all around her, noise rose steadily until it reached a deafening crescendo; a crashing, crazy din.

"Oi, Hannah! Truth or dare?" Lise grinned, showing off the ugly gap between her teeth.

"Piss off, Lise."

"I vote truth. You going to shag Karl?"

"How do you know I know him?"

But of course she knew. Lise knew everything. "My mate Jase said you met. He said you were gagging for it. But I said, 'No, she's a frigid little cow.' Thought you were, until now. So when you going to shag him?"

"I'm not."

"That's a lie as well. So now she's got to do a dare, hasn't she, Kate?"

Her sidekick nodded.

"Dare you to go smash up Superman's chalk before he gets back. Go on – liven up the morning for us, why don't you?"

Lise and Kate giggled, waiting. Hannah hesitated. Suddenly she sprang up, walked over to the blackboard, grabbed fistfuls of chalk, broke them into pieces, and flung them on the floor. Just as she was grinding them underfoot while the others watched her, snorting with laughter, Mr Klark came back into the room.

"Hannah!" he thundered.

The teenagers hooted. Hannah stopped stamping and looked at the rows of faces that stared back at her – gloating, excited faces. She filled her cheeks with air, and then let the breath out in a snort. Mr Klark was sweating now; eyes popping out of his face. The classroom fell silent; the teens looking at their teacher, trying to suss out his next move.

"Right," he said. "You come along with me, Hannah, and explain your criminal damage and insolence to the headteacher."

A crowd of kids, headed by Lise, surged after them down the corridor.

Mr Klark turned on them and yelled, "Sit back down in the classroom!"

The headteacher was called Mr Morm. His nickname was 'Mr Moron'. He was an ineffective man – pot-bellied, with a high-pitched laugh that sounded like a mix between a cackle and a wheeze. No one was scared of him. But he was unpredictable, and Hannah had no idea what he was going to do now.

Mr Morm watched her with beady eyes. "So, wilfully damaging school property and disrupting the class, you say, Mr Klark?"

Mr Klark nodded. Hannah watched the headteacher. She was already beginning to regret her rash act.

Mr Morm appeared to be chewing his tongue and swirling it around his mouth. When at last he spoke again, it was as if from a great height, even though Hannah was at least a foot taller than him. "Do you have any idea how serious this is? Well, do you?" He sighed. "Hannah, your behaviour gives me little choice. There's only one way to teach you a bit of respect for this place and its property. And that's to deprive you of our company for a while."

He paused for dramatic effect. From somewhere behind her, Hannah heard the call of the school bell.

"You're suspended from school with effect from today. I don't want you to show your face here for two weeks."

Chapter 21

"*Two* weeks?"

Hannah winced. Jake spoke very quietly; far too quietly. He leaned over her, hands resting on the top of the chair near her head, breath warming her hair.

"What's up with you? Unable to concentrate? Been out and about too much, have you? Well?"

With each question, he cuffed one of her ears and then the other. Then he pressed down harder on the back of the chair; as if he wanted to send it crashing through the floor, and his daughter with it. Hannah held her breath. She waited. Every object in the room waited with her. Inside her head, fear swirled like fog.

"Stop." It was Hannah's mother who had spoken. And when Hannah turned to face her, she saw that her eyes were clear and still, suffused with light. "Leave her alone, Jake."

Jake fell silent. He stood, looking from Hannah to his wife and back again. Finally, he clutched the material of Hannah's cardigan where it touched the back of her neck, stretching it tight. The sound of the tearing material hurt Hannah's ears. He yanked her to her feet. "Outside!"

They stumbled out into the featureless backyard. Hannah could hear her mother's anxious step behind them. When Jake let go of her cardigan, she backed away from him against one wall of the cramped space.

Banks of grey cloud glowered down at her, moving slowly towards her. Hannah sank to her knees before her father, raising her hands up over her head. She waited. The seconds took an eternity to pass. Eventually, when nothing happened, she looked up. One of her mother's hands was resting on Jake's arm. It seemed as if they were barely touching, so light was its pressure. But as a finger may stop a pendulum swinging, so her mother's hand stopped Jake's movement and his arm hung motionless at his side. For a while Hannah watched her parents stand unmoving, barely touching but still fused together, and time seemed to slow to a stop. No one moved or spoke. At last, she scrambled to her feet.

She was almost at the back door when she heard her father yell, "Hannah! Come back!"

"Jake, let her go." Hannah was conscious of a struggle behind her, and then again she heard her mother's voice. "*Let her go.*"

Incredibly, Jake didn't come after her. She reached the back door and looked back. She could see her parents in the backyard, still standing together, her mother's hand still resting on her father's arm. At the front door, Hannah looked back along the hallway one last time. Now she could see Jake approaching her mother; his face, his hands moving towards hers.

Hannah didn't wait to see what he was going to do next. She flew out of the front door and into the street. She left the door open behind her, moving back and forth on its hinges, swinging in the breeze.

Chapter 22

She was never going back home, she told herself. But Sal wasn't picking up her phone, so finally, wearily, Hannah turned in the direction of Robert's flat, intending to stay there only a short while, until she could get hold of her sister.

She was only a short distance from Robert's place when she saw Karl. He was standing outside a pub, in the centre of a small group. Neon light from a nearby street sign flooded his face and the faces of those around him. Hannah moved faster. But just as she was passing the pub, it occurred to her that she was hungry, and so she hesitated for an instant, breathing in the thick, greasy smell of frying fat that came from the take away place next door, before moving on.

"Hannah!"

As she heard Karl's voice, another voice inside her head urged her on, and the two voices vied with each other until her head was so crammed with noise, she couldn't think, and so she stopped. Karl came towards her through the dark, and it was as if one piece of the darkness had detached itself from the whole and was travelling towards her. Hannah stood, waiting, until he drew level with her.

"Hello," she said, her voice small and flat.

The glowing tip of his cigarette lit up Karl's face.

"What are you doing here?"

"I left home."

"*You?* How come?"

Hannah drew herself up. "I'm sixteen now," she said. "I can do what I like."

"You got somewhere to go?"

Hannah thought of Robert. She hesitated.

Karl grinned. "You best come with me, then."

She opened her mouth to speak, but no words came out. Karl pulled her towards him and kissed her, his tongue moving into her mouth like quicksilver, in and out, leaving its fire to move through her. She leaned against him; felt him all around her, even though she could barely see him. Then she allowed herself to be led towards the loud, laughing group outside the pub.

"Look what I've got here!" Karl said, pushing her into the light.

Hannah, slightly dazed, faced the group. There were three of them, and she only recognised one – Jason. There were two girls, both a couple of years older than Hannah, with hair extensions and heavy eye make-up. Hannah blinked and backed away from them.

Karl pushed her forward again. "This is Jase. You remember him. And Sharon and Jules."

The girls barely acknowledged Hannah; they just looked at Karl. "Where did you pick her up from? The gutter?" one of them said. And then they both tittered.

Karl's good mood vanished as quickly as you could flick a switch. He pointed a finger at the girls. "Watch it, Jules," he said.

"Well, 'scuse me for breathing," the girl said, and turned her back on him.

"Where you taking her?" Sharon asked.

Karl looked at Hannah. "Home with me, I guess." And then he smiled his lopsided smile at her, and in spite of the fact that she was cold, tired and hungry, she smiled back.

The two girls lost interest. "What we going to do now?" Sharon asked. It was only then that Hannah noticed that she could barely stand. She wondered how long they'd all been drinking.

The group looked at Karl expectantly.

"Let's go for a drive," he said.

They surged towards a battered car nearby and piled in.

"I'll drive," Karl told them.

"You can't, mate," Jason said. "You've had too many."

"You telling me what to do now?"

Jason shrugged his shoulders and moved around to the passenger side of the car.

Karl got behind the wheel. "Okay, kiddos, ready for the ride?"

Jules and Sharon giggled. Karl started the engine, kicking the car into reverse, forcing it backwards, and then braking suddenly and changing gear. The car spun to one side, leapt forwards with a screech of tyres, and hurtled through the night. In the back, amid the smell of leather and gin and cheap scent, Hannah closed her eyes and prayed. Beside her, she could hear the squealing of the two girls.

After five minutes, the car stopped. All around her loomed blocks of flats, their windows throwing out squares of light into the darkness. Karl exited the car and lurched towards one of the blocks. He beckoned to the others, throwing one arm over Hannah's shoulders when she caught up with him.

They moved through a dark and grimy hall and up the stairs. Karl's place was on the second floor of the block. There, the party continued. More people joined them. The cramped kitchen was crowded with rapidly emptying bottles of booze, and drunk people. Smoke filled the corners of the small living room. People crushed together on the sofas and queued outside the bathroom, spilling drink on the floor, scattering tobacco from badly rolled joints. In the background, and sometimes in the foreground, thudded the bass beat of a single unrecognisable tune. A boy burned Hannah's arm with his cigarette. A girl dropped ash on her skirt. Occasionally, Karl pressed up against her, asking her if she was enjoying herself, then moved off before she could tell him that she wasn't.

Eventually, Hannah opened the door to a bedroom off the main room. She curled up into a ball on the bed, clutching her knees to her chest. Her mind spun nervously. She covered her ears with her hands. She could still hear Karl's voice in the kitchen, offering people one drink or another: different kinds of drink, but always more of it. She shut her eyes.

When she woke, it was dark, and the music had stopped. Hannah tensed, listening. She couldn't hear anything from the living room. But next to her in the darkness was the sound of breathing: measured, relaxed. She lay listening to it. Finally, tentatively, she put out a hand towards the breathing. It seemed to stop. Hannah held her own breath and moved her hand forward again. She touched the body lying on the bed beside her, Karl's body, and then moved her hand upwards until she got to his lips, exploring the softness of his mouth: the chipped tooth at the front, the raised scar tissue on its left side. She could feel his breath coming fast between her fingers, its heat fanning her. She moved her fingers up from his scar until she felt his eyelashes brush her skin and his eyes blink beneath her. Hannah shivered.

And then Karl moved towards her through the darkness, swift and silent, his breath hot on her face. The mix of pleasure and pain made her cry out as he pushed himself inside her, as he pressed his mouth hard on hers. She shifted to allow him deeper inside her and he moved faster, further, stretching her arms above her head, holding both of her hands with one of his, while with his other hand he held her face to his. And then he pressed down on her arms with his hand, and it hurt where he held her arms but not where he was pushing into her. She moaned into the darkness.

Karl shuddered, his breath coming out in a hard rush. Hannah tried to move him further into her then, but he drew away, and it seemed as if there was a vast space between them in the bed. Neither of them spoke. Hannah turned towards him, unfinished, her body a question mark hanging in the air, but after a while, he fell asleep, and once again the warm air was filled with his breathing.

It was as if nothing had happened; as if she'd dreamt the whole thing. But she knew that she hadn't; that something *had* happened, bigger than anything that had happened to her so far. She lay there for a long time, unable to sleep, listening to Karl's steady breathing and the swift beat of her own heart.

Chapter 23

It was a dark day, late in November, and the windows of the café in which Hannah and her mother sat streamed with condensation. Outside it was snowing – great, fluffy white flakes – but the snow wasn't sticking, and the pavements were slick with melted slush. Inside, the air smelled of bacon frying. Hannah felt warm and comfortable – she wanted to stay there forever, sitting with her mother.

She had only seen her mother a few times since she'd started living with Karl. Of course, she was old enough to do as she pleased. She had already left school. She'd been home only twice since, both times to pick up some things, having checked first that her father wasn't around. Each time she'd been terrified that Jake would appear and try to make her stay. Or that he'd come round to Karl's house at any time and make her go home with him. Her mind was shot through with vivid imaginings of a violent altercation between her father and Karl; her stomach constantly in knots. But Jake had never appeared. In spite of his show of control, it seemed he was happy she was gone.

Things were all right, Hannah told herself – better than they had been at home. She couldn't come and go as she pleased because Karl always wanted to know where she was and whom she was seeing and she didn't like having to lie to cover her tracks. But she had become accustomed to it, and it wasn't so bad, even if she did feel a little lonely at times. Yes, Karl's place was better than home, far better, because she got to be around him, and he made life seem less safe but more thrilling at the same time. Whenever he came near her, she felt this mix, and it was intoxicating. She smiled and shifted in her seat.

Hannah felt relieved that her mother seemed unchanged. Hannah's life might change – must do so, in fact – and yet, selfishly, she wanted her mother's to remain the same.

Her mother watched the snow outside as it turned to sleet and then to rain, and then she turned to her daughter. "So, how are things with you?"

"Okay."

"Only okay?"

"More than that, I guess." Hannah shrugged her shoulders, as if the words meant nothing to her. How could she explain to her mother how she felt? That feeling of falling, always falling, in spite of herself, as if she were being pushed down a smooth surface with few footholds or sent spinning on a glorious ride? Of loving without knowing why, but just revelling in the act of loving, and everything being greater and more magnified as a result? There must have been a point – following their first meeting at the party in King's Cross, perhaps – when she could have stopped herself falling for Karl, but she didn't really think so. And liking didn't come into it; oh, no. She had decided that you must love without knowing why, with everything mixed up and upside down and crazy and just one thing being clear, and that was that you loved.

Her mother put out one hand and stroked Hannah's arm. "You look a little thin," she said.

"I always look that way, don't I?"

"Your dad is most upset that you're not at school any more."

"He can't make me go now, can he?"

Her mother hesitated, swallowed tea. "Diana called the house."

"Right." Hannah really wasn't interested. Her friendship with Diana seemed such a long way off now, and her relationship with Robert even further. "How is she, anyway?"

"She's doing a media studies course at a sixth-form college. Oh, and she's got a boyfriend."

Hannah snorted. "I'll bet that's John. He's so dull. I can't imagine…" She flushed; stopped herself just in time.

"Hannah…"

"Oh, come on, Mum. I knew him at school!" Hannah laughed; a short, nervous laugh.

Her mother shook her head. She stared at some distant point, the space behind her daughter, as if trying to recapture some faraway thing and bring it back to her. "And what about this Karl?" She paused. "Sal tells me there was some violent incident at a fairground.

That he was involved. Was the instigator, in fact."

Hannah's cheeks burned. "Sal shouldn't have told you that. Don't you get it? She's just jealous."

"Did it happen, Hannah?"

"Yeah, but who cares? *I* don't. And you can't talk, anyhow."

Her mother winced. She lit another cigarette, her eyes flicking back to the distance. "You okay for money?" she asked finally.

Hannah shifted. There never seemed to be enough money, what with the number of people who got drunk around the place, and Karl not letting her get a job, and his own hunt for work being so up and down. She hated acknowledging their cash shortage to herself, let alone to her mother. But the need for money was too great, like a craving for a drug. "No – money isn't okay," she admitted finally.

Her mother reached into her pocket and took out a bundle of soiled notes. She pushed them over the table. "Here. That's for your birthday. Buy yourself something nice, won't you?"

"Thanks, Mum." Hannah stuffed the money in her pocket. She wouldn't show the cash to Karl. She'd have to keep it for food and light bulbs and loo roll and depressing, boring stuff like that, but her mother didn't need to know that.

Her mother hesitated, as if she wanted to say something but wasn't sure how.

"What is it, Mum?"

135

"I know… home wasn't perfect…"

Seeing her mother struggle, Hannah felt a sudden rush of tenderness rise in her throat, almost choking her. "It wasn't that bad."

"I know your dad's got a temper, and I know that you think I don't know about Diana's mother…"

Hannah looked up, startled.

"I might be a fool but I'm not blind." Her mother paused. "But what I'm trying to say is that I love you, Hannah, and your dad loves you, in spite of everything, and home *is* home, and if you want to come back…" She cleared her throat. "If you *need* to come back, then you can. There's a place for you. There'll always be a place for you. And I know right now you're with… Karl," she stumbled over his name, "but if for any reason things don't go right with him, then you can always come back. You know that."

She looked at Hannah, waiting for her to speak. But Hannah stood up, so that she seemed to tower over her mother, and in that moment she felt strong and sure, and utterly invincible.

"Thanks, but no," she said firmly. "Things aren't going to go wrong with Karl. And even if they do, I'm not coming home. Not ever." And she turned away from her mother and walked swiftly through the café, and out onto the freezing, sodden streets.

Chapter 24

With her mother behind her, Hannah headed for Karl's place, rushing towards the bus stop and then from the bus back to his flat. As she ran towards Karl, a sense of loss seemed to permeate the air around her, and she breathed it in, and it filled her with sadness.

She ran up the steps to the flat, her heart sinking slightly when she reached the door and realised that she didn't need to turn the key; that Karl was in. She slipped inside and, having put away her coat, made for the bedroom, hoping that he wouldn't hear her.

"Hannah, that you? Come here."

She stopped. He was calling her from the bathroom. Slowly, she walked towards him.

He was lying in the bath, the pale length of his body almost suspended in the water, the dark hairs on his arms and chest standing upright. The coils of the cobra on his upper arm rippled under the water, its forked tongue flickered. "Where you been?" he asked.

Hannah stood, looking down at him. She hesitated. "With my mother."

"What took you so long?"

"I've only been gone a couple of hours, Karl."

"She tell you what bad news I am?"

"No."

"Yeah, right. She give you any money?"

Again, Hannah hesitated. Her hand circled the bundle of notes in her pocket. "No," she said.

"That's a shame. Because we haven't got any. And we're running out of supplies. Vodka, for a start."

"We'll manage." Hannah spoke more confidently than she felt.

He shifted in the water, his penis bobbing up and down as he moved, looking bald and exposed, like a small, pale fish. Hannah giggled.

"What you laughing at?"

"Nothing." She shook her head.

Instantly, Karl heaved himself out of the water, and the water rolled around the bathtub in great waves and spilled over the edge onto the floor. He shook himself, covering her with tiny drops. Then he moved towards her, and her stomach shifted with a toxic mix of fear and excitement.

Karl circled her with his arms. He placed both hands behind her back, pulling her towards him. "Hannah?"

Water soaked through her shirt, making her shiver. "What?"

He moved his face closer to hers so that his breath hit her mouth. Then he kissed her. He leaned into her; she could feel his penis hardening, pushing against her.

"What?" she whispered.

"*Don't. Ever. Laugh. At. Me.* Understand?"

She nodded. He moved his hands up her skirt and pressed them against her thighs, water trickling down them. He pushed her up onto the basin. The hard enamel pressed against her legs. Then he moved one finger inside her, sliding it around her soft insides, while his other hand pressed into her hip. Hannah caught her breath and moaned, and leaned against him, her legs shaking against the side of the basin.

"There," he murmured. "You like that, don't you?"

He continued stroking her, moving further up into her. She caught her breath, pushed against him, moaned again. She could see herself in the mirror by the sink: dark head thrown back, small breasts rising and falling. But her face was indistinct, obscured by steam. She was close now... and closer. She gasped, leaning into him. Karl knew what to do instinctively. And he got better with practice. But just as she tipped over, her insides contracting against him, he pushed up further, deeper, too far, too deep, stabbing her with his finger. Hannah gasped, crying out, and the pain was a bitterness washing through her.

"That's for laughing at me," Karl said. He stabbed again. "And that's for sneaking out and not telling me where you were going."

Hannah slipped from the sink and stood slumped against it. She felt a wetness between her legs. When she put her hand there and took it away her fingers were red.

She remained in the bathroom after he'd left, until she heard the front door slam, and then she moved to the bedroom. She lay there for a long time, curled up, unable to sleep, eyes wide open and unblinking.

Hours later, she heard the door open; footsteps approaching the bed. Karl's breath was ragged and uneven. She heard his boots hit the floor, then a struggle with the clasp of his belt, cursing under his breath. He sank into the bed next to her. He'd been drinking: fumes radiated from him, saturating the air around them and making her head spin. Hannah kept her eyes closed.

Karl reached out one arm and shook her. "Hannah? You awake?" His voice was low and coarse.

She turned from him. "Leave me alone, Karl. You know I hate it when you drink."

He moved over to her, his hand cradling her head and then moving down. "I'm sorry, Hannah. You drive me crazy; you do… I'm so sorry. Let me make it up to you."

His fingers caressed her thigh; his touch so gentle she could barely feel it. She tensed as he moved his fingers across. But he persisted, moving against her again, stroking, rubbing and stroking, softly, gently, so that finally Hannah's body relaxed. She twisted away from him, but she could feel her body betraying her, while her mind clamped down, preventing the release. Until Karl bent his head, kissing her breasts, then further down, moving into her with his tongue. Hannah came quickly then, in short, uneven sobs.

Afterwards Karl buried his head in her chest. "Hannah, I love you. Can you forgive me? Darling…"

She laced her fingers through his hair, and then moved her hands against his temples, rubbing them over his forehead and then down and over his back. She sighed. "I love you too." And she shut her eyes and waited until he slept against her, as she continued to hold him, tears falling down her face in the darkness.

Chapter 25

Hannah opened the plain brown envelope addressed to her in her mother's handwriting. Inside was an invitation on thick white card, with gold edging and raised black lettering. She flicked it over and then back, and then sent it spinning over the kitchen table to rest among the stained glasses and the dirty mugs filled with greying tea. She twisted her own mug of tea around in her hands, warming her fingers on it. It was cold in the flat, and the kitchen was filled with white light that highlighted the dirt on the floor and surfaces and the piles of washing-up.

Karl had got a new job at a warehouse, working shifts, heaving boxes. He'd been in a brighter, lighter mood ever since, and that meant that he'd stopped hassling Hannah about money, about her whereabouts, and she could pretend that the few times he'd hurt her hadn't happened at all. She'd also noticed that he'd been drinking less, though sometimes she wondered if that was just wishful thinking on her part. He'd leave her alone for a couple of days at a time, barely speaking to her, just working, and then coming home, washing, eating, and going to bed. She was conscious of a guilty kind of relief when he did this; a feeling which had never been present in the early days of their relationship, but had crept up on her, slowly and stealthily, since.

When Karl came in, he picked up the invitation from the table. His fingers left dirty marks on the white card. "What's this?" he asked.

"An invitation from Diana, my old friend from school. She's having a party to celebrate her engagement."

"Your posh friend? Why didn't she invite me?"

"I'm not sure she knows we're together. Don't worry – I don't want to go anyway," Hannah added quickly.

"We can both go."

She hesitated. "You wouldn't like it."

"How do you know what I'd like and what I wouldn't? We can both go, I told you. Or – fuck it – go on your own. See if I care."

"You wouldn't want me to."

Karl turned to her. He opened his mouth as if to say something, and then stopped. He shrugged his shoulders. "You want to go, then go, Hannah."

She looked at him, trying to read his mood. He moved closer. There were dark stains on his T-shirt and streaks of dirt on his arms. He moved even closer, and she could smell his sweat, sweet and dark.

"Go, for fuck's sake. Jesus – I know you want to!" he yelled.

Hannah winced and backed away from him.

"Do you have to ask my permission every time you go out? God, I'll be glad to get rid of you for an evening. Hanging round my neck all the time like a noose, you are."

Hannah swallowed hard, blinking back tears.

"I'm going to take a shower," Karl said.

The night of the party, Karl left around six, telling Hannah that he would be working until the early hours. She figured he wouldn't notice if she was gone for a short while. But even so, she was still nervous about going. She stood in front of her clothes, piled together in a messy heap, picking over them unhappily. She had almost forgotten how to dress; she tended to pick out only the garments Karl said he liked. In the end, she found a pale green dress which brought out the colour of her eyes; one that she'd borrowed from Sal a very long time ago and never returned. She combed her hair and put on a bit of mascara and lipstick. Then she slipped out into the night.

The party was in a large stucco-fronted house in Pimlico; white as a frosted wedding cake and at least five storeys high. On the front door hung a large holly wreath, its leaves glowing in the light from the porch. Through the glass Hannah could see the moving, coloured shapes of the guests.

Diana answered the door. Her hair had been curled, making it seem thicker than usual, so that it fell over her shoulders in a twisted, shining mass. Her dress – blue velvet, low-cut – stopped just below her knees, and round her neck a single large diamond swung on a thin chain. For a moment, the two girls stood several feet apart, staring at each other, Diana framed against the light and Hannah in the darkness. Then Diana drew her friend inside.

"Hannah! How lovely to see you! I've been wondering how you've been getting on. Even your mother said she hadn't seen you of late. I'll take your coat. Oh – you haven't got one. You must be freezing."

"How's college life?"

"College is wonderful; I'm having a great time. I've made so many new friends." Diana looked guiltily at Hannah and then carried on. "And now that I'm eighteen, John and I are engaged. We haven't set a date yet, because we're quite young, but he wanted to demonstrate his commitment, so he bought me this." She extended her hand so that Hannah could admire the solitaire diamond that flashed on her finger.

Hannah felt as if her face were painted on, and trying to smile was like cracking through the paint.

"And here he is. John, come here!" Diana pulled a fair young man with a mottled complexion towards her. "You remember Hannah, my old school friend?" She flashed a smile at Hannah. "I'll just get you a drink, Hannah. A glass of champagne, perhaps?" She returned with a glass for Hannah, before floating off again, calling out to various acquaintances as she passed.

Suddenly overcome with shyness, after her mumbled congratulations, Hannah couldn't think of a single thing to say to John. The champagne was fluffy, effervescent – she could feel bubbles filling her insides. She suppressed an urge to laugh nervously.

John looked uncomfortable too, hopping from one

foot to the other, a shine breaking out on his forehead. "Haven't seen you since school," he said finally.

"What have you been up to?"

"Can't complain. Been working for my dad in his brewery. And business is good. Booming, in fact," he replied proudly. He opened his mouth as if to tell her more about it but thought better of it. "Of course, I'm lucky to have nabbed Diana. She really is the most wonderful girl. I'm so proud of her; with college and all that." He paused, twisting his glass around. "How about you? Working?"

"Not yet. But I'm starting a job soon."

"Jolly good. And what's that?"

They were interrupted by a girl handing out drinks, so Hannah didn't have to answer the question. She reached for another glass, watching money parade itself around the room: the immaculate clothes, the fine jewellery, and the tinny laughter that grew more expansive with the champagne. She felt like a child again, who presses her nose against the cold glass of a shop window, longing for the objects displayed within.

She had forgotten John in front of her, until he nudged her. "Here," he said, rather kindly, and handed her a handkerchief.

"Thanks." Hannah turned from him, embarrassed.

"Oh, there you are, Hannah! You've been monopolising her, John." Diana moved Hannah away and steered her towards the other guests. "Here's another face you must recognise."

Hannah stared at Robert. He seemed changed, but then she hadn't seen him for a long while. His hair was a shade darker and his face a touch thinner, and his limbs no longer seemed too long for him; everything about him appeared to have evened out, so that his clothes now fitted him properly. Seeing him, Hannah felt light and buoyant, the champagne coursing more swiftly through her veins.

"Robert!" She smiled. She noticed then how pale he looked; that around his eyes were sallow yellow circles. She wanted to ask him what was wrong, but she hadn't seen him for such a long time and shyness held her back.

He put both arms out to her. "Hannah – it's good to see you."

She couldn't look him in the eye as he held her, tilting her face towards his.

"You look tired, though," he told her. "How are you? Your mother told me you… you're living with someone…"

"And you're at university."

"At Newcastle, right. I just started there. I'm back for the Christmas holidays."

"How is your mother doing?"

"She's stable. The medication is helping a little, they say."

They were silent, staring at each other, while all around them the party swirled, happy voices trilled, and holly shone.

Finally, Robert took hold of Hannah's arm, steering her towards the hallway where it was quieter. "Hannah, is… everything okay? I'm worried about you." He gripped both her hands in his. "Do you need help… anything?" His voice was soft but insistent, and she felt the warmth of his hands spreading to hers. "I called your home…"

"I haven't been there. Not for almost two years, Robert." She shook off his hands and tried to laugh, but her laughter was empty, and she knew he saw through her. She stopped, looked down. "I'm fine, honestly."

"Who is this Karl?"

"How do you know his name?"

"Your mother said—"

"Well, she shouldn't have done. It's none of your business."

"I called her to check you were okay. I was worried. I *am* worried."

Hannah's head was aching now, and it was all Robert's fault. She wished Diana had never invited him to her party. Anger rose through her, and then it left and upset took its place. She looked at him, speaking slowly and kindly, as if to a child. "Robert, I've fallen in love. You must never have been in love, else you'd understand. It's not always easy; at times it's hard, but… but… it makes everything seem… more exciting. I'm not like Diana. I couldn't do what she's doing. I mean, John's a nice bloke and I'd love the money, but being married to him… well, I'd rather be *buried alive*."

Robert's face was impassive, inscrutable. And then something passed over it, unsettling his features. Distaste or disapproval, no doubt.

Hannah turned towards the party. "What's the point? You'll never understand."

"Oh, I understand. More than you think," he said quietly. Then he turned her gently back towards him.

Reluctantly, she faced him. Tears made her eyes shine. "What?"

"He doesn't... he isn't... like your dad?"

Hannah's eyes were green circles with massive dark centres. "Sometimes..." She dropped her voice. "Sometimes he's worse." And then she turned again to the party.

When, later, Robert offered to walk her home, she refused, and he left shortly afterwards. His eyes searched the room for her before he did, and when he saw her, he raised one hand. She should have been glad to see him go, but instead she felt bad, as if it were *she* he was leaving and not the party. A little later, she left too.

Diana showed Hannah to the door. She was swaying ever so slightly, and her words had a noticeable slur. "I'm so sorry that we haven't had much of a chance to speak properly, Hannah. But come visit. Not here, of course. This is John's parents' place. But come to our flat in Chislehurst. Any time." She flashed Hannah a smile, showing off her perfect teeth. But before she shut the door, she called to her, beckoning her back up the steps. "I wanted to talk to you about something," she whispered.

"What is it?"

Diana flushed. "It's a bit awkward, you know. But I'm not sure when I'm next going to see you. Only... John and I... we..." She leaned towards her friend; her pretty features all twisted up. "Can I ask you something?" she murmured. "I feel terrible admitting this, but the physical side of things... it's a bit... well, disappointing, to be honest. Maybe because he's my first. Well, almost my first; the first was... never mind. Only, I almost wish I hadn't had the comparison. I keep telling myself it doesn't matter so much. But still..." Now her eyes rested on her friend. "I know I shouldn't ask you how it is with Karl..." Her colour deepened, her eyes a question. "But is it good?"

Hannah bit her lip. "Yes... it can be..."

Diana nodded. "That must... make up for a lot, don't you think?"

It was Hannah's turn to blush. "I don't know, Diana. Honestly, I don't know."

Her friend seemed reassured by this, because her voice resumed its usual perkiness. "Come see me, Hannah. Any time." And she squeezed her friend's arm and sent her off into the night.

Chapter 26

Karl rolled off Hannah and lay back on the crumpled, twisted sheets. The stillness of the room settled upon them.

They'd been holed up together in the bedroom for two days, and the real world – the world of work and money and such mundanities – had ceased to exist. But now, after forty-eight hours, Hannah was sick of the room with its stained walls and grubby sheets. Her body ached where Karl had pulled her around and up and back. Often he'd thrust into her from behind, which was what he liked most: the brutal anonymity of it. And even now, as Hannah lay back in bed thinking about that, it brought a blush to her face: the way he did it, bending her over and spreading her open, then pushing himself into her. Sometimes it felt as if he wanted to split her in two, and she'd cry out – and then he'd smother her mouth with his hand, and it hurt but then it didn't, and it was a good kind of hurting. In spite of herself, she'd arch back into him. And afterwards there was aching, even a bit of bleeding, but she felt fuller of him than she'd ever been, as if at last she could lose herself in him.

It had been Karl's decision to shut them both up in there. He wanted to get her pregnant, he said, and she told him she wanted it too, but a part of her, that she hid from him, didn't want it at all; was afraid that he would then use it to keep her in the flat forever. She didn't tell him that she doubted she'd get pregnant anyway because her periods seemed to have stopped altogether, and not for that reason. She'd been to the doctor, and he had done some tests and confirmed that she wasn't pregnant. He'd noted that she was a little too thin, but he hadn't been able to find anything else wrong, and finally he'd said that this could happen when a woman was anxious, and he'd looked at her with a face that seemed to have soaked up some of that anxiety and asked her what she was anxious about. And she'd just looked at the floor and hadn't said a word.

Hannah thought about all this as she lay next to Karl, and then she thought that it didn't matter, none of it mattered, and so she pushed it out of her mind; tidied it away. But the moment she'd done that, another, more pressing worry came to the surface; one that she couldn't let go. Money. Only two weeks ago she'd realised that they'd run out of soap and toothpaste, and as she had no spare cash left, she'd been forced to nick both from the corner shop. She'd felt adrenaline flood her veins as she'd lifted the goods from the shelves. She'd seen her pasty face distorted by the globular mirror above her head that shone down on her like the moon; a silent witness. But she'd got out without incident that time. Then four days ago, she'd gone again, for bread and baked beans, and that time it was even worse. A cold sweat had soaked her as she'd left the shop, and she'd had to run and hide. She'd stood in an overgrown alleyway near the shop, drawing on a cigarette. She'd been pretty sure that the shopkeeper had seen her nicking his stock but had pretended not to notice. She didn't know if there could be a third time. She didn't think she could do it again, so she had to raise this with Karl.

Karl was sleeping. He seemed less intimidating with his eyes closed. But still, Hannah felt her stomach bunch up as she leaned over him.

"Karl?"

"Hmm?" He opened his eyes, bleary with sleep. "What is it?"

"I think... I need to get a job. We... I can't go on... with no money. It's too hard for you. It's not fair."

Karl sighed and turned on his side, away from her. "Hannah, didn't I tell you? I don't want my girl going out working. *I* can look after you. Don't you ever listen? Are you deaf or something?" With each question his voice grew louder and louder, the words reverberating around the room, bouncing off the walls.

Back down, Hannah told herself, but she couldn't. She just *couldn't*. "I think I should, Karl. And if I did, we could go out more. You could buy more things for yourself—"

"You don't have any skills, Hannah. You can't type; you know fuck all. *Fuck* all. How you going to get a job?"

Inside her, knots were thickening and tightening, as if someone were pulling at them, drawing them together.

"Can't I at least try?"

He glared at her like he was going to pull a knife on her.

She felt as if she were sliding downhill fast. "Please?" The knots knitted themselves up still further, but still she couldn't stop. "Karl?"

Then it was as if something inside him exploded, and he hit her, and the knots inside her seemed to undo themselves and her whole body went limp like a doll's. He told her afterwards – when she was crying and he was hugging her – that he was sorry, but he said over and over that it was all her fault.

And perhaps it was, she thought later. It could have been prevented. She shouldn't have pushed him. She'd have to learn not to push him too hard, too quick; else, as he often told her, she'd find out the hard way.

Chapter 27

Eventually, Karl did allow Hannah to get a job. When his job at the warehouse fell through and they ran out of booze and had no money to buy more, that's when he capitulated.

The day Hannah was due to start work at the checkout tills in a local supermarket was mild and sunny. All around her she could feel spring gradually revealing itself, like a shy young girl. The new grass by the road was pale and fresh, drops of dew still clinging to it. Trees were slowly unfurling their leaves, spreading themselves to the sun. The air smelled of growing green things. Hannah herself felt brighter than she had in days. She raised her face to the sun as she walked, like a frail flower which had just crept up from the dark earth.

At the shop, she made herself known to the supervisor – a round, cheerful woman with heavy jowls and dimples. "We'll get you sorted on the system and then you can start right away," she told Hannah. She pointed to a girl with honey-coloured skin and a mass of golden hoop earrings that gleamed and shifted in the light. "That's Della over there. You watch her for ten minutes and you'll soon learn what to do."

Della's fingers moved quickly and efficiently over the till. Her nails were long, curved like talons, and painted metallic blue. Hannah couldn't help staring at them, until finally Della asked, "What you staring at?"

Hannah told her that it was the nails.

Della grinned; a slow grin that lit up her face and flared her nostrils. "You like them, honey? I'll bring you some in if you like. They're fake, though. Stick-on made to look like acrylic, but don't say I told you so. My husband thinks they're one hundred per cent kosher. He'd die if he found out." She smiled and carried on ringing items through. "You got a husband?"

Hannah shook her head.

"A boyfriend, then?"

"Yes."

"He good-looking?"

"Oh, yes."

"He good to you?"

Hannah hesitated. "Sometimes," she said.

"Sugar, that's not enough. You've got to make sure he's good to you all the time. You hear me? *All the friggin' time.*" Della grinned again. "You want to try?" she asked, gesturing at the till.

A grumpy-looking woman came in and bought some bread and a bottle of gin. Hannah ran them through. It was easy. The easiest thing she'd ever done. She turned to Della, smiling.

"Is that it?"

"Sure is."

"You don't get bored?"

"I just think of the money. And that makes it all better."

Hannah followed suit, and when she got back to the flat that first day, she was in a good mood; a better mood than she'd been in for ages.

It was like that for one week. Then, the following week, as she'd promised, Della did Hannah's nails during their lunch break. She painted them the colour of spring grass, and on each thumb she painted a white daisy. The smell of the nail polish reminded Hannah of Sal; how she used to paint their nails at home, and the music they'd listened to while they dried. Hannah hadn't seen so much of her sister of late – Sal had invited her over to Maeve's many times, but Hannah had only felt able to go occasionally. Karl made it difficult for her to leave the flat, so she'd not seen Sal that often since she'd been going out with him. She told herself that Sal was jealous, but deep down she knew she wasn't. She just disapproved of Karl. And Hannah wasn't in any rush to be interrogated by her disapproving sister. She wasn't sure her relationship with Karl would stand up to Sal's scrutiny.

After Della had finished with the nail polish, she nodded, and her earrings shook and shone. "Like the colour, honey? It brings out the green in your eyes, don't you think?"

Hannah smiled. All afternoon she admired her nails as she watched her hands move around the till, and the knots in her stomach relaxed.

Karl wasn't in the flat when she came back, and Hannah sat waiting for him in the gathering gloom. Eventually she heard the front door slam, and then footsteps in the kitchen, the fridge door open and then close again; a bottle open with a clunk. She came into the kitchen, and watched Karl lift the bottle to his mouth and tilt his head back. She watched his hair fall back from his face, and his throat move as he swallowed. She started to tell him about her day then, but he didn't respond so the words dried up. Soon the monotonous drone of the television was sucking the life out of the room and into its small, bright screen.

Hannah wanted to disappear and go to bed. But just as she was sliding like a shadow along the side of the television, Karl said, "Come here."

She came towards him, slow and hesitant. She didn't want to be in the room with him. She would rather have been at work, or even at home with Jake. Anywhere but there.

"Show me your hand."

She tried to move her hand away, but Karl grabbed it and pulled it towards him.

He bent one finger right down towards him. "What are these?"

"Nothing. Just nails. Della did them."

Karl pressed down on one of the nails. "Who's Della? Some new friend at work? You don't have any friends, Hannah." As he spoke, he broke off the nail.

The pain made Hannah catch her breath.

"They're ugly," he continued, as he broke off another nail, "and they make you look even uglier than you do already." And he continued to snap off the nails until all of them had come off.

When he'd broken the last one, and the floor was covered in pieces of plastic, Hannah backed away from him, sucking the ends of her fingers. He got a look upon his face then, and she thought he might hit her again, even though she'd been so still and small and quiet around him these past few days, she didn't see how he could. He didn't. He made as if to come after her, and then thought better of it and sank into the sofa instead.

Afterwards, once she'd realised that he wasn't going to do it, not that time, she wasn't even glad. She just felt wash over her an exhaustion so deep that her knees were weak with it. It occurred to her then that she was tired; sick of the fear that he might do it, and the telling herself that she'd have to leave if he did. And tired, too, of the relief when he didn't do it and she didn't have to leave after all.

Chapter 28

The next day, Della asked about the nails and Hannah said that she didn't think they suited her. She knew that Della was wondering what was up because Hannah looked so nervous and her nails were so sore, and she was biting them all day long, which made them worse.

But when Hannah started getting into work late every day after that, and once with a black eye, Della came to her and asked her straight up what was wrong. Hannah told her she'd tripped going up the stairs, stumbled, and caught the edge of her eye. She couldn't tell her that Karl had lashed out at her again; that she felt guilty leaving him in the mornings, which was why she was late. That he seemed to hate it when she did leave, and so she'd linger and let him delay her, peel off her clothes as she struggled out of bed, pull her back to him. And that when she finally got to work, all she could think about was the fact that he hated her being there, and that was why she was so restless. At first, she'd tried to think of the money, but after a bit she couldn't do that; she'd just think about Karl, and then the guilt and anxiety would come back.

Things continued like this for a while, and then one day a well-dressed woman came up to Hannah's till. "Anyone in there? I said I'd like a plant bag," she said after Hannah had rung through her items. She shook an ugly purple plant at her.

Hannah flicked her hair back, eyes glazing over. It seemed a huge effort to pick up the bag. "Sorry. Here you go." She handed the bag across to the customer.

The woman barely managed to fit the plant into the bag. She gave Hannah a tenner. "Could I have some small change with that?"

"Change?"

"Yes, if it's not too much trouble."

Hannah handed the woman her change.

"That's not enough."

"It's correct, I promise."

"No, it isn't."

"Yes, it is."

"You calling me a liar?" the woman demanded.

Hannah looked at the woman: at her lips that were all puckered up, the lipstick bleeding into the corners of her mouth; at her tightly permed hair. Suddenly she hated her, with a hatred that was thick and dark and strong. She drew herself up. "Yes, I am."

"*What?*"

"I gave you the right change. You saw it. So you can go..."

"Go what?"

Hannah sighed. "Go away," she said in a small voice.

Ten minutes later, the manager called Hannah into her room. The room was small and stuffy and smelled of mould. On the desk, a garish vase held a bunch of plastic flowers. When the manager shook her head, the loose folds of skin beneath her chin shook. "I can't have you behaving like that. You've had a few warnings already about your timekeeping. You've got to go, Hannah."

Hannah thought about Karl: how, though he couldn't hold down a job, it was one rule for him and another for her. He hated her working, but he liked the money she made doing it. She looked up at the manager with panic in her eyes. "You don't understand. My boyfriend... he is going to flip out."

But the manager just shook her head again.

Hannah left the store at two in the afternoon. It was windy out, and as she walked back, she felt as if the very act of walking was a struggle; as if she were forcing herself against the wind. At one point she stopped, and everything seemed to stop around her, and she could feel only the stickiness of the fear that clung to her. She stood for what seemed like hours while the wind made everything move around her. She stayed still until she knew that she simply couldn't face Karl; knew it with a knowledge that was part of the true order of things. And so she turned and, walking with the wind this time, headed off not to Karl's flat, but in the opposite direction, to another place entirely.

Chapter 29

Hannah came out of the cinema and lit a cigarette she'd stolen from Karl that morning. The small crowd leaving the cinema surged around her and down towards Leicester Square. The coloured lights in the square blinked and trembled in the twilight.

"You should quit," Robert told her, not unkindly.

"I only just started. You're just like my dad, always telling me what to do."

"I hope not."

"Surely you have a vice, Robert?"

"I think so. Well, it's not exactly a vice, but it may very well be my downfall."

His eyes shone at her, and Hannah looked up at him and smiled. She hadn't seen Robert since Diana's party and now she warmed with the familiarity of his features: his fine, crooked nose; his fair hair, which was longer than she remembered; his large, expressive eyes, more golden than green. "What is it, then?" she teased.

He smiled back. "I'm sure you can guess."

It had been Robert's idea to see the film. When Hannah had turned up at his flat, he'd asked her what was wrong, but she wouldn't tell him, and after a while, when she still wouldn't talk, he'd said she'd feel better for an outing and had insisted on the cinema. When he suggested the West End, Hannah was worried about taking the time away from Karl, but Karl was now working in a bar until late, and the Tube journey had been quick enough. And the film had taken her mind off Karl: sitting in that dark room, staring at the screen and the gorgeous faces and scenery, she'd been transported to a brighter, better world. But when the credits began to roll, that world faded and died and she was left with this one, and her disappointment at this hung in the air about her, like the smoke from her cigarette.

Robert held out Hannah's coat so that she could put her arms into the sleeves, and then wrapped it around her. The coat almost went around her waist twice. He smiled. "Just like *Breakfast at Tiffany's*. That last scene," he said, touching her arm.

Hannah felt the smile in his eyes playing over her face, and the skin on her arm respond to his touch. She wanted to lean into him, but she stopped herself.

"Shall we go eat?" he asked.

She bit her lip. After a while, she could taste the metallic taste of blood on her tongue. She hesitated, looking anxiously at her watch. "I really need to get back."

"Come on, let's eat."

"Robert, I *can't*."

But Hannah knew that Karl wouldn't be back yet, and so she finally let Robert steer her in the direction of Chinatown and a tiny restaurant with steaming windows. As they shared a bottle of wine, Hannah felt herself relax. Robert talked more than she did – about his university, his studies, his mum. She slurred her words more frequently now, and occasionally became breathless. She was always exhausted. Her sister, Robert's aunt, was looking after her while he was at university, but now he was home for Easter and working in a restaurant in the holidays to get some extra cash. He told Hannah about the bad habits of some of the diners. He made her laugh. She'd almost forgotten how to laugh.

When the bill came, Robert picked it up. "I'll get it. I'm earning now."

Hannah wanted to tell him that she was earning too, but after what had happened earlier that day it would have been a lie.

Robert took her arm as they walked out of the restaurant. He smiled at her. "I like taking you out," he said.

Hannah took in the traffic clogging up the vibrant Soho streets; the theatres with their coloured lights; the people in theatrical outfits, laughing, pouring out of teeming pubs. She wanted Robert to take her to his place, where it was quiet and safe. "I'd better go back now," she said instead.

If he was disappointed, he didn't show it. "Come to the park; let's walk a bit first."

Hannah let him lead her around the crowds in Trafalgar Square and down through Piccadilly Circus to Green Park. Just before they came to the park, they passed the shiny windows of the Burlington Arcade and Hannah caught a glimpse of the luxuries there: shimmering jewellery, piles of cashmere, small silver trinkets. They seemed so close that she could have reached out and touched them. Then they moved on into the park and through the avenue of great trees that crossed it, down towards Buckingham Palace. As they walked, they could hear the wind move the leaves above their heads, with a roar like that of a giant waterfall. Halfway down, they came to a bench. To their right, they could hear the muffled roar of traffic.

"Let's sit here for a while," Robert said. "Don't worry – I'll keep you warm."

He pulled Hannah close, so that her head rested on his shoulder. Neither of them spoke. Something stayed Hannah's tongue; kept her quiet through the chaos of the city. Then Robert pulled her face towards his and kissed her. She moved into him, remembering that bright afternoon by the pool, as the warmth from the kiss moved further down her and her blood rose to meet his. And then she didn't think at all. Finally, he pulled away. She leaned into him, wanting his kiss back, wanting that, and then more than that.

"Kiss me again," she whispered.

"Talk to me first."

She turned from him, eyes on the vast avenue of trees before them. In the darkness, their outlines were blurred, as if they were melting into the sky around them. "About what?"

"Karl."

"What about him?"

"He hasn't… touched you… has he?"

Hannah laughed; a brittle, sarcastic laugh. "He touches me all the time."

"You know what I mean."

His words felt like needles pressing into her skin. "You mean has he hit me?"

"Has he?"

She fixed her gaze on the trees. She could feel Robert staring at her. "No."

"I don't believe you."

In front of her, two children, a boy and a girl, were running around the trees. The boy was chasing the girl, and he was gaining on her now, and at any moment he'd catch her. Perhaps if she, Hannah, carried on speaking, he wouldn't. And then the girl would get away; she'd get away.

Hannah's voice rose. The wind took hold of her words, throwing them to Robert, making them seem louder and angrier than they were. "Stop hassling me. You're always hassling me. Why don't you just leave me alone?"

"Is that what you want? You just have to say it, and I will at least try."

Hannah burst into tears.

He pulled her to him. "I'd struggle to do that. I'm not sure I'm capable of it." He held her and stroked her hair until her sobs subsided. Finally, he spoke again. "Leave him, Hannah."

"I can't," she whispered.

"Hannah—"

"I *can't*. I've got nowhere else to go."

"Sal? Your mum? *I'll* help you."

Hannah shook her head. Calmer now, she turned away. The children had gone. She sighed. "If you want to help, you can stop hassling me. You're *bullying* me."

She regretted it the moment she'd said it, even before he stood up and moved away. It was the second time she'd seen him angry, and this time his anger seemed colder, and it left her feeling worse.

But all he said when she caught up with him was, "I don't know how you can call me that, Hannah, when you live with... what you live with..." The anger left his voice and it swelled with concern.

"We're not at school any longer, Robert. You can't rescue me from this one. All you can do is let me go back."

"Hannah—"

"You can't stop me."

He took hold of her arm.

She turned on him. "Let me go!"

Still, he kept her tight to him. Finally, in desperation, she scratched at his hand. He cried out, lifting it to his mouth.

Instantly, Hannah raised her own hand to her face in horror. "Robert, I'm so sorry." She put out a finger and touched his hand. She could feel the skin rising around the scratch.

He drew his hand away from her. He wasn't angry now, just upset, and that made her feel terrible. "I'm sure you've given Sal far worse. Come on, I'll drop you at yours."

"You don't have to."

"It's dark. I'll take you."

By the time they got to Karl's flat, the wind had risen further. It raced around the building, pushing against Hannah, pulling her back with it, beating the stunted trees on the street into submission with its breath.

Hannah looked up at the flat. There was a light on. She shivered. How could she have been out so long? Her heart thudded nervously. "I'd better go up," she said to Robert.

Then Robert was hugging her, and she no longer felt the wind or anything at all; only the length of his body pressed up against hers and his arms circling her and his breath in her ear. Warmth spread over her, and she moved into him. But he couldn't kiss her again – not here, not now – and the warmth was too much. And so she pushed him back. Inside her head she was screaming as she strained against him.

Finally, she hissed, "No!"

Robert let her go. "Call if you need me; if you're in trouble, right?" he whispered. "Any time." And he turned away.

Hannah shivered in the wind. She raised one hand

to his back in a conciliatory gesture, even though he couldn't see it, and then she turned and walked into the block of flats.

Chapter 30

Hannah trod the last stairs softly, hoping that Karl had already gone to bed. The light in the hall was so dim she could barely see the door of the flat in front of her – it was just a dark oblong fringed with light. She pushed against it, but it wouldn't move. She tried the lock, but her key wouldn't turn. And again, but still it wouldn't turn. Suddenly she wanted nothing more than to be in that flat with Karl. She banged on the door, leaning against it. "Karl!" she called. "Karl!"

No response.

She scraped at the door with her nails. "Karl, let me in!" She hammered again.

Suddenly the door swung open, and she stumbled into the flat. Before she could draw herself upright, she was flung against the wall, banging the back of her head.

Karl was in front of her now. He grabbed both her hands and raised them above her head, pressing her against the wall. "Where have you been?"

Hannah's head started to spin. "Nowhere."

"There was a man outside with you. I saw him."

"There wasn't anyone, Karl."

He pulled her left arm towards him and then twisted it behind her back. "Don't lie to me," he hissed. "Who is he?"

Hannah gasped. "A friend."

Karl took her chin in his hands and raised her head to his, bringing his mouth close to hers. "Liar," he hissed.

"Karl—"

He shook her. "Don't 'Karl' me!" he shouted. "That's the last time I let you out of my sight, you hear? Soon as my back's turned, you go sleep with the first man you meet!" He shook her so hard her teeth rattled, and her eyes moved back in her head. Then he reached around and overturned the coffee table. A glass hit the floor and smashed into bits.

She shut her eyes. "Karl, *please!*"

Just at that moment, the phone rang. Karl looked back towards the sound, distracted. He hated to ignore the phone. Hannah prayed he'd answer it. And he did. She leaned against the wall, panting. She had to move, and quickly. Karl had his back to her now. This was her chance. She turned and ran out of the flat towards the stairs.

Hannah heard a door slam and footsteps behind her as she reached the stairs. She ran down the first flight, and then looked back. He was gaining on her. She started down the second flight, but just as she got to the landing, she felt herself falling. Quickly she pulled herself up. Karl was moving towards her, but she was in the entrance hall of the block now. Just four more steps and she'd be out of there. *Four, three…* He reached out for her, missing her. *Two…* He missed her again. *One more. Just one.*

She'd done it. She hit the cold air and carried on running, out, out, and away from him, into the night.

Chapter 31

Hannah kept on running until she reached the end of the road. Only then did she look back. Karl had stopped moving momentarily. She could see his dark bulk silhouetted against a street light, like a black bull's against the sun.

"Hannah!" he yelled. He raised his hand to beckon her back, and the gesture seemed almost welcoming, though it was the same hand that had been raised against her a minute before.

She hesitated. The yellow street light seemed warm, even comforting compared to the darkness around her. Then she turned and ran, and her name was flung out to the wind and swallowed up by the dark.

She carried on running, fear driving her forward. She knew that Karl wouldn't give up. But her right knee was sore where he'd pushed her down the stairs; her left arm bruised and tender where he'd twisted it. It started to rain. Fearful that he would hear her shoes clattering on the pavement, she took them off so that her bare feet trod the streets noiselessly. Occasionally she would pass the glow of a street light, shining through the wet, making the faces of passing strangers gleam. Once she passed a group of girls, laughing and smoking. They looked around the same age as her, but otherwise different in every conceivable way.

Hannah reached City Road and stopped. She turned into a doorway and sank down to the ground, bringing her knees up to her chest and her head to her knees, listening to the drumming of her heart.

A woman with a kind face said to her, "You should be at home, love."

Gratefully, Hannah took the cigarette she offered and drew on it, blowing blue smoke out into the rain. Her body relaxed with the nicotine hit. It was raining harder now – a gutter near her had flooded, spewing up rubbish. People passed, some holding newspapers or plastic bags over their heads. It was as if the whole world were drowning.

Suddenly she thought she could hear Karl's voice calling her from some distance away. Terrified, she turned and hammered on the door in front of her. No response. She hammered harder. Still nothing. Karl called again. He was closer now. She flattened herself against the doorway, shrinking from the light of the neighbouring shop. He passed her, angry eyes peering into the blackness ahead of him; into nothing. Hannah headed down the street in the opposite direction and then took a left off it, onto another street. After a while, when she was sure she had given Karl the slip, she let herself into a phone box and with shaking fingers reached for a coin in her pocket.

"Hello."

Hannah could barely make herself heard over the music at the other end of the line. "I left Karl," she told her sister.

"What?" Sal yelled.

"Karl's awful."

"I told you so."

Hannah cut the call. She couldn't deal with Sal and her breezy superiority, not now. She thought instead of Robert and winced with shame. She couldn't face Robert either. His concern would be tempered with judgment, as it always was. She hesitated, and then she found herself calling another number, breathing hard as she imagined the phone ringing in the familiar space; her mother's slow, abstracted step as she moved towards it.

"It's me. Hannah."

"What do you want?" Jake's voice was as hard as a fist hitting her face.

Her mother took the phone. Her voice was softer. "How are you, sweetheart?"

"Ask her what she wants."

Hannah could imagine Jake slumped on the sofa, her mother next to him, the blue light of the TV flooding the room. "I left Karl," she sobbed.

Her mother's voice dropped to a whisper. "Oh, sweetheart—"

"Don't call her that!" her father yelled. "You spoil her rotten, that's what it is. That's why she's got herself into this mess in the first place."

Then her mother's voice, even lower. "Hannah, come home. You hear me?"

And Jake saying, "Give that thing here." A struggle at the other end of the line; her mother's fast, strained breathing; and then Jake yelling, "Hannah, you get yourself back here! You hear me? Now." A sharp click as the receiver was replaced, and then nothing.

Hannah was shivering and her feet were aching. At least her mother wouldn't judge, she told herself. She would understand. The rain was driving into her eyes, almost blinding her. She braced herself and, turning her face into the rain, headed home.

PART 3
CARLA

Chapter 32

Sal poked her shining head around the door. "Ready?" she asked her sister.

Hannah woke with a start. In her dream, she'd been running through undergrowth that was dense and lined with thorns that clung to and tore at her legs. Overhead, trees with knotted branches blocked out the sky. Someone or something was behind her, steadily gaining on her, crashing through the twisted undergrowth, crushing it underfoot. And then the crashing stopped, and she felt clammy fingers on her skin, arms wrapped about her in a suffocating embrace, and she was falling through darkness that was endless and terrifying...

It was Sal's voice that had broken her fall. And now, with difficulty, Hannah raised herself from her sister's sofa. She was shaking, her skin clammy and slick with sweat.

"What's up with you?" Sal asked, exasperated. "You can't go out looking like that."

Sal's hair had been swept back from her head with copious amounts of hairspray, so that it framed her face in a stiff, sticky mass. About her hung the scents of freshly applied nail polish and hand cream. Her face was heavily and quite skilfully made up: peachy-pink lipstick coated her lips; blue-black mascara covered her top and bottom lashes. Her skin was a light golden brown from numerous sunbed sessions, with only occasional patches of red and white where the strict tanning regime had not been entirely successful.

But Hannah was not looking her best after six months at home with her parents, interrupted by occasional nights at Sal's place. Her hair needed a cut, her skin was sallow, and even her green eyes, usually luminous, were dull and lifeless. It was as if she had reduced herself to her lowest level, as if only by doing so could she survive.

Sal didn't have much sympathy: not only was she having to share her wardrobe and make-up collection with Hannah, as she had abandoned at Karl's place the few belongings she had, but Hannah's state reminded Sal of their mother's, and that disgusted her. She simply couldn't understand how Hannah could have got herself into such a mess over a man. All men were losers, Sal thought, and Karl was the biggest loser of the lot. She'd told Hannah what she thought of him and yet she had gone out with him anyway. How could she be that dumb? She had even accused Sal of being jealous when she'd dared criticise the man. Hannah didn't know what was good for her, that's what it was. Like she didn't know that the best thing for her now was to get up, get dressed, go out and get drunk.

"C'mon." Sal dragged Hannah from the sofa and into the bathroom, making her sit down on the loo. She cleaned her face with wipes and her ears with cotton buds, and then applied foundation evenly, hiding the dark circles under her eyes with a smooth peach-toned mask. Then she covered her face with a heavy powder that made Hannah sneeze, made up her eyes using her new mascara, applied blusher to her cheeks, and finally fixed her lips, painting over their edges to make them seem fuller and coating the lipstick with a colourless lacquer which would, she said, keep the lipstick on, "in case you get lucky. Which isn't likely, but you never know. You may find a man who doesn't care for conversation. Come to think of it, that's not that difficult. Few of them do." She turned her sister to the mirror and admired her handiwork. "Brilliant," she said. "Now you can go and party."

Hannah looked at herself in the mirror. She looked garish, artificial, like a sick doll. She sighed.

Sal pushed her out into the night, double-locking the door and leaving her in the street while she went back to double-check that it had been locked.

Hannah breathed in the cool air. She felt curiously light-headed, as if the evening weren't really happening to her; only to the crowds around her who scurried about their business – a living, eating, breathing mass. The sky was a pale orange, lit by the lurid glare of the London lights. It didn't seem like the sky at all, just as the trees, which reared from the gloom, misshapen and monstrous, didn't seem like trees. She was unsure why she was out at all, until she remembered: it was her birthday and the purpose of the evening was to celebrate by going out and getting drunk.

"Hannah, what you dawdling for? *C'mon.*"

Obediently, Hannah followed Sal down the street.

Sal managed to find seats in a corner of the bar next to the club they were going to later. "Sit down," she told Hannah. Five minutes later she reappeared with two drinks covered with pink foam, and tiny parasols emerging from the froth. "Drink fast, Hannah. We don't want to queue up at the club too long."

As Hannah drank, a stealthy excitement stole over her limbs, dispelling the torpor that had kept them prisoner for days, making them feel freer and lighter.

Sal weaved through animated faces and returned with more drinks. "Here – you have the stronger one," she told Hannah magnanimously, passing her the drink that was a darker pink. "It's your birthday, after all."

Sal's generous impulses were always calculated, never instinctive, and yet at least she acted on them. That was something. Hannah warmed to her sister and to the run-down bar in which they were sitting, with its dishevelled clientele, while the drink spread its artificial warmth through her like winter sunshine.

"Good to see you relaxing for once," Sal said, looking at Hannah with relief, as if she were a mathematical puzzle that she, Sal, had at last, to her great satisfaction, cracked. "Jesus, you've been a pain recently. I've told you and told you. Don't you ever listen? All men are mean and shitty, just like Dad."

"Not all men," Hannah protested.

"Here we go. *All* men, Hannah. Why, who you thinking of? Don't tell me you're still hung up on that loser."

"No."

"You sure?"

"Yes."

"You don't sound it."

"I *am*." Hannah shivered, as she always did now whenever she thought of Karl. It had been months since she'd last seen him. He'd given up trying to come after her because her father had yelled at him whenever he called. Once he'd knocked on the door and Jake had opened it and punched him in the stomach so hard it had made Hannah (who'd been watching from the upstairs window) double over in sympathy. Certainly, it had given the neighbours something to talk about. But still, at times Karl's face appeared before her with a clarity that terrified her. Just that morning, in the bathroom after her shower, when the steam had cleared from the mirror she'd seen him staring back at her: eyes hard as stones; the scar to the side of his mouth rising like red wire from his pale skin. She'd had to clutch at the sink to stop herself falling over. But she didn't tell Sal any of this. With an effort, she smiled at her sister. "Robert's not mean and shitty."

"If you like that type," Sal sniffed.

"What type?"

"The type that's glued to their books all day long." Sal drained her drink and tapped her glass. "Mind you, you may be on to something there."

"What do you mean?"

"Well," Sal frowned; she was concentrating hard, for her, "I think he'd be quite good in that department... you know. Not too selfish. Maybe not selfish enough, in fact." She spoke like the expert she was – a girl who might not have known much about men, but who certainly knew all there was to know about sex.

Hannah almost choked on her pink drink. "Thinking of trying him out?"

"Why? You saving yourself for him, Hannah?"

"Hardly. Haven't seen him since Easter."

"Well, then."

"You going to follow him to Newcastle?" Hannah demanded.

"All right. No need to get so jumpy." Sal yawned, suddenly losing interest. "I've got better things to do with my time. Let's go."

They stood in the queue for the club, clutching their arms to their sides and shivering. The line was filled with wired teenagers; eyes fixed on the bouncers. All around them, people chewed gum, bickered and spat.

Finally, the doors of the club opened, and the crowd surged forward, sweeping Hannah and Sal past walls lined with leather, along an illuminated floor, and then through a set of doors onto the dance floor. Sal moved with determination through the mass of bodies to the bar, raising herself up using the rail that ran along the bottom, so that she was head and shoulders above the other clubbers. She got served quickly that way. She handed a tequila shot to Hannah, then bought two more shots and led her sister to some seats at the side of the dance floor. Lights swept over them. 'Fools Gold' was playing. Ecstatic faces were raised towards the light.

After a while, Maeve joined them. Another girl was with her – Shaz – and a boy called Mark, who had sunken eyes and a greasy forehead.

"Your hair's gone green," Hannah said to Maeve.

"Nah – still pink. It's the light playing tricks on us."

Shaz sat next to Hannah. She was wearing white, which the light had turned an unearthly glowing blue, the colour of an electric flytrap. "Nineteen. Congratulations. Still one year away from the downhill slide." She grinned, shaking her corkscrew curls.

"A toast to Hannah!" Sal called out, raising her glass. "Happy birthday, sis!"

"Happy birthday!" the others echoed dutifully and drained their glasses.

"Make a wish," Sal told Hannah.

"What's the point? It won't come true."

"Make one anyway," Shaz ordered.

"What shall I wish for?"

"We can't tell you that, moron."

Hannah was silent for a moment, looking at the

young people dancing, the shifting kaleidoscope of moving light, and then at the expectant faces around her.

"What did you wish for?" Sal demanded.

"Money. A lot of it."

"Cash!" they all chorused.

"Definitely won't come true now you've told us," Shaz told her surlily.

"Fame and fortune for Hannah!" Sal cried.

"I'll settle for fortune," Hannah laughed. "And a fresh start."

The group cracked their glasses together, drink spilling over the sides and down their hands as they drank. And Hannah looked at the circle of laughing faces, breathed in their fume-filled optimism, and was happy.

"Who's for a dance?" Sal asked. "C'mon, Maeve, Mark." She pulled them towards the shining dance floor. "Hannah?"

Hannah shook her head. Eventually, Shaz followed them with an apologetic little shrug. Hannah leaned back and watched the way Sal's body curved with a suggestive, pliant movement, swaying rhythmically in time to the music. She felt the evening fill with a fizzing energy, with hope and promise and all things that begin beautifully and go on and on without end. She shut her eyes. Light danced beneath her lids.

"Having fun?" The voice was low and melodic; pleasing, as if each word were a different note that the speaker was testing on some secret string, again and again, until the harmony came out absolutely right.

Hannah turned. There was a figure sitting behind her in the darkness. As she watched, the figure rose and a tall woman came into the light, her hair short but expertly shaped; her clothes tight-fitting, revealing more than they concealed; her body like a sculpture, so well defined each curve of flesh, each muscle beneath the skin.

Hannah stared at the stranger as a person might stare at an exquisite work of art. Every movement this woman made was precise, calculated. It was as if her whole body were directed towards a single purpose; one that was unseen and unchangeable, and that she had made completely her own. The woman saw her staring and smiled, moving away, to return with a drink.

Hannah tasted the drink. It was cloying and sweet and made her throat close slightly.

"Good, isn't it?"

"What's in it?"

The woman put her finger to her lips. "It's a secret."

Hannah found herself following the alluring tone of the woman's speech, and in doing so ignoring its content, so that, even if she had been told what was in the drink, she wouldn't have remembered.

"I'm Carla," the woman said.

She held out her hand. In spite of the warmth of the club, her hand felt cold in Hannah's, and the tips of her long fingers even colder. Twisted golden bracelets lined Carla's wrist and swung around it as she moved. Golden rings hung from her ears. Her lashes were false, and long like spider legs. Her skin was pale but her lips dark; a large gash in her face, like an open wound. Hannah couldn't tell what colour Carla's hair was because of the strange light in the club which, as a vampire sucks blood from flesh, sucked the vibrancy out of any colour there, distorting it and altering it entirely. Carla moved her face forward, exposing the parts of her that had been in the dark – the hollows beneath her high, finely delineated cheekbones; the defined ridge of her lips – so that everything about her came suddenly to life and her eyes glowed like those of a panther. The only part of her that remained in shadow was her deep cleavage. She rested one painted nail on the glass in front of her.

"You're Hannah, right?"

"How did you know?" Hannah asked.

"Some would call me psychic. But no: I heard you talking to your friends." Carla smiled, and with her right hand picked at the trim on her top. Hannah's eyes followed her hand, the delicate caress of her fingers. "You're the one who wants to earn some cash, right?"

"How did you know?" Hannah repeated.

"Again, I heard you talking." Carla's eyes moved over and through every part of Hannah, slow and appraising. "What do you do now?" she murmured.

Hannah shifted in her seat. She gripped its soft

material and began stroking it with her fingers, up and back, drawing comfort from it. "I've been doing a few jobs on and off: waitressing, bar work, so…"

"And what do you *want* to do?"

The question made Hannah panic. The dreams she'd once had were all childish fantasies; she didn't dare reveal them to Carla. And Karl had stripped her of her belief that she could do anything at all. Or her father had done before that. Or her mother. Perhaps none of them had. Perhaps it was her own fault. Sal seemed focused enough. She'd already finished her beautician training and had started work in her first salon. "I… I'm not sure," she said at last.

"But you know what you want, yes?"

For the first time since they'd met, Hannah sensed the slight accent moving through Carla's speech, beneath its undulating, musical quality.

"Yes."

"You know what I do?"

Hannah shook her head.

"Guess."

"I can't."

"I'm an artist."

Hannah gazed at Carla. She envied her self-possession. She seemed as powerful as a goddess, larger than life, able to exploit its rich possibilities that lay open to her, while Hannah felt small, worthless, as powerless in the face of her circumstance as an ant in the shadow of a giant foot. She sighed.

Carla leaned towards her. Her scent was rich and potent, laced with the bitterness of fresh sweat. "Come and model for me, then. I'll reward you handsomely in return." She smiled, displaying perfect teeth that glowed in the light. "Give me your arm."

"Sorry?"

"Your arm."

Hannah held out her arm. She felt Carla's hand grip it, fingers pressing down upon her skin, as Carla removed an ink pen from her bag and wrote her number on the underside of Hannah's wrist.

"Now you have my number. Use it."

Carla smiled at Hannah and then disappeared, and where she'd been sitting there remained only empty space, filled with nothing but the hypnotic beat of the club.

Chapter 33

Weeks went by. A constant restlessness needled Hannah. One afternoon she was at Sal's place, having been looking for work in the pubs nearby. Her job enquiries that day having proved almost entirely fruitless, she told herself that she'd try again the following day and turned on the television. She sat, watching a gardening programme, fascinated by the exotic blooms of different species of orchid, their petals curling over and around each other at night, tight as fists, then unfurling slowly, their dark hearts turned by the heat and light of the sun. Without questioning the impulse that drove her, she reached for the piece of paper that she kept in her purse, onto which she had transferred Carla's number.

The muted, breathy voice at the other end of the line seemed at once utterly alien and intensely familiar. "Yes?"

"Carla – it's Hannah. We met some weeks ago, remember?" Hannah couldn't understand why her voice was trembling. The hand that held the phone trembled too; one nervous finger tapping its side.

Carla invited her to her place that day, throwing out the invitation with a kind of studied carelessness, as if she wasn't bothered if Hannah came or not. But when Hannah said she would come, Carla laughed, and the laugh caught in her throat so that it sounded like a low, thrilling murmur. And to Hannah, her voice was as alluring as a siren's, so that when she finally left Sal's place, her feet beat the streets in time to its music.

Hannah turned left into Cleveland Terrace and so to the square that ran off it. She walked almost around the entire square before she came to Carla's building – white stucco that had seen slightly better days – then pushed at the door when the buzzer sounded.

Walking into the hallway made Hannah feel as if she were entering a cave – she almost expected to see stalactites hanging from the ceiling, or to find the walls covered with moss. In a recess on the landing were several houseplants, their leaves trembling slightly. From an unseen source to their rear, water dripped. Classical music drifted down the stairs: unfamiliar, sweet and tender, filled with longing. Hannah climbed the stairs and hesitated at the threshold of an open door, listening to the music coming from the space inside. Finally, she walked in.

A heavy floral scent drifted through the room she found herself in. The curtains were only partially closed, and through the gap filtered the late-afternoon light. In the shafts of sunlight, dust motes danced. On the walls were several paintings, all a mass of twisted, abstract patterns. Hannah thought she could make out female shapes depicted there, but they were distorted, mixed with strange symbols that jarred like dissonant notes. The eyes of a marble bust stared at her from one corner of the room. On a gilded plinth sat a cage, and in it a small black bird, with a dark beak. The bird was silent, its head cocked sideways, listening to the music which rose like the tide to fill the room, spilling through the open door and down the stairs.

Carla was standing in front of a fire that burned in an ornate black marble fireplace. Soft firelight fell on her face. She was wearing a dark velvet dress that clung to her curves. In one hand she held a glass; in the other, a cigarette; and, like the bird's, her head was cocked sideways. She moved towards Hannah and drew her to the fireplace. "Do you like my canary?" she asked, raising her voice to compete with the music.

"I thought c-canaries were yellow," Hannah stuttered.

"He's an onyx canary. Naturally very dark, just like this marble." Carla reached around and caressed the fireplace surround.

Hannah could feel her cheeks burn with the heat from the fire. She took a step back.

"It throws out quite a heat for a gas fire, right? The flame is supposed to be quite low – some annoying regulations, apparently – but I managed to get around those."

Hannah watched the fire twist and flare. Above the fireplace was a vast antique mirror with cloudy glass. Above that, the high ceiling of the room was covered with intricate moulded plaster.

Carla slipped away and returned with a glass of champagne. "Take this," she told Hannah. "And sit down." She pushed her down onto a hard chesterfield.

Hannah soon finished her drink, and Carla fetched her another.

"Close the curtains, please," she said, when she saw that Hannah was now standing and trying to look out. She adjusted the curtains slightly.

After two glasses of champagne, Hannah felt giddy. She leaned back on the sofa.

"Now you're starting to relax," Carla told her. "One more piece of music and we'll begin." The music she put on next was softer, sadder, more beguiling; surrounding her so that she seemed the embodiment of its sadness and its spirit. "You know what this is? It's called *D'amor sull'ali rosee*. It's Leonora singing, see? She's asking for Love to comfort Manrico, her lover, who is in prison. It's beautiful, hmm?"

Hannah nodded, but the truth was, the music made her so sad she couldn't bear it. She closed her eyes.

"Don't dare go to sleep. We haven't even started yet!" Carla laughed, and this time she didn't keep the laugh locked up in her throat, but released it, so that it filled the corners of the flat. The canary, agitated, hopped up and down inside its cage. "Another drink? But I *insist*."

She took Hannah's empty glass and pressed a refill into her hand. The last of the sunlight that had managed to filter into the room glowed with a rush of ecstatic energy before fading to nothing, and the music flared up gloriously and then softened, dying out.

"I'm going to arrange you now so that I can start to paint," Carla told her.

"Don't you need light to paint? It's quite dark in here."

"I prefer to paint in semi-darkness. Like Caravaggio. You know him?"

Hannah shook her head.

"You know very little, it seems. He was a very violent man, but a brilliant painter. Lean this way and put your arm here. And adjust your shirt a bit."

Hannah winced when Carla's fingers rested on her collarbone. They were cold, as they'd been in the club when they'd first met.

"I'm not going to hurt you," Carla whispered. Gently, she unbuttoned the first two buttons of Hannah's shirt, moving it back over her shoulders. She stepped further back and stood in front of her, frowning. "Maybe a little more."

"Shall I take it off altogether?"

"No, no, but just more buttons, if you're sure…"

Carla seemed confused, and that made Hannah more confident. She shrugged her shoulders. "If it's easier to paint," she said. She turned away from Carla and unbuttoned her shirt fully. She turned back, her small breasts partially visible.

Carla surveyed her critically. "You are a little too thin."

"Karl didn't mind it."

"Who's he? A boyfriend?"

At the mention of his name, Hannah shivered.

"You're better off without him, aren't you?" Carla's voice was low and musical.

Hannah nodded. When Carla said it, she almost believed it.

Now Carla moved Hannah's left arm so that it cast a shadow on her skin, and Hannah submitted to the rearrangement. Carla's fingers rested on the curve of her stomach. They now felt hot, and Hannah caught her breath. Carla drew away, disappearing to return with an easel and then busying herself with her paints. Soon the smell of paint filled the room, making Hannah queasy. Even the canary was quiet. Carla stopped talking, but while she concentrated she hummed to herself; a tuneless hum, like the sound of live electrical wires.

After a while, Hannah's limbs began to ache. It was difficult to keep the same position for such a long time. She could almost feel the push of blood through her limbs, and she longed to move with it. Her hair fell over one side of her face and tickled her cheek. She reached up and drew it back. Her arm tingled.

Carla stopped painting, a deep frown on her face. "I told you not to move!" she hissed. "Useless girl. How can you be painted if you don't sit still?"

"I'm not very good at sitting still."

Carla stood back from her work. "I've an idea. To

make you quiet."

"What's that?"

"That would be for another day. For now," she sighed, "I've had enough." She looked at Hannah. "I'm tired. You're tiring to paint."

Hannah was crushed. Tears started up in her eyes. "Does this mean...?"

"Does this mean what?" Carla was putting her paints away with swift movements.

"You... you're not going to pay me?"

"You think I'm going to *pay* you?"

"To model. You told me..." Hannah's voice faltered.

Carla looked at her in astonishment. "*Did I?* With what money? I'm an *artist*, Hannah. No, you'll have to do more than you've just done for me. Then I'll pay you." She moved over to Hannah, bending down to her. With one finger, she raised her head so that their eyes met. Carla's eyes were alight, but with what – amusement, anger, sympathy – Hannah couldn't tell. And then she smiled, and the pronounced curve of her mouth dominated her face. She moved her mouth down to Hannah's and brushed it with her lips. "Come model for me again. I'll make you feel beautiful, yes? Pay you a little. And then, when you're ready, I'll introduce you to Charlie. And Charlie, Hannah, *Charlie* will make you rich."

Chapter 34

The next time Hannah modelled for Carla, she unbuttoned her shirt without being asked to do so, and she managed to stay still for longer: for fifty-three minutes, in fact. She was scared to move, but in the end she became uncomfortable, as she'd done last time, and she allowed her head to tilt back.

Immediately Carla made an exclamation and threw down her paintbrush. It clattered onto the floor, startling them both. "You *must* sit still."

"But it's hard," Hannah protested. She hesitated. "You did say you had an idea to help."

A small smile played around the corners of Carla's mouth. "So I did." She moved over to Hannah, silent and stealthy, like a cat, and placed a hand on either side of her, staring into her eyes. "Let's try this," she murmured. And then she kissed her.

Through the shock, Hannah felt her body respond as Carla's tongue explored her mouth. The blood rose through her, though whether with heat or nerves, she couldn't tell. She gasped, drawing away.

"Don't move," Carla whispered.

She knelt in front of Hannah, her fingers playing along her neck and down over her breasts. Hannah's heart hammered in her chest, her eyes widening in shock. Her body tensed, her back arching slightly.

Carla looked at her and smiled. "I think you want more, right? You know I would never hurt you."

Hannah watched Carla scanning her face. She held her breath as Carla slipped her shirt down over her shoulders, and as the fingers of one hand moved over her stomach the other hand moved beneath her skirt, between her legs. She felt Carla's tongue on her nipples, her fingers slid inside her, stroking her softly at first and then with more pressure in an insistent rocking rhythm. Images of Karl flashed through Hannah's head, and her muscles tensed with the memory. She held her breath.

Carla paused. "Do you want me to stop?"

Hannah couldn't move; couldn't speak. It was as if Carla's voice were coming from a great distance away. Carla continued to work Hannah with her fingers, and the memories faded, and Hannah's mind went blank. She closed her eyes.

"I think you like it. Do you like it, Hannah?"

Carla's voice was a soft murmur, her laugh, low, musical. Hannah could smell her scent – its mix of sweat and roses. She held her breath, feeling her body flood with pleasure. Almost immediately afterwards, she rearranged her skirt, reaching for her shirt, suddenly overcome with embarrassment and shame.

Carla laughed, putting out one hand and snatching the shirt away before Hannah could pick it up. "I still want to carry on painting, Hannah. And I know now you'll keep still for me."

Hannah began to model for Carla two afternoons a week. She had to sit for hours at a time, trying and often failing to keep her body still, while letting her mind wander in time to the music. She'd sit for what seemed like an eternity until she started to ache all over; until finally she heard Carla say, "That's it," and she was allowed to get up.

Carla didn't touch her; not after that one time. Nor did she ask Hannah to remove any clothes. Once Hannah had finished modelling, Carla would feed her. Her food always tasted strange and smoky, and when Hannah asked what made it taste like that, Carla told her that it was the spices she used: the cumin seeds, cinnamon sticks, cardamom pods, coriander seeds. And Hannah sat transfixed, listening to the unfamiliar ingredients trip off Carla's tongue.

When Sal asked Hannah how her job hunt was going, Hannah didn't tell her about Carla; didn't admit to her sister that she'd found her trips to Carla's so distracting that the search had stalled. Instead she told Sal that she'd got a part-time job at a stationery shop in Central London. She was deliberately vague about its whereabouts, hoping that Sal wouldn't be sufficiently interested to seek her out, and she wasn't. Yet Sal was a little confused by her sister's changing appearance. For Hannah was looking far less angular; smooth layers of flesh covered her bones, making her look rounder and softer, as snow covers a stony landscape and softens and buries its imperfections. Sal couldn't understand why that would be so: Hannah couldn't be making enough money to afford fine food, and Sal in fact never saw her eat at all. The food at home no doubt hadn't changed: their mother had never been a great cook, and Sal was sure Jake had never so much as switched on the oven.

One day, when Hannah went round to Carla's flat, she was surprised to find that the easel wasn't set up in its usual place. She turned to Carla, puzzled. "Aren't you painting today?"

Carla shook her head. Then she took hold of Hannah's hand and drew her to face an antique full-length mirror in the hallway. She stood behind Hannah, a hand on each of her shoulders, caressing them. Hannah stared at her reflection in the mottled, rippled glass. Her cheekbones were less prominent now, and her eyes had lost their listlessness and were luminous once more.

Carla looked at Hannah's reflection too and smiled. "Better. A lot better," she whispered. She removed her hands from Hannah's shoulders and smoothed out her hair, which glowed with a soft sheen where the light hit it.

For the first time she could remember, when Hannah saw herself in the mirror, she no longer felt ungainly, awkward and ugly. For just one moment, she felt like a Queen. But then Carla moved away from her, and she was herself once more: Hannah – subject, slave to circumstance, ugly and ordinary.

Carla moved across the room and picked up her coat. She turned to Hannah. "Let's go," she said.

"Where?"

Carla didn't answer; she just walked out of the flat. Hannah followed.

Carla strode ahead. She led the way through the square, past its gardens where daffodils glimmered in the dark grass, and then across the main road, dodging the rushing traffic, then down a short alleyway, stopping at a period building at the end of it. She pointed to the steps down to the basement of the building. "Down here."

Hannah followed her finger. There was a door set in the basement wall of the building, a door the colour of gunmetal.

"You go first," Carla told her.

Hannah walked down the steps. They were coated in wet, with a light layer of green, slightly slippery, and she almost fell towards the door. "It's locked," she said.

"They're expecting us."

"Who?"

Carla didn't answer; she just knocked on the door. Her fist made a hollow, metallic sound, and the basement stairwell reverberated with it. They waited. Then they heard footsteps, the sound of metal ringing on stone, and at last the door swung open.

Hannah had to peer closely at the face that presented

itself to her through the gloom, to determine to which sex it belonged. Finally, she distinguished a male face that had once been ravaged by acne and that still bore the scars of the spots that had at one time raged upon it. The nose was prominent, the eyes sunken, and the mouth just a thin line on the lower half of the face.

Carla moved forward. "Thanks, Will." She turned and beckoned to Hannah, who was lingering outside, putting one hand on her arm to draw her forward, her touch gentle but insistent. Her voice undulated slightly. "Come in, my dear."

Will drew back into the darkness to let them in. The air inside the basement hallway was close and stagnant. As Hannah followed Carla deeper inside, her steps faltered. They had stepped into a large, cavernous room with walls of exposed brick that were encrusted with limescale and dripping with moisture. The room seemed dank and unsavoury, rather like a dungeon. In the middle was a bar with strips of neon light above it that lit up rows of glass bottles and the liquids they contained, so that they shimmered and shone like a pile of jewels. Hannah moved towards this glimmering oasis, hypnotised by the dance of light on the glass.

Will caught up with them. "Make yourselves at home," he told them. "And let me get you drinks."

"Where's Charlie?" Carla demanded. She spoke as if she were accusing Will of a crime; of having hidden the person they most wanted to see. Hannah had never seen her so aggressive.

"He had to step out. He'll be back in five minutes."

They sat on two of the stools that lined the bar, while Will filled their glasses with wine. After a while, Hannah heard the metal door shut with a crash.

"Charlie," Carla said. She seemed to be holding her breath, each muscle finely tuned to the sound.

The curtains separating the space from the hallway leading to the external metal door were flung back and a man entered the room as if he were an actor mounting a stage. His step was quick and confident; his arms flung wide, stretched towards them, palms open, as if he intended to embrace them. He wasn't a tall man, but he seemed far taller than he was, no doubt because of his charisma: everything about him seemed to shine. There was a golden ring on his finger, a glowing bangle around his wrist, and his eyes were large and gleamed like amber. But his other facial features were small and indistinguishable, and his face itself rather round, with too much forehead, which had a shine to it too. Hannah wanted to get up and walk into this man's arms, so charming did he seem; so wreathed in smiles.

Charlie reached them, laying one bejewelled finger upon Carla's arm. "Carla! Sweetheart! I am *so* sorry I'm late. I got my driver to drive in all the bus lanes, I was that desperate to get to you, but you know how it is." He smiled more intensely and shrugged his shoulders, then turned to Hannah and grasped her hand. "Finally, I get to meet the elusive Hannah."

Hannah moved back involuntarily, expecting her bones to be crushed, but Charlie's hand was soft and covered hers completely. It squeezed rather than shook.

Charlie put his head on one side and grinned at her. "And isn't she lovely? Well worth the wait."

"I told you so." Carla smiled.

"You've done well, Carla. She will do," murmured Charlie. "She will indeed." He took a deep breath in. "But hold on – I'm getting ahead of myself, and your glasses are empty!" He looked horrified. "Is that any way to carry on? Jesus, where has Will gone? Let's get you some more drinks." He darted behind the bar, resting both hands on its surface, looking proud and confident. "What will you drink, Hannah?"

Hannah froze, unable to think of a single drink. She was relieved to see Charlie busy himself behind the bar and produce a bottle of champagne. He whistled as he set about opening it.

"Charlie!" Carla protested. "It's far too early for that."

"Nonsense – this girl is a cause for celebration, as you well know, Carla. Plus, it's never too early for champagne."

Carla sniffed her drink delicately, almost suspiciously, while Hannah took a gulp of the frothing liquid, feeling the bubbles tickle the back of her throat.

"What shall we drink to, then?" Charlie asked. "Any ideas, Hannah?"

Hannah hesitated. Why did people always have to

drink *to* something, she thought? Wasn't it enough just to drink?

"Hannah likes to drink to the pursuit of wealth," Carla said.

Hannah flushed.

"And not to that of love? Or happiness?" Charlie was chuckling, deep and throaty, his face turning pink with amusement. He raised his glass. "Here's to the pursuit of pleasure," he said. "And to my new watch," he added. He turned to Hannah. "Want to see it?" Without waiting for her response, he undid one cufflink and drew back his sleeve. On his wrist, nestling in thick, fair hair, was a golden watch. The numbers were picked out in tiny diamonds, and there was a larger diamond to the side. "It's a vintage solid-gold Rolex. Set me back a fair bit." Charlie took off the watch and held it out to her. "Do you want to try it on?"

Hannah, emboldened by the champagne, slipped the watch onto her wrist, and held it up to the neon light, which made the diamonds sparkle. "It's lovely!" she breathed.

Charlie laughed. "It's just a toy, really. Yet another toy to keep me amused. Along with my collection of Porsches. I need these distractions, Hannah. They stop me from getting bored, and when I get bored, I get bad. And I get bored easily, don't I, Carla?"

Hannah saw Carla incline her head slightly, but she couldn't read the expression on her face, which was in shadow.

"Have more champagne, sweethearts," Charlie told them. "And something to go with it? Crisps, caviar… coke, perhaps?" The shine on his forehead deepened to match the gleam in his eyes.

"Charlie!"

"Oh, lighten up, Carla."

Carla made a hissing sound in her throat. "Can I have a word?"

Obediently, Charlie followed her to one end of the bar and bent his head, listening to her, one hand resting on one of the four metal poles that ran up from the bar. Watching them, Hannah had a sense that something momentous was about to happen; something that would make her life bigger and better, as she'd always hoped it would be. When Charlie and Carla separated and came back to her, so that they no longer looked like some strange two-headed creature and resumed their separate identities, she could feel her heart drumming against her ribcage.

Charlie stood in front of her, looking like a man who had struck gold. "Where are you living now, darling?"

"At home, with my parents."

"And do you want to leave home?"

Hannah thought of Jake, and of her mother, and of the stagnant circularity of it all. "Oh, yes!" she breathed.

"Right, you'll move in with Carla. And you'll begin work very soon. If not tonight, then soon."

"Work?" Hannah faltered.

Carla stood over her, her breath sour with the champagne. "Dancing, Hannah."

"But I… I can't dance. I mean… not well…"

"Come along one evening and Carla and I will… put you at your ease," Charlie told her. He was brisk and business like now, already tidying up the champagne glasses and wiping down the bar. He grinned widely at Hannah, showing a mouth full of teeth that were yellowing slightly. "One thing's for sure: you'll be paid very handsomely to dance here. *Very* handsomely indeed."

Chapter 35

"What sort of dancing?" Hannah asked Carla a few days later, as she moved her few belongings into Carla's spacious flat. Doing so made her giddy with excitement and relief. She'd had to wait to pack up until both her mother and Jake were out. Although Michael was frequently away from home, he was around when she was packing, but that didn't matter as she was by now mostly invisible to him.

"You'll see. When we go back to the club," Carla told her, taking her bag from her and directing her to her bedroom: a smaller room at the back of the flat. "Don't put them there," she said, as Hannah started emptying the bag and depositing clothes on the bed. "I don't want clothes lying around the place, making it look untidy. Here." She opened a dark antique mahogany wardrobe that loomed over the bed. A spider scurried from its depths as Hannah filled it with clothes. "You won't be wearing these much longer anyway."

"Why not?"

"Because you'll be getting new things."

Hannah's eyes widened. "New clothes? What for?"

"To fit in; look the part."

"But I don't have any money for new clothes."

"Charlie will give me the money."

Carla was about to leave the room when Hannah

called to her. She turned, waiting, eyebrows raised.

"Do you work at the club?" Hannah asked.

"In a sense. I organise the dancers, and everything behind the scenes. And Charlie is front of house. We are a team."

"And how many dancers are there?"

"Oh, I don't know – about thirteen in all. But they rotate; there's only seven or eight maybe dancing in one evening. And there's a hierarchy of sorts."

"What do you mean?"

"Well, some of the dancers make more than others. A few are… prized. They do… other things, apart from dance. And they're rewarded amply for it. We hope that, if you're able and willing, you might be one of those precious few."

Hannah looked puzzled. "I still don't understand," she said.

"I just told you." There was an edge to Carla's voice.

Hannah so wanted things to be clear. She could feel her voice rising, and the tears with it. "But I still don't see where they dance. There isn't any stage."

Carla turned on her in a fury. Her voice was harsh; her face had clouded over. "Stop pestering me with questions!" she cried. Then at once she calmed down and shook herself, as if coming to a sudden recollection of who she was, and whom she was with. "Hannah," she said again, but this time her voice was softer and slower. She drew close to Hannah and put a hand on her shoulder.

Hannah flinched.

Carla caressed her shoulder in a gentle circular movement. "Come," she said, drawing Hannah towards her, slowly and gently, hands stroking her arms. "Patience is its own reward, right? It will become clear very soon, I promise."

One evening shortly after that, Carla told Hannah, "Tonight, we will go to Charlie's. But first, I must find you something to wear." She went through her own wardrobe, finally removing a silk shift dress – silver, with thin straps, the hem just below the knee. "Here – I think this will fit you. It ceased to fit me a while ago."

After she'd put on the dress, Hannah let Carla make her up, which she did slowly and carefully, as if she were painting a picture on her face. And when Hannah looked at her reflection, she looked quite unlike herself, and she wasn't sure if this made her beautiful or not.

When they got to the metal door in the basement well, Hannah was surprised to see a neon sign over it which read, simply, 'Charlie's'.

The light from the sign made Carla's face look as if it were bathed in moonlight. "It's very different by night," she breathed. "Go on – go in."

Hannah stepped inside. Will was nowhere to be seen. Two large, bulky men stood in front of the curtains which led to the cavernous place where they'd been drinking before. Swathes of plush velvet hid the limescale-encrusted walls. At the back, Hannah could now see a raised black stage. It was empty, with only two spotlights throwing circles of light upon it, which moved through the black space, glowing a bright white, like magnesium flares. There must have been nearly forty people in the room – most of them sitting at tables, drinking, and staring at the stage. The bar with the band of neon light above it was the only thing that remained unchanged; that and Charlie behind it, genial and jocular, smiling at the room and the people in it.

Carla led Hannah to one of the tables. "Wait there." She smiled as she left her; a slow, sensuous smile that made Hannah's eyes burn.

The air was laced with expectation and anticipation, as before a performance. Now Hannah saw Charlie coming towards her. She tensed as he kissed her; as she felt his breath upon her neck, his hand upon her back.

"Hannah!" he whispered. "You've surpassed my expectations. You look stunning. But I thought you might need to relax a little bit tonight, while you suss out what's what. So here's a little gift – just to give you a little boost, you know." He smiled and winked at her and laid a small packet on the table in front of her, almost tentatively, as if he were offering a piece of bread to a bird. Then he clapped her arm twice, with exaggerated joviality, and was gone.

Hannah opened the package. Inside was a pill. She hesitated, one finger resting on it. She thought of Sal, of her sister's tight and narrow mind. Sal wouldn't approve of all this, not at all. She'd told Hannah a couple of horror stories – having experimented herself, of course. But it was always one rule for Sal and another for Hannah. And Hannah was curious. Her sister's face bloomed inside her head and then left it as suddenly as it had come, leaving in its place a dark, open void. With a shaking hand, Hannah popped the pill in her mouth and swallowed it.

The air around her seemed to crackle with static as Carla reappeared to sit by her side. Finally, three girls appeared onstage, scantily clad in clothes that revealed every smooth curve of their bodies. They twisted in time to the music, their movements subtle at first but becoming more exaggerated and daring as the music strengthened. Their flesh glimmered in the light as if it were dusted with diamonds. To Hannah they seemed like the most glamorous creatures she'd ever seen. The stage seemed to pull her towards it like a magnet, and she would have moved forwards were it not for Carla's restraining hand. The rhythmic charm of the music moved through her, flowed along her limbs like a golden stream, and her head was full of flowering certainties. She looked at Carla and saw a being brimming with beneficence and bounty. She was filled with gratitude for her own good fortune.

The dancers moved together, their bodies a shining mass. Then one of them, with blonde hair, came towards one of the tables nearby and started to remove her costume with slow, languid movements. Her eyes stared glassily ahead; her fingers trembled slightly as they picked at the fastenings of her clothes. The stage filled with amber light as the two other girls swayed to the hypnotic beat of the music, like trees in a breeze. As the girls' bodies were slowly revealed, desire filled the space around Hannah and the girls seemed to bask in it, to reflect it back, and to become more powerful still, drawing themselves up proudly. Hannah watched the blonde-haired girl move around the tables in slow motion, as if in a film, and marvelled at how deftly she managed to avoid the hands that sought her out. After that she wasn't aware of anything at all: it was as if she were floating far above the scene, unable to connect to anything or anyone, conscious only of the rush of blood around her body and its beat in time to the music. She closed her eyes, and the darkness seemed to pulsate; to push at her.

Suddenly she felt a hand on her arm, pulling and tugging at her. The hand wouldn't let her be. Hannah opened her eyes – with difficulty, for their lids were heavy and it seemed that the easiest thing to do was to keep them shut forever.

Carla was leaning over her. "Hannah, are you all right? *Hannah!*" She shook her again. "Oh, damn Charlie," she muttered. "He always goes too far." She almost lifted Hannah out of her chair, her grip surprising in its strength.

Hannah could still feel the music inside her. Her legs wanted to sway in time to it, but instead they bent and crumpled beneath her. "But I want to dance," she murmured, the words slurring slightly.

"Another time, okay?"

The cooler air outside was like a slap in the face. Carla managed to drag Hannah into a black cab, its interior dark and warm as a womb, engine purring contentedly. Hannah lay across its back seat, her head on Carla's lap. Carla spoke to her tenderly, resting her hand on her hair.

Once the cab had pulled up outside the flat, Carla helped Hannah upstairs to her bedroom, handed her a glass of water, and sat on her bed while she drank. "I'll get you more," she said as she made to leave the room.

Hannah raised her arms, beckoning to her. "Stay a bit, Carla," she whispered. "Keep me company."

Carla sat back down on the bed and held one of Hannah's hands. Hannah let her head slide back on the pillow as Carla's face swam before her own; as she felt Carla's hand reach out and caress her face. She smiled. Her head was still filled with the light and music of the club. All thought had abandoned her, and she felt only relief at its release, and then there was only pleasure, its pursuit and its capture – though it was pleasure that came at a price; that she struggled to find, to follow, to hold; for it died as quickly as it came.

Chapter 36

Hannah sat at Carla's dining table, one finger running around the rim of a champagne flute, another tracing a pattern over the intricacies of the gleaming Italian marble that formed the surface of the table. She hadn't been back to Charlie's club since that night two weeks ago. In fact, she hadn't been anywhere at all in that time – Carla had told her that she wasn't quite ready for the club; that she should rest and wait. Hannah was starting to find Carla's flat, although beautiful, rather oppressive. She longed to be some place, any place, just not where she was. Carla never seemed to want to take her out, telling her that she was too busy – she had to work, to paint – but she never seemed to want Hannah to go out on her own either, even for a walk. Although Hannah found Carla fascinating to talk to – she had learned so much from her, mainly about art and music and important things like that – the novelty was beginning to wear a little thin. Add to that the fact that, when Carla was in a bad temper, she'd fly at Hannah for no reason, so that Hannah often found herself treading on eggshells around her, fearful of causing offence, trying to make herself as meek and unassuming as possible, in order to reduce any chance of upsetting her new friend.

"Shall we go to Charlie's this evening?" Carla asked

Hannah suddenly.

Hannah's eyes flew open in shock, and she rose from the table in delight. "You sure? I thought after last time… I embarrassed myself, you said…"

"Well, it won't happen again, will it? Promise?"

"I promise," Hannah told her.

"What will we be doing at Charlie's?" Hannah asked her companion as they walked. She thought hopefully of the pill she had taken last time.

"Didn't you say that you wanted to dance?"

"I did, but I'm not very good…"

"Well, then."

"But the girls… they removed their clothes, didn't they?"

Carla smiled. "They did."

Hannah hesitated. "The money might be nice, but I'm not sure…" Her voice trailed off. She still didn't have any money. Carla paid for her food, even bought her clothes, but she didn't give her her own cash. Hannah wanted cash more than anything.

"That's something you must think about, isn't it? You can't live with me indefinitely if you don't pay rent."

"But… I still model for you sometimes. You did say you'd pay me a little for modelling, and then I could get another job…?"

Her voice tailed off when she saw Carla's face. Sudden anger had distorted it, making it look ugly.

"I never promised I'd pay you," Carla spat. "And a menial job – which is all you're fit for – how would that give you the money you need to pay me rent?"

Hannah drew back. Doubt gnawed at her like a tumour. Tears stung her eyes.

Carla took hold of Hannah's arm, and moved closer to her, whispering, "Hannah, you did find the dancing very beautiful, did you not? And did you think that it was less appealing, or the girls less alluring, simply because they removed their clothes? All those people watching those women wanted them so much, and they couldn't have them; did you not think that that made the women even more powerful?" She pulled Hannah's face towards hers and kissed her mouth gently. "No one is allowed to touch them. They want to, so much. They try, but they seldom succeed. And what's your experience of people – men – who can and do touch women, Hannah?"

Hannah flinched, but Carla pressed on.

"How do they touch them? Do they do so with love, with tenderness, hmmm?"

Hannah covered her face with her hands, and Carla dropped her voice so low that it was barely audible.

"And wouldn't you like to be as desirable, as unattainable as those women, and to have those men *not* touch you but want you anyway, and to reward you handsomely just for that? Well?" Carla continued. "And if you continue to excel, wouldn't you want to be able to join the elite, those few girls who are paid so well for what they do that they can do anything they want with their lives – *anything* at all? Well, wouldn't you?" Carla drew back. "But it's up to you, after all, Hannah. If you won't even dance, I can't afford to have you live with me any longer, and I don't think Charlie has any other work for you. But you can always go home, can't you?"

Hannah remained where she was and, with one heel, rubbed at the inside of her shin. Carla drew away and started walking down the street, her heels making clicking sounds on the tarmac.

"Carla!" Hannah called.

Carla carried on walking, so fast she was about to disappear. Hannah panicked. Carla was so sure about things; so happy with her life as she had made it. Hannah couldn't just watch her go.

"Carla!" she called again. "Wait!"

At last Carla stopped, and Hannah ran after her. When she caught up with her, her cheeks were pink.

"Okay, I'll try it," she said.

Carla smiled at her. "You won't regret it, I promise."

Chapter 37

Charlie and Carla were talking animatedly at the bar, their heads so close to each other that they looked as if they were fused together to form a single unit, like those belonging to a pair of Siamese twins. Finally, Charlie detached himself from Carla and came towards Hannah, raising his arms in greeting to some of his clientele as he passed. He placed both hands on Hannah's shoulders, pulling her towards him, and hugged her. Being hugged by Charlie was like being enveloped by a warm cloud: confusing, but not altogether unpleasant.

"Sweetheart, welcome back!" he exclaimed. "Come with me."

He drew Hannah into a small room that opened off the main space. The room was in darkness, and when Charlie switched on the light, Hannah could see that it was windowless, and rather dingy, with tired furniture and peeling paint.

"Sit down and make yourself comfortable," Charlie told her. With one plump hand, he pressed Hannah down in front of a table scattered with paper. He swept away the paper, making space. "I always have a little coke before I start business." He started laying out lines. "Now… first things first. Did Carla talk to you about money?"

Hannah nodded.

Charlie rolled up a twenty-pound note and bent his head over the coke. "What did she say?"

"That I'd earn it. And how."

Charlie passed the rolled-up note to Hannah, "Your turn."

After Hannah had bent over the white lines, Charlie pushed a sheet of paper across the table to her. He pointed at the bottom of it. "Sign here."

Hannah hesitated. "What is it?"

"A contract. Some people say there's no point having them in this business, but I think differently. I like to have my affairs arranged properly. I'm an ordered person, Hannah. A *very* ordered person." He smiled. "Go on, sign."

"What am I signing?"

"Carla didn't tell you?"

"Tell me what?"

There was a knock on the door. "Come in!" Charlie called.

One of the dancers walked in – a girl with long, thin hair, a narrow face, and a pointed nose like a whippet's.

"What is it, Sarah?" Charlie asked impatiently.

The girl hesitated.

"Can't you see I've got someone with me?"

"You said you had something for me?" the girl said. Her eyes darted around the room, and finally rested on the coke; her hands twisting over and around each other.

"So I did," Charlie said absent-mindedly. He drew a small packet from his pocket and handed it to the girl. "There's half a gram. Now, go on – go!" He ushered her out of the room and turned back to Hannah. "Sorry about that, sweetheart – she gets a little nervous without it. Now, where were we? Yes – the contract. I can't believe Carla didn't tell you about the contract. Well, it's just setting out what the deal is with the dancers. Some girls earn more, others less. Usually, I take around half a girl's earnings to cover the cost of running this place – heating, electricity, rent, things like that." He made a vague gesture in the air. "But in your case, because when I saw you, I thought, *Well, finally, here is a girl who has class, brains; a girl who is one of the special ones, who will get them to fork out –* know what I mean?" He paused. "In *your* case, I said to Carla I'd only take thirty per cent and I'd give her thirty as well."

"So, I get less than the other girls?"

"Yes, but, Hannah," Charlie got up from his desk and moved around the room, "did Carla mention to you our plans for your future?"

"She said something about… the elite?"

"Ah, yes. Those girls are few and far between. They are rewarded handsomely. Because they are *exceptionally* good at what they do."

"And what's that?"

"That's a conversation for another time. Let's not get beyond ourselves, Hannah. Let's start with the dancing. That pays well enough." He stood behind his desk and bent over the coke again, hoovering up another line with a loud sniff. "But just as an aside – a sweetener, if you like – do you have any idea what one of those fortunate girls earns?" He grinned; rested both hands on the edge of the desk. "A thousand pounds a night! A *thousand* pounds," he repeated, smacking his forehead. "Jesus, that's a lot of money. Can you imagine what you'd do with that sort of cash? Bet that's more than you've ever dreamed of, hmm? Well, isn't it?" He continued to pace around the room. "A thousand pounds a night; five nights a week – that's *five* thousand pounds. A proportion goes to me, admittedly, but still, that's a great deal of cash, Hannah." His eyes were shining through the dark. Now he came around to her and bent down so that his face was level with hers. There was a sheen on his forehead where the light fell upon it. "But *you*, Hannah, a prime piece like you – well, we're talking serious amounts of cash. I'd say maybe fifteen hundred a night. Maybe even more. Maybe as much as two thousand…"

The smell of Charlie's aftershave – sweet, heavy – made Hannah's head spin. "*Two* thousand pounds?" she breathed.

"That's right. And if that happens – *when* that happens – are you going to begrudge Carla and me some of the bounty, eh? Especially when our lovely Carla is putting you up. Did you think she was doing that out of the kindness of her heart, Hannah? Well, did you?" He laughed; a deep, hoarse laugh that bounced around the dark corners of the room. "She's too wily to be driven purely by her preferences, that one," he murmured. "Sign the contract to become a dancer now, and then we'll celebrate."

After Hannah had signed the contract, Charlie folded it very carefully and put it in his pocket. Just as she was leaving the room, he turned her to face him, drew her to him and kissed her on her forehead. His lips left a patch of wet there.

"You're nervous about the dancing, right? Don't be. You'll be fantastic. You go to Cathy. You can't miss her – she's got long red hair. Get her to give you some clothes and tell her to give you something Charlie wanted you to have, okay?" And he pushed her away with a little wave.

Hannah found Cathy almost straight away. "Charlie said you had something for me."

Cathy, a bleary-eyed girl with hair the colour of peeled carrots, eyed Hannah suspiciously. She handed Hannah a dress and heeled shoes and a small packet. Then she held out her hand. "What 'bout a pill as well?"

"What sort of pill?"

Cathy's fingers uncurled to reveal a couple of pills sitting in her palm, like two eggs inside a nest. "Want one?"

Hannah reached for the pills, but Cathy swiftly

closed her fingers over them.

"Promise first," she hissed.

"What?"

"That you won't tell Charlie. What he don't know won't kill him."

Hannah shrugged her shoulders. "Sure. Cheers, Cathy." Quickly, before Cathy could change her mind, she stuffed the pill into her mouth. Then she locked herself in the bathroom, changed, and laid out the coke Cathy had given her. It seemed as if outside that room a bigger, better world was waiting for her, pressing its mighty weight against the door so that it creaked and groaned. Just one more line… and another… and she was ready to face it. With shaking legs but a glorious emptiness of her head, she opened the door.

When Hannah finally walked up onto the stage, she couldn't see the faces watching her. The neon band of light around the bar was all she could make out in the darkness. Her body was the only other lit object in the room; a body bathed in golden light, that was gorgeous and absolutely her own. Her head was empty save for a singing confidence. The world had retreated. She was the world and everything in it – all that existed was her body that swayed and circled in time to the music.

With one hand she unfastened the buttons at the side of her dress, allowing it to fall at her feet. She could hear shouting – but she ignored it, for it was such a long way away – and continued stroking her skin, touching her breasts in the way *she* wanted, for they were beautiful. She wet her fingers and moved them over her nipples. The shouting was more insistent now, like a pressure at the side of her head. But she would ignore it, for she was without thought or weight or design; only existing in the moment, as she had always wanted. She drew her hands over her hips, swaying to the slow murmur of the music, then moved them down the insides of her thighs, while her mind remained bright and hard as a diamond. No one else had touched her like her own hands could do: so lightly, as if she were playing herself like a musical instrument. An aching started between her legs as her fingers moved over and up to the tops of her thighs. A tantalising yearning seemed to fill the room and the space around her, coming from her and at her at the same time. She loved it, and she, Hannah, was the cause of it. She loved herself. She threw her head back and then around in one slow, sweeping movement; feeling her hair fall against her back. The music was inside her now; it was the pulse inside her veins. Soon she would no longer be able to contain it. She moved across the stage towards the void beyond as one in a trance. Everything – her body, the music, the stage – seemed part of some glorious whole; perfect and complete. Then, just as she could no longer contain the music within her, it stopped suddenly, and silence took its place. Shocked, she stepped out into the silence… and collapsed to the floor below the stage.

Hannah felt someone tugging at her arm. "Hannah,

get up. Charlie wants to see you!" Cathy threw her discarded dress at her.

Stepping into her dress, Hannah stumbled to the bar. Dancing on the stage was already a distant memory.

Charlie was standing in front of one of the girls. His outline was blurred, and Hannah could barely see him in the murky light. His arms were gesticulating wildly, stabbing the air. He seemed like some hyperactive dwarf. Then, as she drew nearer, he was Charlie once again: charismatic, avuncular, the maker of miracles. "Hannah!" he cried, turning to her. "You were fantastic! Truly incredible." He handed her a shot glass, resting his arm on her shoulders. "Drink this. It's tequila. High quality, mind you." He paused while she drank. "There was just one thing – one *tiny* thing. You were stunning, darling. But the thing is, you're not on your own out there, Hannah. You've got to *interact* with the punters. You've got to *please* them. Then they'll give you what they've got. You earned no cash tonight. Next time, all you've got to do is to get off that stage, move faster, and closer to them, and you'll get all they give, right? You got me?"

Hannah nodded.

"Interact, sweetheart, right?" Charlie reached inside his pocket and took out a few notes. "Here – take these, or Carla will be mad at me."

Hannah did so. The notes were slightly damp. She closed her eyes. Behind the lids, moving patterns pulsed.

Behind her, she could hear Charlie shouting at Cathy. "What you give her? *Idiot!* It was her first fucking time!" Then his voice faded, and she could hear another: a familiar voice calling her name. She moved towards it.

Carla helped Hannah out of the club, and into a cab. Back at her flat, she made her get into her bed. She handed her a cup of hot tea and, with a damp cloth, cool and comforting, wiped Hannah's face. Hannah closed her eyes, remembering her mother and how she had once cared for her in a similar way. She surrendered to Carla's undivided attention, imagining that it was her mother's hand moving over her forehead with a slow caress. She felt herself being pushed back onto the pillow; heard a voice saying, "There, go to sleep now. You'll feel fresher tomorrow."

But in the middle of the night Hannah sat up, clutching her chest, nervy heat radiating from her.

A man had been chasing her in her dreams, through ill-lit and unrecognisable city streets. Once she had turned around and caught a glimpse of him: he was wearing a coat with a hood, and she couldn't see his face, so he appeared just like the figure in the nightmares she used to have as a child. Except that this time she thought she recognised the voice that was calling out to her, getting closer and closer until it seemed to be shouting in her ears.

Then she knew. The man was Karl. The voice was

Karl's. She bent her head over her arms and started to cry.

Carla had been sitting by the window, her figure lit only by the soft moonlight that cast its silver sheen over the room. Immediately she got up and moved towards Hannah. "What's the matter, darling?"

"I was running away, but he was still *there*," Hannah sobbed. "He came after me. I couldn't get away from him. I tried, but I couldn't run fast enough."

Carla placed one hand on her head and smoothed out her hair. "Who?"

"My ex. He was… *horrible* to me."

Carla began to massage Hannah's head. "Shh. Forget him. You're safe now. With me."

Hannah shut her eyes as a tingling sensation started up at the sides of her head. She tried to blot out Karl's cruel words, his blows. She remembered how she had touched herself when she was dancing, except she wasn't dancing now. She held her breath as Carla moved her mouth down, over her breasts, her tongue circling each nipple. She felt Carla's fingers parting her legs, and then sliding into her, making her wet. Then her hands were warm on her hips, so warm, pressing down on her hips so that Hannah couldn't move, so that she had to let Carla's tongue claim her, move down, press against her, and into her.

Hannah gasped, pleasure fanning from the sides of her head, coursing through her, increasing, becoming steadily higher, higher, bringing her up with it, until she couldn't get any higher and she was looking down into a dark space, and then she fell into the emptiness.

Hannah cried out as Karl's face bloomed in the darkness of her mind. She opened her eyes, but she could see only Carla's face looming in front of hers, could feel nothing but her hot flesh pressing against her own.

Chapter 38

The heat of the room seemed to be getting to Charlie: his cheeks were flaming red, and he kept wiping his forehead with a large handkerchief. All over his face beads of sweat stood out; the light from the intricate glass chandelier overhead making them shine like jewels.

Watching Charlie made Hannah uncomfortable, and she left the table to stand at the open window. She was on the first floor of a grand building in Mayfair, the private dining room of a smart hotel which Charlie had hired for this gathering. Hannah could see the lights of the city blinking in the darkness below her, and beyond them, the lightless space that was Hyde Park, a vast and misty nothingness. Hannah stood breathing in the cool night air, enjoying the open space in front of her. Behind her the party was in full swing: she could hear the clink of glass, the clash of cutlery, laughter rising to the ceiling, and, over and above it all, Charlie's voice urging everyone to drink more, to eat more, and generally to have the time of their lives.

Hannah had been at the club around six months now. She felt more at ease than she had done at first, and she was extracting cash from the punters, though perhaps not at the rate of some of the others. She still struggled to get on with the other girls. Some were barely civil. Only the day before she'd had a fight with Cathy over the safe space assigned to their belongings. Hannah had noticed that a few of the girls were treated differently from the rest. She thought that this must be the hierarchy Charlie and Carla had alluded to. A dark-haired girl, whom the others referred to as Raven, and an auburn-haired girl they called Rosa seemed expensively dressed, even stylish. There were a couple of others that stood out too. Hannah seldom saw them dance – they merely flitted to and from Charlie's office. They were impossibly aloof. She hadn't managed to speak to any of them. When she'd asked Carla why they danced so seldom, Carla had stonewalled her.

Hannah felt Carla behind her now before she saw her reflection in the glass to one side; she sensed the change in the atmosphere that came with her strong perfume and made the air around her close and sultry, like the air before a storm.

"Come away from the window, dear. You'll catch a chill." And Carla closed the window, shutting out the city and drawing Hannah back to the party; to the cocaine, the chaos, and the crowd.

Hannah saw Charlie beckon to her from one end of the table and point at an empty chair beside him. Others were also taking their seats. Hannah sat down, as Charlie stood up and banged his champagne glass with a fork.

"Everyone, be quiet!"

The noise in the room subsided.

"Now," he continued, "as you know, Carla and I arranged this special dinner at this exquisite hotel to celebrate the third anniversary of the club, which, I have to say, is doing better than I ever dreamed possible."

Everyone cheered.

Charlie beamed fondly at the group, which consisted mainly of women. "I wanted to thank each of you. All of you have made my dreams real." He stopped to wipe his eyes with his handkerchief. "I know everyone here has benefited from the success of the club, but without you, that success would not have been possible. So I want to drink to every single one of you. You're... you're..." he struggled, reaching for words, "like the family I never had. And as my family you mean everything to me. And this evening is on me, so carry on enjoying yourselves."

Raven was the first to raise her glass. "Hear, hear!" she called out. Hannah looked over at her. She was flaunting a Chanel bag. A diamond bracelet glinted on her wrist. The other guests cheered too and raised their glasses. The chandelier above their heads vibrated with the noise.

"And now!" Charlie called out when the hilarity had subsided somewhat. "A toast to Hannah. Most of you have met her already. She first came to us some months ago. She was broke, weren't you, darling?" He pressed her to his side. "And – I will say it – looking a tad *under the weather*. But now look at her! Doesn't she look gorgeous? And she's doing fantastic." He chuckled. "So I want you all to congratulate Hannah!"

The room continued to cheer. Arms were stretched out, glasses raised. The massive chandelier overhead glowed like a second sun, making faces shine.

Hannah adjusted her dress, rose unsteadily, and raised her glass. Her head was spinning a little, and the faces in front of her were slightly blurred. "Thank you, all of you. Without you, I don't know where I'd be. Still at home, probably, with very little to show for myself." She looked around at the other girls. She'd been drinking vodka, and it brought a rush of feeling to her head. Her voice, which had been unsteady at first, gradually grew in strength. "You're all like sisters to me, and Charlie… he's the real dad I never had." She swallowed. The coldness of the girls, and even her recent fight with Cathy, were forgotten. And Charlie was her golden guardian angel.

"And what does that make Carla?" Cathy called out.

Hannah looked over at Carla. She was sitting to her right, her face cool and still, her eyes assessing the room and everyone in it. She appeared now as Hannah had always wanted her to appear: as a benign benefactress to whom she owed everything, and by whose divine intervention her life had been turned around. Hannah raised her voice, so that it was as clear and steady as a bell's. "To Carla!"

"To Carla!" they all echoed.

Carla barely acknowledged the toast. But Hannah

was conscious of her sitting by her side, saying nothing, just watching them all – detached, incurious, and impossible to read.

Later, some of the girls started to dance, in a loose-limbed, suggestive manner, though they remained fully clothed. Cathy stumbled over to Hannah and began apologising for their fight the other night. Then, in the middle of her apology, her nose started bleeding and Hannah had to accompany her to the bathroom to help her clean up, and then to wipe up the blood that dripped upon the bathroom floor. Afterwards, Cathy insisted on laying out a couple of lines on the closed toilet seat as a thank-you for 'sorting her out'.

When Hannah came out of the bathroom, Charlie accosted her, laying one hand on her arm protectively and muttering something about "a proposition. I've got someone to introduce you to, darling. Do not leave without meeting him."

Later, when Charlie came over to her again, there was a man by his side: a man with a pale, pockmarked face. On his neck was a tattoo of a small eye.

"Hannah, meet my friend, Rees. Rees is a *very* close friend of mine. We go back a long way. You make sure he gets the golden treatment, right, Hannah? You hear me?" He waved his hand in the air and left Hannah and the man together.

Hannah stood in front of Rees, swaying to the music. "What does he mean by that?" she asked.

Rees grinned. "You're gorgeous, you know that?" he

whispered, leaning into her.

Right at that moment, Hannah actually believed what he was saying, but still she was conscious of wanting to move away from him; of her relief when a couple of the girls, who had opened the windows and were leaning over the balcony, calling to passers-by on the street, then called to her to join them. But when she did, they spoke at her too fast, their speech blurred and incoherent, making no sense.

The party continued through the night. When Hannah looked down at her watch it was one; she looked again, and it was three. The room emptied out and then it filled again. Time ceased to have any meaning or design, while all around her people continued their pursuit of pleasure, their words merely disembodied sound which floated around the room, up above the heads of those gathered there, and then escaped out of the open window and into the night.

Chapter 39

A couple of weeks later, Raven came over to Hannah to tell her that Charlie wanted to see her.

"What about?"

Hannah thought she saw a small smile move over the dark-haired girl's flawless features. But she shrugged her shoulders. "How would I know?" she asked coolly.

Hannah hadn't been into Charlie's office for a while, and she'd forgotten how small it was. Charlie had had the room redecorated since she'd last been there, but the blue walls and gold woodwork had, in Hannah's eyes, done very little to improve it.

Charlie rose to his feet. "Hannah – just the gorgeous girl I wanted to see. How goes it, my darling?" He sat down again, waving Hannah to the chair opposite him, picked up what looked like a lump of molten plastic and started playing with it, kneading it again and again. He spoke almost casually. "You remember Rees, whom I introduced you to at the party a while back?"

Hannah remembered Rees's thin, pitted face. She nodded.

"Well, he's taken quite a shine to you. And he wants to take you out."

Hannah looked suspiciously at Charlie.

"No, nothing like that. He's not like that, Hannah,

I assure you. He just helped me out with a business matter, and so I said I'd let him take you out for dinner as a thank-you. I'll be accompanying you as a chaperone. He won't lay a finger on you, promise – unless you want him to." Charlie leered at her, then sobered up when he saw her face. "So, as I said, he's keen to enjoy your company, just for the evening, and even if I'm around too. And guess how much he'll pay you for it?"

Hannah shook her head.

Charlie slapped his thigh gleefully. "*One thousand pounds*," he said triumphantly. "And as much coke as you want, by way of a bonus."

Hannah's eyes widened. "A thousand pounds, just for my company?"

"That's right! Incredible, isn't it? But he is *that* taken with you, Hannah. And you are worth every penny of it – *every* penny, my darling. So… what do you think?" Charlie was bobbing up and down in his seat like an energetic genie.

"What's in it for me?"

"Well, I won't take a cut."

"I don't believe you."

"I promise," Charlie protested. "Rees is a good connection. I'm… how to say it? I'm *cultivating* him."

Hannah thought about it. Why not? It was quite flattering, in a way, that a man would pay that much just to have dinner with her. How far she'd come from her ugly duckling schooldays. A thousand pounds was a lot of money – money that would help get her away from Carla; from them all. She shrugged her shoulders. "Whatever, Charlie. Sounds like fun," she said.

"Where you going?"

Carla's question was soft and sweet, but Hannah wasn't fooled. She turned back to the mirror and adjusted her hair, then reapplied her lipstick.

"Out," she said, smiling with equal sweetness.

Carla's reflection appeared behind hers. She put out one hand and, with a gesture Hannah now found proprietorial rather than protective, smoothed out her hair. "Where?"

"Nowhere special."

"Who's taking you out?"

"A friend of Charlie's."

"Who?"

Hannah sighed. She might as well tell her; Carla would find out eventually, as she always did. "A man called Rees."

Carla's face paled. "Rees," she repeated, making the 's' a long hiss. "*Already?*"

"What do you mean?"

"I told Charlie you weren't ready; that I didn't want this."

"What do you mean?" Hannah repeated. "Ready for what?"

Carla just shook her head.

From the street below, the sound of a car horn

travelled up to them. Hannah moved from the mirror and looked out of the sitting-room window. Far below, she could see a red convertible glittering like a giant ruby in the light from a street lamp. Through the open sunroof she could see its driver's fair head; a small, circular bald spot in the middle of it. "I have to go."

"Hannah, please!"

But Hannah had already let herself out. Delighted at having escaped Carla, she took the stairs as quickly as she could, calling up as she did, "Don't worry – I won't be back late!"

As she opened the building's front door, the warm night air fanned her face. She breathed it in, and with it, all the promise the evening held, and all the freedom and the joy. She moved to the red car, opened the passenger door, and then slid inside, leaning back on the soft leather.

"Where's Charlie?" she asked, after Rees had greeted her with a kiss on each cheek.

"Urgent business to attend to, he said. He was so upset not to be able to make it – so very upset."

Charlie's absence should have made her feel nervous, but Hannah felt relieved to be rid of both her minders for one night.

As if to emphasise this, Rees leaned over her and whispered, "We'll have fun anyway, won't we, Hannah?" He winked at her, and Hannah was sure she saw the tattooed eye blink too.

Hannah smiled. She intended at least to try. And

Rees wasn't looking as bad as she'd remembered, with his smart black pinstriped suit and his white shirt, and his hair all combed back from his head. She ignored his pockmarked face and the fact that, when he'd leaned towards her, something within her had recoiled silently.

Rees started up the engine. "Where do you want to go?"

"Where did you have in mind?"

"Didn't you want to choose?" He grinned.

Hannah froze. She could go anywhere; any place she liked. All kinds of options ran through her head.

"I know a place," Rees laughed, and he put his foot on the accelerator.

As the car drew away and into the night, the breeze lifted the hair from their heads. When they reached the Westway, they picked up speed and the air rushed past them with a sound like running water, and the headlights of the cars around them became a fluid blur. The lights of London fanned out below them, blinking through the blackness, and it was as if all the dirt and the shabbiness, the noise and the ugliness of the city had disappeared, leaving nothing in their place but a pile of jewels. Hannah closed her eyes. She would go wherever the evening wanted to take her. Her body relaxed completely and became limp and lifeless, giving itself up to the car and to the man in it.

After about ten minutes, the car slowed down and then stopped. Hannah opened her eyes. They were parked beside a curved semicircle of lights. In front of them a red carpet led up to a set of revolving doors. Rees tossed his car key to the doorman and manoeuvred Hannah out of the car and through the doors, weaving her past several well-dressed people in the lobby and towards another set of doors at the end of it. She could hear the tinny rattle of machines, excited cries. The noise brought a surge of blood to her head. She put out one hand to open the doors.

"Easy," Rees said, drawing her hand away. "Here first." He turned her to the left and led her towards the bathrooms. With a furtive glance around him, he pushed Hannah into the gents'; locked them in a cubicle. There, he laid out coke neatly, making sure that every last grain of powder was caught in the lines, and waited for Hannah to take her share before he did. Then he laid out more.

"I'm okay, really," Hannah said, wiping her nose with one hand. The spinning had started up in her head again. It had been happening a lot with the coke lately. She'd have to learn how to control it; else, like a car locked in a deadly spin, she'd crash spectacularly and that would be the end of her.

"C'mon, Hannah – we only just got started." Rees made a gesture as if to push her head down.

Before he could do so, Hannah bent over the coke.

"Now," he said, taking her arm, "let's go."

The casino bloomed before them like a forest of flowers. Hannah stepped towards it, lured by the brilliant light; by the sound of money falling from slot machines, like the drum of heavy rain.

As the evening progressed, they won and they lost and there seemed to be no pattern to it at all – or, if there was a pattern, Hannah couldn't recognise it. At regular intervals, Rees went to the bathroom and returned refuelled, his determination to pile up his winnings redoubled. And through it all, the noise of the casino seemed to rise steadily. After some time, the coloured lights around them seemed no longer brilliant, but garish. The spinning in Hannah's head made her feel as if she were on a fairground ride, with the lights and music of the fairground all about her. The roulette board in front of her was spinning too – red, black, red, black, red – and now it was a blur, turning so fast it seemed as if it would never stop. And it didn't look like a board any more, but the smooth circle of a spinning fairground car, and she was in it, and Karl was there too, and soon they were going to lift off from the ground altogether and rise up, up into the sky…

She leaned against Rees. "Make the wheel stop," she whispered.

"Be quiet, will you?" he said, pushing her away.

Slowly, the board stopped. Hannah was just in time to see the ball take a final skip and a jump and land on black before she had to shut her eyes. She could still see the colours circling beneath her lids.

"What's up with you?" Rees asked. "How can a

person be lucky with you mumbling and playing up like that? Jesus."

"Can we go somewhere quieter?" Hannah whispered.

She opened her eyes in time to see Rees smile.

"Follow me."

Rees moved up some stairs and down a quiet corridor. He took a left into a large room. Its walls were covered in red-and-white wallpaper, striped like a candy cane. Drops of coloured glass, like fruit drops, hung from a chandelier above their heads. Hannah longed to reach up and pluck off one of the drops, pop it in her mouth and let its sweetness melt on her tongue.

Rees shoved a glass of water into her hand and pushed her down onto a long sofa. "Drink," he told her. "You need to sober up. I'll kill that Charlie, selling me shit like that. God knows what was in it. Feeling a bit peculiar myself."

Hannah's head was full of live wires, fizzing and twisting. The sofa was as soft as a bed, softer than the seat of Rees's car, and she lay back into it. She still felt relieved to be away from Carla and her place, even if it meant spending time with this man.

"You just lie there and relax," Rees whispered, sitting beside her. "There's no need to go back in for a bit."

After a while, Hannah felt one of Rees's hands moving around her ankle. She shifted slightly, away from its pressure. She was glad when Rees moved back and lit a cigarette.

"What's up with you? You seem a little jumpy,

sweetheart. Charlie did warn me you could be a little…
wired." Rees put one hand on her leg again, moving it
higher and lifting her skirt.

Hannah tensed.

"If you would just try and relax, Hannah. I am just
what you need right now, believe me." His hand was
resting on the inside of her thigh now, tracing a slow
circle on her skin.

"Please, Rees—"

"C'mon, Hannah – that was the deal." Rees moved
away from her briefly to extinguish his cigarette.

"What deal?"

"The grand for the evening, remember? Don't say
Charlie didn't mention it."

Hannah flushed. "He didn't explain…"

"He never does. But that was the deal. Oh, come
on, Hannah. Lovely as you are, your company alone
isn't sufficient to make me cough up that much cash.
You must realise that. You've been working at the
club for a number of months now. Open your eyes,
sweetheart." He smiled; moved closer, so close that she
could feel his breath on her mouth. "I don't have to
tell you how many pretty things you could buy with
my money, do I? So why don't you relax and just let
it happen?" He put one hand behind her neck, while
the other rested on her thigh, fingers pressing into her
flesh. "I tell you what, I'll add fifty per cent on top,
just for you," he murmured. "Beginner's luck, we'll call
it." He moved his hand from her thigh, reached into

his pocket and drew out a wad of notes. "Just you relax and let it happen, and I promise you Charlie doesn't have to know a thing about the extra." He placed the money on the table in front of them.

The sofa was so soft, and finally Hannah yielded – to the pliancy of its cushions; to the insistent pressure of Rees's fingers. She closed her eyes and waited, while the wires in her head twisted and fizzed again, almost painfully this time.

Chapter 40

Hannah stood outside the revolving doors of the department store, waiting for her friend. The air smelled of tar, as if the roads were melting beneath the scalding breath of the baking summer's day. Crowds surged outside the store and made the streets swell. The traffic moved slowly, creaking and groaning. Even the trees seemed tired; their leaves, covered with a film of dust, drooping to the cracked pavement. Hannah watched a child drop an ice cream, then send a fractious wail into the humid air, while a trail of sweet, sticky liquid oozed along the street. People pushed past her, restless, impatient, longing to be in a cooler space, spending money.

Hannah was irritable too. Since their first encounter, she had seen Rees several times. After the second time, Rosa had come up to her unexpectedly and asked if she was okay, but Hannah had just nodded, and Rosa had asked no further questions. Hannah was still dancing too, and she was exhausted both by the late nights at the club and by the nervous tension and guilt seeing Rees generated. She told herself that she still got a kick out of the dancing and out of the desire she generated in the punters, but she didn't. And the money was insignificant compared to what seeing Rees gave her. She certainly enjoyed the fact that she was now making a little cash of her own (after Charlie and Carla got their shares), but when, like now, the coke had worn off, she just felt like shit. She stared at her reflection in the glass doors – she was sure she looked as bad as she felt – and looked impatiently at her watch.

Minutes later, a voice called out to her, and she turned towards the sound. Diana was crossing the street, waving at Hannah, eyes still fixed on the traffic so that she might work out how best to avoid its onslaught. Safely across, she picked her way through the crowd until finally she reached her friend. She breathed a sigh of relief, as though she had completed a demanding obstacle course, and ran a hand through her blonde hair, which she wore long and back from her head in the style described as 'windswept'.

"Hannah! So lovely to see you," she exclaimed, as she took her friend by the arm and led her into the store and up to the café situated at the top. "How long's it been?"

"I last saw you at your engagement party, I think. You look well, Diana."

"Thank you. And you, Hannah, you look *so* smart." Diana fingered Hannah's shirt. "Gorgeous," she whispered. "Armani?"

Hannah nodded.

"Exquisite," breathed Diana. "So," she said, when she'd sat down, a decaffeinated coffee in front of her, "how *are* you?"

"Okay. How's John?"

"He's lovely. So kind." Diana beamed. "Things are very… settled between us. Though, I must admit, it was a bit of a let-down at first, you know. After the excitement of the wedding…" She broke off and turned to Hannah with reproach in her eyes. "Why didn't you go?"

"I couldn't. Karl…" Hannah corrected herself quickly. "We were away."

"I heard you split."

"I… it didn't work out." Saying that brought Karl back – his forceful kisses, his cruel words, the soreness Hannah had sometimes felt after he'd been inside her. Her stomach heaved and shifted.

"Are you okay, Hannah?"

"I'm fine."

"Where was I? Oh, yes, well, you have the wedding, and that was all rather fun – a huge organisational feat, of course, but fun – and then the honeymoon – we went to Florida – and then…" Diana looked at Hannah and her eyes were blank, like sheets of glass. "And then… nothing."

"Nothing?"

"Well, you have a child, of course. We haven't started trying yet, but we will. And then you have another child!"

Diana rolled her eyes at her friend, and Hannah rolled them back, and suddenly they were schoolgirls again and life was like the playground.

"What are you up to, then?"

Hannah knew she was curious – *very* curious. She'd seen Diana staring at her shiny jewellery, her gleaming watch, and her smart clothes, wondering where it all came from. But she wouldn't tell her; not yet. She'd keep her guessing awhile. "Oh… things," she said vaguely.

"What things?" Diana persisted. "Where did you get all this, Hannah?"

"What?"

"*This*." Diana waved her hand at Hannah's outfit. "Don't say you got hitched to some rich man. You were always so anti the idea."

"Let's go shopping and then I'll tell you."

Diana followed Hannah out of the café and into the store. She watched in astonishment as Hannah paid for a pair of gold Chanel earrings and a Versace handbag. Finally, having seen Hannah buy a dress from Gucci that even she, Diana, could not begin to afford, she could no longer contain herself. She grabbed her friend and spun her round.

"*Where* are you getting all your money from?"

Hannah grinned. The earrings, the bag and even the dress were all for Carla; pre-ordered and paid for with Carla's credit card. Carla had given Hannah a debit card, but she pored over her statements like a hawk. Although Hannah was saving a little, she was never able to spend much without Carla knowing about it. But Diana didn't know that. Her pretty face was a puzzle; envy now replaced with a look of complete bafflement. How delighted that made Hannah feel! How thrilling to be standing in a posh department store with her old friend and to feel that, in material terms at least, she was at last her equal. It had all been worth it – the late nights, the grief Carla sometimes gave her, even the awkwardness she'd felt on calling Cheryl to ask for Diana's new number, the old hatred that had risen in her throat like bile when she'd done so – just to see that. In that moment, even tired and sober, she was happy.

"What is it you do?" Diana's voice was softer now, pleading.

"Don't worry – it's all above board. I'm a dancer."

Diana's eyes widened. "A ballet dancer?"

"Not quite."

"What, then?" Clearly, Diana wasn't going to give up.

Hannah hesitated. "Let's have a drink and then I'll tell you."

They went to a bar inside the department store. Orchids lined the marble drinks counter.

After two glasses of wine, Hannah leaned over and whispered in her friend's ear. "I dance in a club," she said.

"What's the name of the club?"

"Charlie's."

Diana digested this for a moment, sipping her drink. And then, finally, her eyes narrowed. "You're a *stripper*?"

Hannah shifted uncomfortably. "I prefer 'dancer'," she said.

"You're joking, right?"

"No."

"You let men touch you? Paw at you?"

"No, *no*. They're not supposed to."

Diana stared at Hannah as if something were wedged in her throat; with a mixture of fascination and horror. Then the horror took over. She drew back. "That's disgusting," she said.

Hannah drained her glass. Two spots of colour stained her cheeks. "I knew that would be your reaction, Diana. But you know what? I don't give a shit. I always wanted to have money, just like you, but unlike you, I'm making my own cash. And I get to be *free* as a result." She hesitated. She knew she should stop there, but rage and jealousy took over and she couldn't help herself. "You're *swimming* in cash, always were, and you never had to lift a finger for it. The downside is, you're trapped in a dull marriage. I'd be expiring from boredom, literally *expiring*, if I were you." In her anger, she used the expression they'd used as schoolgirls when complaining about Mr Klark's maths class. Hearing herself say it brought her up short.

"There are other choices, you know," Diana told her.

"I don't see you making them." Hannah sighed. She regretted having told Diana a thing. Had she really thought she was ever going to win her friend over? Hardly. She'd only just got around to telling Sal about the club, and her sister hadn't been bothered at all. Perhaps she'd been emboldened by Sal's reaction; lulled into a false sense of security. Hannah could feel her nose stinging; the first sign that she was upset. But she wasn't about to apologise for her life. Why should she? "Jesus, Sal always said you were stuck-up, and she was right."

Diana gathered her things together in swift, angry movements. Finally, she stood up.

As she turned away, Hannah caught hold of her sleeve. "Diana?"

"Let go – I'm going home."

"Don't tell my father about this, okay?"

"Why would I tell Jake, Hannah? He no longer visits Mum, thank God. I haven't seen him in ages. And nor would I want to. He's nothing but a big tart, just like his daughter." And Diana stormed out.

Chapter 41

Shortly after Hannah had seen Diana, Charlie accosted her just as she came down from the stage. Hannah was exhausted; she seemed to need more and more coke to perform properly these days. She tried to move past Charlie, but he held on to her arm.

"How's it going, Hannah? Rees tells me he hasn't seen you for a couple of weeks."

"I wasn't well. I told him last time. I—"

Charlie's eyes gleamed in the lights of the club. "Tell me, not him, right?"

Hannah nodded. "I'll see him next week, I promise."

"Good. Because now that things are settled with Rees, I have somebody else I would like you to meet. This person is close to my heart. And very wealthy, this individual, very wealthy indeed. Not that the two are connected," he chuckled.

Hannah felt as if something were blocking her throat. She tried to swallow but her mouth was dry. "Can we talk about it another time, Charlie? I'm... shattered."

Charlie hesitated, then took a step back and grinned. "All right," he told her. He pointed a finger at her. "But you meet Rees again soon, right? And after that you meet Jerome."

That night, Hannah woke in the middle of the night. Her pillow was cold and damp with sweat. She was struggling to breathe, as if she were trapped between the four walls of the room, its ceiling moving towards her head. She sat bolt upright, shaking, only to find that the walls of Carla's flat were as far away from her as they had always been, and the ceiling was way above her head.

Again she felt a presence in the room. She peered through the gloom and saw a familiar figure sitting motionless by the window; the glow from the street lights giving a soft outline to its shape. So still and silent was Carla, so patient did she appear, that it was as if she were waiting for something or someone; as if she were prepared to wait for a very long time.

Hannah should have been glad of the company, but it just disturbed her more. She lay awake for a long while, watching Carla and wondering what or who she was waiting for, until at last sleep claimed her once again.

After meeting Diana, Hannah was wired and nervous whenever she danced, anxious eyes peering out into the blackness in front of her.

Eventually, though, the memory of her friend's reaction faded, and life carried on as before, except that during the day she felt even more tired, for two of the girls had left rather suddenly and so the others had to work even harder to make up for it. Hannah began to look forward to her next encounter with Rees, because she wasn't needed at the club for several days afterwards.

Then one night, when she was onstage, some impulse made her look not out into the room, but down near the stage, to the part of the room which was partially illuminated by the spotlights. And there she saw a familiar face. Its skin was deathly pale, its eyes like gunshot holes, and there was a look on it of pity and fear so absolute, so certain, that it terrified her to see it. But hidden beneath that was the very desire she coveted, the reward for all the pain, that she saw on all the other faces that stared at her.

Hannah stiffened as if she'd been shot, and stumbled offstage, ran to the dressing room, and sat down, breathing heavily. The space was empty but still redolent with the scent of girls; the comforts of perfume and powder. She drew her legs up to her chest and put her arms around them and her head between her knees. She smelled of fresh sweat laced with fear and the recent thrill of the dance. She breathed and waited.

She didn't have to wait long. The banging on the door was deafening.

"Hannah, I know you're in there! Open the door!"

"Go away, Robert!"

"I just want to talk to you. Let me in." His voice was softer now. But when she didn't answer, he raised the tone. "Why won't you speak to me? Jesus, I'm not going to hurt you!"

Hannah swayed backwards and forwards on her chair. She could hear Robert's breathing from behind the door. She covered her ears with her hands. "Go away!" she sobbed. "I don't want to see you."

Finally she moved to the door. She couldn't hear anything now but the pump of the music from the club. Slowly, tentatively, she opened it. When she saw Robert on the other side, she tried to shut the door in his face. But he was too quick for her, moving around as she tried to close it. Once inside the room, he took hold of her.

"Let go!"

He dropped her wrists. She pushed hard against him to force him away, but he didn't budge, as if he were a tree rooted deep in the ground. He was taller than she'd remembered and seemed to fill the room. She looked up at him. His face was still the same: cheekbones high and fine, eyes bright, mouth full and strong. In spite of his height and his strength, he wasn't really so frightening.

Hannah dropped her hands, speaking more softly this time, her one thought now being to make him leave, for his own sake as much as hers, for Charlie would be furious if he found him there. "Who told you where I work? You must leave. At once. *Please*, Robert." She forced herself to speak slowly and with dignity, to hide the embarrassment that was tightening her throat and heightening the colour in her cheeks. "I want you to go."

Robert paced across the small room. It took him only a few steps to do so, and within seconds he was back in front of Hannah. On his face was a tenderness that was almost painful to see. His voice was gentler now. "What are you doing here?"

"You saw what I'm doing, Robert. You looked like you were enjoying it, too."

"Why didn't you come to me? I'd have helped you out. I'd always help you out."

"What with? *Ideas?*" sneered Hannah.

"But..." With one gesture, Robert took in the tiny, windowless room.

"I'm sick of your disapproval, Robert. Sick of you trying to control me. You sit there in your ivory tower, thinking you can spew out judgements on the rest of us. I've met people here who are worth ten of you, and who have made me rich – richer than I ever thought possible. Far more so than you, with your scruffy clothes and that run-down home of yours."

When she saw him wince, she stepped back, winded with shame.

"Which people, Hannah? That seedy man I saw flitting around the punters, who I'll bet owns this place?"

"At least Charlie's making something of his life!" Hannah yelled. "At least he's working!"

"You call what you do work?"

"And what do *you* do, Robert? Sit around and study?

You can't live on air!"

He put out his hands and touched her arms.

"Leave me alone!" she cried.

When he spoke, his voice was soft, and pity broke out over it. "I just want you to be okay. I… I care about you, Hannah. When Diana told me you were stripping—"

"It's not like that." Hannah was sobbing so hard she could barely articulate her words.

"God – first Karl, and now this. Next thing you know, you…"

"What, Robert?"

"Nothing."

"If I disgust you so much, get out. In fact, get out anyway, or I'll call Charlie. I don't want you here. Go back to college and your poncy intellectual friends. I don't want to see you again!"

When Robert still didn't move, the sadness on his face made Hannah even angrier. Who was *he* to pity *her*? How *dare* he?

"Get out!" she screamed.

"OK, I'll go." Robert held up his hands. He walked towards the door, then at the threshold, he turned back. "But if you think I'm trying to control you, Hannah, you're more deluded than I even thought possible. Look around you. Look at who's really out to control you. At your so-called friends."

"Get out!" she spat.

But the moment Robert had gone, Hannah wanted

him back, if only to *make* him understand. Maybe he would, after all. What was it he'd said to her once? *I understand more than you think.*

With those words running through her head, Hannah left the dressing room and moved through the club. Once she reached the exit, she slipped out, telling the bouncers she needed some air. She moved up the steps to the street. She had a sense of wide-open space around her, even though she couldn't see very much at all, for the moon was hidden by the clouds and the street was dark. It was colder outside than she had expected, and she shivered as her feet moved through the fallen leaves with a rushing sound. She called for Robert and then listened.

Some distance away she heard hollow footsteps retreating. She moved towards them. "Robert!"

She stopped abruptly. He was standing beneath a street light, the soft yellow light surrounding him, lighting up the pile of leaves that had collected beneath the light and glowed at his feet, like a small fire. He was turned towards her, waiting.

"I'm in student digs in Newcastle, just off Leazes Park Road," he told her when she came close. "Come find me there. If you need to stay with me you can."

Hannah shook her head; blinked in the yellow light. "I *can't*," she told him. But as she said it, something broke inside her and she took another step towards him.

He put both his arms around her. She could feel

his breath on her face; its warmth cutting through the cold around them.

"It was good to see you," she said. Her voice was muffled because she spoke into his shoulder, but she knew he'd heard her because he hugged her still tighter. And when he pulled her face towards his and kissed her, she was reminded of all that was good about her past life: of Sal's sporadic support, of her mother's kindness, of all the times when things had seemed somehow all right, or as right as they could ever be. Then she remembered where she was now, and it seemed she was in a foreign place: alien and bewildering.

Robert's arms were resting on hers once again. This time she didn't try to move them. "You won't come with me?"

Hannah shook her head.

"You sure?"

Hannah didn't trust herself to speak. Her eyes filled with tears.

"If you need me, Hannah, call my lodgings. Any time."

Hannah could hear the hypnotic music of the club drawing her back to its source. She told herself she hadn't wanted Robert to stay; he didn't fit in with her life now. And there was something else; something she only acknowledged to herself as she stood at the top of the steps down to the club. He disappointed her, she realised. She was disappointed in him because he was so obviously disappointed in her. He clearly thought her disgusting. He had been so horrified at what she was doing at the club that he couldn't bring himself to be anywhere near her. She had forgotten already that it was she who had asked him to leave.

As Hannah stepped inside the club, she brought herself up short. How dare he think less of her simply because of what she was doing for a living? Who was he, anyway? She wasn't going to let him run her down like that and affect how she thought of herself. No way. She'd been a fool to even think about it. She shook her head as if to emphasise the point, and then she slipped back behind the stage.

Chapter 42

Hannah's meeting with Jerome was delayed, Jerome having been called away on 'unavoidable business'. But he'd come back, Charlie assured Hannah, and then they would meet. Hannah was dreading it. When she wasn't at the club or meeting Rees, when she was trapped in Carla's flat, watching the naked branches of the trees spread out like nerve endings against the sky, Robert's words would come back to her. *Look at who's really out to control you*, he'd told her, and for the first time she looked, and she didn't like what she saw.

One night, as the rain spattered against her bedroom window in angry bursts, Hannah decided to count out the money she'd managed to save. She wasn't earning much, she concluded – not nearly as much as Charlie had promised she would all those months ago, and he and Carla took the majority of it from her. She stuffed her money back inside the shoebox, closed the box, and pushed it under her bed. Then she went to find Carla.

Carla was sitting on the sofa in the sitting room, listening to music. She'd finished a new painting – a still life – and was examining it now. One slender finger tapped against the gilt carving on the sofa, moving in time to the rhythm of the music. Next to Carla sat the canary's cage, covered with the black cloth that she spread over it in the evenings. No sound came from within. The flames from the gas fire in the grate brought out the gold on the chair and on the lamp stand, and cast a soft light over Carla's face, making it seem warm and welcoming.

Carla drew Hannah down next to her. "Listen to his exquisite arrangement of the notes," she said softly. "It's so perfect, so ingenious. I never tire of hearing Bach."

Hannah sat silently, trying to listen. But the conversation she was planning to have with Carla kept sliding through her head. "Carla?" she said at last. "How come you're not painting figures any more?"

Carla turned to her in surprise. "You've been too busy to pose for me, Hannah. Charlie says you're in demand now. He tells me he has you meeting... Jerome next week." Her upper lip curled slightly as if she'd just tasted something unpleasant.

"Are you going to look for a new model, then?"

Carla sighed. "I have grown quite fond of you, Hannah. Though sooner or later I will have to accept that there *will* be a vacancy." She lit a cigarette and sent the smoke, in a curving spiral, towards the ceiling.

"If... *when* you find somebody... where will she stay?"

"I'm sure Charlie will find a place for her. He sorts everyone out, does Charlie." Carla turned back to Hannah. "Oh, Hannah, you needn't worry. I'd never move you out to make room for a new girl. I'm *far* too fond of you. This is where you belong. Here, with me." She smiled; a long, slow smile.

Hannah took a deep breath. She was as nervous now as she had been all those years ago when she'd seen Karl on her way to school. She remembered his smell, its sweet toxicity, washing over her. Now she breathed in Carla's heavy, sensuous scent. She remembered the last time Carla had touched her (some time ago now); how expertly she'd brought her to a climax, even though they'd both been drinking. With difficulty, she brought herself back to the present. Carla was holding her hand now, her fingers pressing into Hannah's palm. Hannah could feel her own hand, slightly damp, encased in Carla's smooth, dry skin; fitted neatly within it, as a soft clam fits within its shell. It would take some effort to remove her hand, she thought; it would be almost impossible. Speech was the easier option. And so she started speaking.

"Carla, you've been so kind, so generous to put me up. But really, I think... it's time I lived on my own. You know," her eyes slid away from Carla's, "stood on my own two feet. I've never done that before. And now... now I've got a little money..." She swallowed; her throat was dry, and the heat of the fire was making her flush. She waited for Carla to speak.

"You want to leave here?" Carla asked in surprise. "You'll *never* afford a thing on your own. Where would you live, for a start?"

"I... I don't know. I'd find somewhere."

"Listen to you," Carla mocked. "You're clueless, Hannah. *Utterly* clueless. Do you have any idea how difficult it is to get an attractive place to stay in this city, and how *expensive* it would be?" With every word, her voice rose. She pulled at her cigarette.

"I'll find somewhere," Hannah replied. But a sense of her own inexperience overwhelmed her. "It's not that I'm not grateful to you for putting me up, and for everything else. You've been..." She chose her words carefully. "You've been such a good friend to me. It's just..." She shrugged her shoulders helplessly, with each second that passed more determined that she should go; that she *must*.

Carla shook away Hannah's hand. She put out her cigarette and stood, arms folded, her back to the fireplace. There was an ugly sneer on her fine face. "Well, you *are* ungrateful. You're an ungrateful little bitch. If it wasn't for me, do you know where you'd be?"

"With my sister. Or at home, I guess," Hannah faltered.

"That's right. With that grim father of yours, that violent brother and that hopeless mother."

"She's not hopeless! Don't call her that!"

Carla came to stand in front of Hannah. "Hopeless, Hannah, from what you've told me. And, no doubt, you'd still be fending off that wet boyfriend of yours. The one who came to see you the other night."

Hannah looked up in surprise. "How did you

know?"

"Charlie told me. And you'd never have got your job, or any money, or got to live here." Carla swept out her arms to take in the room in all its glory.

Hannah's words were slow, soothing. "It's a great place to live, Carla. I just need to be on my own for a while. I don't want you to have to look after me. I don't want *anyone* to look after me. That's not what I need..." She stared at Carla's face. Her features were tight and frozen.

"That's fine, Hannah. I'll tell Charlie and we'll arrange for you to work out your notice."

"Notice?"

"If you're not living with me, you're not working for Charlie. It's as simple as that."

Hannah faltered. She hadn't anticipated that Carla would cut her off. *Why?* She'd always accepted that Charlie was greedy, but Carla? She'd thought her motivated by art, by aesthetics, by noble, altruistic impulses. She sighed. "I would still give you the money. You know, the thirty per cent. You can still have it, even if I don't live here."

"It's not about the money."

Hannah frowned. She really didn't get it now. "If it's not the money, what is it?"

Carla drew closer to her, bending down so that her face was level with Hannah's. "I like having you around, Hannah. I enjoy your company. We have such fun together, and we'll continue to have fun. You interest me, and precious few people do. So it's quite simple, you see. Why don't you stay, just until I find another model?"

Hannah felt almost relieved. It was just her company Carla was craving. She was lonely, that was all. Just like Robert's mother, just like Hannah's own mother sometimes, just like the hundreds and thousands of other isolated people living in this city. And if leaving Carla meant losing her job, well, she didn't have much choice, did she? "Okay," she said.

"Fantastic." Good humour restored, Carla leaned forward and kissed Hannah on the mouth. She held out her hand and once again covered Hannah's hand with her own, drawing her towards her. "Come," she said. "Now that's settled, let's make supper."

Chapter 43

Now, when Hannah was with Carla, she was edgy and frustrated; in the club, the dancing had become routine, and the coke only gave her the briefest and most transient of hits. She could no longer lose herself onstage – it was becoming impossible to successfully blank out the people in front of her. She was only too conscious of her audience; an audience that was raucous and irritating, with a mind and purpose of its own. And she no longer felt beautiful when she was dancing; no longer desirable when she saw who, in fact, did the desiring. So she thought of the money, always and forever the money. The one real reason for doing any of it.

Just as she was about to go home one night at around 3am, Rosa came up to her in the dressing room. Her large, tawny eyes seemed wilder and more scared than usual; their pupils dilated. Hannah wondered idly what she had taken. She gave her the briefest of nods before continuing to change. She had given up hoping to make a friend of either Rosa or Raven.

"Charlie wants to see you," Rosa told her.

"*Now?*"

"He wants you to meet Jerome."

"I know," Hannah sighed.

"He wants you to meet him tomorrow."

"Tomorrow?"

"Yes. Jerome pays. You should know that. Rees is small fry by comparison." Rosa leaned into the mirror and began to remove her make-up. "I told Charlie I wouldn't see Jerome any more. That's why he's desperate for you to meet him."

"Why won't you see him?"

Rosa was tying up her shining hair, winding it round and round so that it made a circular coil at the back of her head. "Because he's a mean bastard," she told Hannah. "And he's into all kinds of weird shit." Her eyes flicked to Hannah and then back to her own face. "Just watch your back, is all I'm saying." She leaned back from the mirror and sighed. "Oh, fuck it. You don't know how to." With an eyeliner pencil she scribbled down a number on a piece of paper and handed it to Hannah. "If you get into trouble, find a phone and call this number," she told her. "But do not tell anyone I've given it to you."

As Hannah walked into Charlie's office, she passed a girl who was just leaving. Painfully thin, hip bones jutting out from her trousers like the sharp edges of knives, cheeks hollow and sunken, she looked terribly young. Her eyes were heavy and clotted with make-up.

"Who is she?" Hannah asked Charlie when she'd sat herself down.

"The new recruit. Jenna. I have high hopes for her. I'm hoping she'll follow in your footsteps."

"How old is she?"

"Seventeen."

"She's fifteen at the very most."

"What are you saying? She's lying?"

"'Course she is."

"Hannah, I tell you what. You keep to your business, and I'll keep to mine. You've been seriously jumpy these past few days. What's up? Carla getting on your tits?"

Hannah flushed. She inhaled on a cigarette, the smoke burning the back of her throat.

"I'll bet I haven't hit so wide of the mark," Charlie chuckled. "You sick of her?"

"A little."

"I'd send Jenna to relieve you, but Carla doesn't like fair girls, only dark ones. Unless her tastes have changed, which they haven't in the years I've known her." Charlie grinned lasciviously. He seemed very drunk. And high on something or other – God knows what. Coke, probably, though recently he'd been taking a lot of speed too, and MDA – in short, anything he could get his hands on. He was sweating heavily now, and his cheeks were red, even though it was cool in the room. "Like I say, fair girls are not to our Carla's most exquisite taste. I'd say you've stopped her exploring new talent for a while, Hannah. She's clearly *fixated* on you."

The spinning was starting up in Hannah's head again. She shut her eyes, put her fingers to her temples, pressed hard. That was it. That was why Carla didn't want her to go. Wouldn't let her go. "Do you think… do you think she's fallen in love with me?" she asked faintly.

Charlie's laughter was coarse. "Carla doesn't do romance, Hannah. You should know that by now. But I'd say she's *obsessed* with you. Can't get enough. You get my drift? But what's the matter, my darling? Do I shock you? Don't act the innocent with me. I'll bet you've had a little dabble, am I right? Pleasure's pleasure, no matter the source."

"How did you meet Carla?" Hannah asked faintly.

"Let me see… it was almost five years ago." Charlie counted on his plump fingers. "That's right. I hadn't bought this place yet. I was working front of house at another club; an altogether less salubrious establishment in a far grubbier part of town." He leaned towards her. "If I tell you something, will you promise not to tell anyone?" He was slurring his words. Even at the best of times, his eye contact wasn't good, but he *couldn't* look her in the eye now. "She came to work in the club as a stripper. And she was *really* good at it. She's always great at everything she does, is Carla. I've got great admiration for the woman. But that's by the by. But she got kicked out of that club after a couple of years."

"What for?"

"She was… how can I put it?" Charlie searched for the right word. "Causing trouble. She was, you know, involved with one of the other girls, and it got nasty. The girl kept coming to work with bruises." He coughed. "Carla was a lot more volatile then. The management suggested she leave, so as to keep everyone sane. And she did. But she asked me to go with her, and we opened this place together. She helps me with the business, Hannah. She's a good talent spotter as well. She finds me the girls. You're the first one she's put up, though. She didn't like any of the others. They weren't classy enough for her, no doubt. She's got quite particular tastes, has our Carla."

The spinning intensified. Hannah felt faint, as though all the blood had gone to her head. "I have to leave. I have to... she has to let me go. I feel trapped. I can't breathe..." She rose unsteadily to her feet.

Instantly, Charlie was by her side. "Jesus, Hannah." He pushed her back down into her seat, pressing his face into hers. His breath was salty and sour. "Do not say a word to her, okay? Carla will kill me if she knows I said anything about her past. And you must know what Carla's like when she's angry. Christ, she's scary when she's mad. You just leave when she's ready to let you go, and not before, you hear? It's hardly killing you staying there, is it? Not as bad as some places you've stayed, I'll bet!"

Hannah thought of Karl. But as far as she could tell, Carla was just as threatening as Karl, only different; her sinister nature laced with charm, sugar dripping with poison. She shook her head.

"She'll tire of you soon enough." Charlie wiped his

forehead. "Jeez, you had me worried there. You have to keep on the right side of Carla, okay? She's no good when she's rattled." He shook his head. "Anyway, let's leave Carla for a while," he went on. "I know she likes to be the centre of attention, but I have something more important to discuss. Tomorrow – Jerome."

"Will… will he pick me up from Carla's?"

Charlie coughed. "I'd rather they didn't interact, Hannah. He winds Carla up a little." He widened his eyes, slurring the words. "You'll have to trust me on this one. He'll reward you. Handsomely. All you have to be is your charming self. Meet him at seven o'clock in the foyer of the Savoy. And mind you be there on time."

Chapter 44

Hannah was late getting to the Savoy. It wasn't her fault – the traffic crawled along Oxford Street and towards the Strand. By the time she arrived in the foyer of the smart hotel she was breathless, agitated.

A thickset man dressed in a tight-fitting but immaculate suit that hid his slightly protuberant belly strode forward when he saw her and gripped her arm. "Hannah, I believe." The man spoke in a sibilant whisper. A ginger beard gleamed on his chin. "You're working for Charlie, right? I didn't know what to expect but you have outshone your description, my dear." He spoke with the trace of an accent. When he smiled at her she glimpsed the steely glint of a golden tooth. "Let's go get a drink," he said.

Hannah allowed herself to be steered in the direction of the spotless, expensively decorated hotel bar. There, she shifted on her seat, while Jerome assessed her. His eyes were like small slithers of ice.

"What do you want to drink?"

"Mineral water."

Jerome summoned the waiter. "JD on the rocks and a vodka martini please."

"I said I—"

Her companion slammed a palm down on the table. The glasses on its surface jumped and shivered. He leaned towards her, and when he spoke Hannah saw that flash of gold again. "You do as I say, and everything will be fine, *comprendo?*" He raised his glass. "Now, what do we drink to?"

Nothing is worth this, Hannah thought. The small ball of fear in her guts grew steadily.

"To future prosperity," Jerome said. He drained his drink and signalled to the waiter to bring another. "Tell me, Hannah, is Rosa a friend of yours?"

Hannah was relieved she didn't have to lie. "No."

Jerome's voice darkened. "I have complained to Charlie."

"Why?"

"What she called me I cannot repeat. Not to a lady. I thought she was a lady too, but alas..." He removed his jacket, lifted one arm, and rolled back his shirtsleeve to reveal a scratch on his forearm. "She's quite something, that one. A real spitfire." He grinned, his forehead beading with sweat. "I'm hoping that you prove to be – how shall I put it? – more malleable."

Hannah took a large swallow of her drink, feeling her throat burn. "Are we going for supper after this?"

"No, only for a nightcap."

"Where?"

Jerome blinked in surprise. "Charlie must have told you. About the arrangement, and my expectations. I have very exacting standards, Hannah."

"He didn't tell me anything."

"Didn't you ask?" Jerome started to chuckle, and the chuckle turned into a laugh that made his cheeks flush scarlet. "I tell you what. Let's have another drink here first and get you properly in the mood, okay? Deal?" He summoned the waiter.

Hannah swallowed nervously. Her fingers curled around the piece of paper Rosa had given her, which she had slipped into her pocket earlier that evening. "May I... just use the bathroom?"

She saw Jerome hesitate, then nod almost imperceptibly. Hannah walked at speed into the lobby, found a payphone and took a coin from her purse. With shaking fingers she removed the piece of paper from her pocket and called the number written on it. No one picked up.

When the answer machine kicked in, Hannah started speaking. "Rosa, *please*. You have to help me. You said you would. I'm at the Savoy. I... I've got to go to his room, I think. Jerome's room. I... don't know his room number. I'm scared. Help, Rosa!"

When she returned her second drink was sitting on the table.

"I'm glad you came back, Hannah." Jerome winked at her. "You should know that I reward my friends handsomely, but you should also know that things don't go so well for those who double-cross me."

The second martini slipped down more easily. "So... you never told me where we are going for this nightcap," Hannah said to Jerome. She knew now, of course. She knew where they were going. But she might as well play dumb; play for time.

Jerome looked at her curiously. "To my room, of course."

Hannah took her time drinking the second drink, until finally her companion began to fidget. He called for the bill.

"Drink up," he said. "I can't wait forever."

Jerome's room was on the seventh floor. When Hannah walked in, she was struck first by the smell of burning matches, and then by how dark the room was. She could barely see her own hand in front of her. She only felt Jerome beside her; felt his warm breath on her cheek, his hand around her waist.

"You make yourself comfortable, my lovely. And then the fun can begin."

Hannah heard the bathroom door close with a soft click. She sank down on the bed, leaned over and switched on the bedside light. On the bed in front of her she saw a pair of handcuffs. They were lined with studs. She picked up the cuffs and pressed down on one of the studs with one finger. The pain was almost satisfying. A small drop of red rose up on her skin. Hannah pressed her finger down on the white bedspread; left a red stain on it. Her heart began hammering in her chest.

Suddenly there was a knocking at the door. Hannah dropped the cuffs.

"Room service," a voice called.

"Get that, will you?" Jerome yelled from the bathroom.

Some instinct made Hannah turn off the light. She opened the door. There was a man behind a trolley, his figure framed against the lit hallway. Hannah gasped as he reached out and grabbed her with one hand while he covered her mouth with another.

"Run!" the man hissed in her ear.

Hannah ran. Behind her, the door slammed shut. She and the stranger raced towards the lifts. Just as the lift doors closed, Hannah heard footsteps thud towards them along the hallway.

She sank against the wall of the lift, staring at the man in front of her. He looked familiar, with auburn hair and very pale skin. "Who *are* you?" she asked.

The man grinned at her. "I'm Rosa's brother, John. She calls me whenever she's in trouble. Except this time she said *you* were in trouble. Anyway, she gives me the room numbers and I go get her. Luckily your man Jerome is a creature of habit – he always takes the same room."

"How do I know you're who you say you are?"

"You've got to believe me, lovely. What choice do you have?"

Outside, they ran until they came to a side street off the Strand around the corner from the hotel. John gestured to a small blue Fiat parked on the left. "Get in. I'm taking you home."

Hannah directed him to Carla's place. As they

drove, weaving unsteadily through the London traffic, Hannah caught glimpses of a saffron-coloured band of light at the fringe of the skyline, where there was a break in the buildings clogging up the horizon. She kept searching for this bright golden band between the buildings, but by the time they turned into the streets adjoining Carla's, the band had disappeared altogether, and the sky was dark and the clouds heavy.

John parked outside Carla's. Hannah looked up at the flat. A light was on. She swallowed nervously. She imagined Carla sitting, waiting for her, cigarette in hand, face like a mask. She hoped that her vigil had been cut short by sleep.

"You can leave me here. Thank you."

"You sure?"

Hannah nodded. "And please thank your sister for me. I... I didn't expect that."

"I look out for her. That's what family does."

Hannah thought of Charlie and Carla, and then of her own parents. She could feel her eyes sting with unshed tears.

John reached into his pocket and pulled out a joint. "She gets mixed up in some pretty crazy stuff, my sister does, but then I can't talk." He tapped the joint. "There's worse where this came from. I sort out all sorts. So if you ever need me to sort you out some shit, let me know." He offered Hannah the joint. She shook her head, and he leaned over her and opened the car door for her. "Chivalry ain't entirely dead, you know," he told her. "If you need me again, you know my number."

Hannah came to the last flight of stairs leading up to Carla's flat. The open door formed a golden oblong of light that shone into the hallway. She stood in the darkness at the foot of the stairs, her head pounding.

A figure appeared in the doorway, framed against the light. "Come up here!" Carla spoke in a hoarse whisper. Suddenly, she shot down the stairs.

Hannah felt her arm being gripped painfully as she was dragged back up. "Let go!" she hissed. Carla's grip on her arm was like a vice.

"What time do you call this? I've been worried sick!"

"It's not even eleven o'clock."

A stinging slap on her face almost winded Hannah. All fight left her, and she gave herself up, trembling, to her captor, allowing herself to be dragged into the flat.

"Who were you with all this time? Jerome? Damn Charlie. *Damn* him." Carla drew Hannah into a sudden embrace. Her arms were hard and muscular, and Hannah felt as if she were surrounded by an electric fence. "Did he hurt you? You poor darling. Come sleep in my bed tonight."

Carla led Hannah to her bedroom. But at the door Hannah whispered, "Please, Carla, I'm exhausted. I need to sleep now."

"I only want to make you feel better, Hannah," Carla dropped her voice, "in that special way I have. You do like that, don't you?" She smiled, moving towards Hannah.

"I need to be alone, I said."

Carla held up her hands. "As you wish."

Quickly, Hannah moved into her own bedroom. In the bathroom next to it she leaned over the tap, drinking the clean, cool water. It was like diving into a deep, dark pool – the world seemed to right itself as she drank. Then she hurriedly began piling a few clothes into a large bag. She emptied out the shoebox and stuffed her savings into the bag. Then she opened the door. Carla was standing on the other side of it.

"I'm leaving," Hannah told her. She could feel her legs shaking beneath her.

Carla folded her arms, effectively barring Hannah's exit from the bedroom. "Charlie won't like it," she said, with a decisive shake of her head.

"I'll deal with Charlie."

"No one can *deal with* Charlie." Carla's smile was sinister.

"You can't stop me trying."

"Hannah!"

Carla took a step towards her, reached out her hands but Hannah ducked and ran across the living room, past the canary's cage, the heavy curtains, the marble bust. Coated in darkness, these inanimate objects seemed alive, as if they were listening to her footsteps. She unbolted the front door of the flat and moved down the stairs. With Carla's steps behind hers,

Hannah increased her speed, reaching the bottom of the staircase a full flight ahead of her pursuer. Before Carla could turn a corner in the staircase Hannah turned back on herself, heading not out to the front, but to the back door of the building, which she knew led to a large garden. She leaned against the staircase by the back door, waiting.

Carla ran through the hallway, flung open the front door and ran out. Hannah unhooked the key to the back door from the safe space where it was stored and opened it. She stepped out into the dark garden and moved through it and out of the gate at its end, looping back around to the street, but further down from the flat. From there, she continued along the street until she slipped into the shadows of a neighbouring alleyway and disappeared.

Chapter 45

It was almost midnight by the time Hannah reached the club. Music was pounding inside it. The stage was lit. She could make out Cathy and another girl curving in time to the music.

"What happened to you, love?" Will called out. "You look like shit."

Hannah ignored him and made straight for Charlie's office. She hammered on the door, then opened it without waiting to be invited in. Charlie was with Jenna, their heads bent together. At first Hannah thought they were going through paperwork, and then she realised that they were just doing coke.

"Am I interrupting something?" she asked, rather too sweetly.

Charlie looked up. Something – guilt or embarrassment, maybe – moved over his features. Whatever it was, he hid it quickly. "No, no, of course not," he told her, and ushered Jenna from the room. "What's with you, sweetheart? You're not looking your usual self these days."

"I don't want to work here any more. I don't want to live with Carla either."

"Come on, Hannah. We spoke about this."

"And I want my money," Hannah said.

"What money?" Charlie asked in surprise, sitting

back with a cherubic grin on his face.

"You haven't given me anything for Rees or for the club for the last few weeks. And then there's Jerome," she added.

"Oh, that." Charlie's grin became apologetic, sycophantic. "Jerome won't pay out."

"Why not?"

"Because you didn't dish out. He already called me. You gave him the slip." Charlie pointed one stubby finger in her direction. "Don't try to screw me over, Hannah," he hissed softly. "You *will* fail. Jerome is not a happy man, that's for sure."

Hannah sighed. "Just give me the other money you owe me," she told him, "and I'll go."

Charlie's eyes protruded in shock. "You'll go? *Where?*"

"I... I don't have to tell you."

"But Carla and I – we're your *family*," Charlie protested.

"No, you're not."

"You can't just quit. What about your notice?"

"What notice?"

"Any girl has to work a week's notice before she goes."

"I don't want to do that."

Charlie leaned back in his seat and yawned. "And I don't want to give you any money. Leave me, leave Carla, by all means. But I won't pay you for it."

Hannah took a step forward, before a sudden wave

of sickness overwhelmed her, and she sank into the chair opposite him.

"That's right," he laughed. "Don't even think of going anywhere near me. This place is riddled with people willing to leap to my defence."

She watched him watching her, and he seemed no longer charming, but devilish and sly.

"Get back to work, Hannah," Charlie told her. "Carry on working. And then you'll earn your money."

By the time she went onstage, Hannah's legs were so weak she could barely dance. She stood in the spotlight, filled with nausea and nerves. In front of her, for the first time, the crowd separated, and she could make out each individual face. Then the faces ran into each other and became indistinguishable; a leering, pulpy mess. With a supreme effort of will, Hannah approached the nearest table. She removed her top as if she were in a slow-motion film, acutely conscious of the small bruises that had already appeared on her upper arm from Carla's grip. She felt ashamed of her body because she had lost so much weight. As she began taking off her skirt, she thought of Carla, and of Rees, and finally of Jerome. She tried to drive these thoughts away and to think only of the money she was able to earn. She felt a man grope at her skirt, his sweaty hand touching her leg; his fingers trying to hold on to her elbow.

"No touching," she whispered, but her throat closed

over the words. Soon it became almost impossible to move, let alone remove any more clothing.

One of the men nearest to her leaned over to his companion and said, "What's up with her?"

"Looks like she's on drugs."

"Far too skinny. Look at them bruises."

"You going to give her any cash?"

"No way, mate!"

They laughed, as if at some private joke, until one of the other men at the table called out, "Go on – piss off!"

Hannah froze. Finally, she turned her back on the men, swaying slightly.

When she got to the bathroom, she threw up. Then she changed into the clothes she had come in, grabbed her bag, and made her way to Charlie's office, walking rather unsteadily.

Charlie was with Jenna again. This time, they weren't taking coke, and Hannah was in time to catch just what they were doing, because she opened the door without knocking. Charlie sprang away from Jenna the moment she opened it, but he knew she'd seen him.

"I want some money, Charlie."

"Hannah," Charlie protested, "we've been through this. The night is young. Get back to work."

"I want the money I'm owed." Hannah's voice rose. "If you don't give it to me, I'll tell people just how old Jenna is and what her employer's been doing with her."

Charlie's shining face whitened. "You wouldn't."

"Give me my money, Charlie."

Charlie sighed. Finally he shuffled behind his desk before handing her a bunch of notes. "Take this. That's all you're getting for now."

Hannah took the notes. The wad was slim. She was being given a fraction of what she was owed but she knew that no amount of blackmail would get her more. *At what price freedom?* she thought. She turned away.

"Where are you going?" Charlie demanded.

She blinked. "Back to Carla's, of course."

"Do you think I'm stupid? I know you gave her the slip too this evening."

Hannah flushed. "She was doing my head in. But I'll head back to hers now; I promise."

"Well, I'll tell her you're coming, so she can expect you." Charlie pointed at her. "And I'm expecting to see you tomorrow. Don't you try any funny business, okay?"

As Charlie reached for the telephone, Hannah backed away from the room. She slammed the door behind her. She looked back just as she had crossed the club and was preparing to leave, half-expecting the bouncers to stop her. But the men stood still as statues in the half-light, while the door to Charlie's office remained closed.

Chapter 46

When Hannah came to a payphone she dropped her bag and dialled a number. The phone seemed to ring for an eternity before it was picked up.

"Can I talk to Sal?"

"We ain't heard from you for a while." Maeve didn't sound too pleased to hear from Hannah now. Her voice was bleary with sleep. "What you doing up at this hour?"

"Where's Sal? I need to talk to her."

"Didn't she tell you?"

"Tell me what?"

"She went away."

"*Where?*" Hannah demanded.

"Lemme see… Thailand first, she said. Then Nepal. Or maybe it was Nepal first."

"She's gone *travelling?*"

"Yeah."

"When did she go?"

"Three weeks ago, I think."

"How did she get the money?"

"She saved up. Took 'er a while." Maeve chuckled. "She tried to get hold of you to tell you she was off—"

"What about Jake? He let her go?"

"Couldn't stop her. Yer dad's ill, anyhow."

"Mum said it wasn't serious."

"Dunno."

Hannah sighed. "How long's she gone for?"

"She didn't say. As long as the money lasts. Mebbe two weeks, mebbe ten. Who knows?"

The emptiness inside Hannah intensified, until she could no longer contain it and it spilled over and out of her. She stood holding the receiver, imagining mountain air so clean it hurt to breathe, and a bright foam-filled sea whipped by a wind that seemed to fill her ears so that she could barely hear Maeve saying, "And how about you? I heard what you was up to."

When Hannah spoke again, her voice seemed to come from a great distance away. "I quit."

"Seriously?" Maeve sounded as if someone were tickling her; she was chuckling and chortling. "What happened? Nah, don't tell me: you saw the light."

"I gotta go, Maeve."

Hannah cut the call. She remained in the phone box, blowing on her hands to warm them. It was still freezing out: spring was hiding. When she left the box, her footsteps rang out on the pavements and her feet tingled with cold. She didn't want to go home. That meant there was only one place left she could go. Thrusting her hands deep into her pockets, she headed north in the direction of King's Cross.

Chapter 47

In a corner of the station, where two yellowing concrete walls met, Hannah crouched wearily. Above her head, single bars of strip lighting ran across the ceiling, filling the space with sickly yellow light. Around her a few people had settled, waiting for the first train, their breath misting the cool night air. Hannah put her bag under her knees and brought her head down between them so that her whole frame was bent over the bag, protecting it.

She had fled Charlie's over an hour ago, but the first train wasn't due for a while. She was so tired, she was scared she'd fall asleep and miss it. She concentrated on staying awake, sipping a vending-machine coffee that tasted of sugared tar and rubbing her eyes to stop them from closing.

When Hannah finally made her way onto the platform, the clouds drew back to reveal a faint circular moon. Dawn's first light cast a silver sheen onto the tracks, and they glimmered faintly. With the light, at last, the train drew in. Hannah, relieved to be on it, leaned her head back against a seat. She closed her eyes as the train pulled out of the station, and eventually its steady, soothing motion sent her to sleep.

Three hours later, a guard making his rounds found

Hannah slumped across two seats.

"Miss!" he called loudly. "Wake up!"

Stirring, Hannah shrank back, for, though his eyes were kind, his teeth were stained and yellow and reminded her of Charlie's. "Are we there yet?" she asked him, handing over her ticket.

"Where you going?"

"Newcastle."

The driver yawned. "Another fifteen minutes. Train just left Durham."

Hannah pressed her nose against the window. A clutch of churches towered above the houses in front of her, their spires pinning the clouds against the sky. For a while, chaotic graffiti lined the tracks and then disappeared, to be replaced with swathes of green and brown dotted with fir trees and grazing sheep. Then the ground dropped away as the train crossed a bridge. To Hannah's right a smooth river flowed beneath the vast arch of another bridge. Its bricks were a faint greenish hue, and the river water looked yellow and sluggish.

When Hannah stepped off the train, her legs twisted with cramp. A man sold her a can of Coke at a tatty newsagent outside the station. "How do I get to Leazes Park Road?" she asked him. She scribbled down his directions and set off along the road he pointed out.

The air was so cold, it hurt her lungs. The wind carried scents of damp wood and river water. Hannah walked up Clayton Street, past the clock on the corner of Westgate Road, past Grainger Market, left and through Eldon Square, across Percy Street, and then left again up Leazes Park Road, climbing all the while. At the end of Leazes Park Road she stopped, her heart beating hard with the climb. She felt as if she were on top of the city. In front of her was a low wall, and behind it she could see trees, barely in bud, their stark, bare branches etched against the cloud. To her right, dark chimneys of factories dominated the skyline. To her left lay Leazes Terrace; a long line of identical houses.

A sign above an opening in the middle of the terrace indicated student lodgings. As Hannah turned into it, she felt the first drops of freezing rain fall on her face. She walked down to the courtyard at the back. A door to her right opened into a white corridor. She stepped through a set of doors, and down another corridor. Finally, she came into a large, old-fashioned room with tall windows. Rain spattered the glass. The air smelled of coffee. Groups of students lounged at the sides of the room, eyeing her curiously. Hannah hesitated. Finally, she walked up to a student sitting on a scruffy sofa nearby – a boy with a sallow complexion and a mass of messy hair as unkempt as her own – and asked for Robert.

"Tall boy with yellow eyes?"

She nodded. She shifted uncomfortably from one foot to the other.

"You seen him today?" the student asked his companion, a girl with rosy cheeks and a crop of acne across her forehead.

The girl shook her head.

The male student thought for a while, scratching his head. "Tell you what – the library's the best bet, knowing him."

But the girl was pointing to a far corner of the room. "He's over there," she said.

Hannah's heart jumped. She hadn't been expecting to find Robert so quickly, and among all these people. She'd hoped to see him in his own room, where they could talk, just the two of them. She swallowed nervously.

"Are you okay?" the girl asked.

But Hannah was already walking away from the two students towards Robert. As she walked, students turned and stared at her. The smell of coffee, close and bitter, seemed stronger than ever. Up ahead, Robert sat at a table, his back to her. His back was strong and straight, his hair a dark gold. Even though he was sitting, she could still tell how tall he was. As she watched him, with one hand he smoothed back his hair in the gesture she remembered so well. Moving towards him, a million questions seethed through her brain. How would he react on seeing her? Would he still pity her? She couldn't bear that. What if she couldn't look him in the eye? What if...? Eventually, she slowed down and stopped some distance away from him. She shut her eyes and stilled her mind. Finally, she opened her eyes.

Robert wasn't alone. A girl was sitting opposite him; a very beautiful girl with hair as dark as Hannah's, but not messy and twisted like hers – it spread over her shoulders in smooth dark waves. And the girl's skin wasn't pale, but a caramel colour that lit up her face and neck and made them glow. To one side of the girl sat a pile of textbooks, their titles indecipherable. The girl didn't notice the stranger standing some distance behind Robert, the girl with hair the same colour as her own; she was too busy talking, rather animatedly, to her companion. Hannah saw her reach over and caress Robert's forearm, a smile playing around the corners of her mouth, and as she did so, Hannah's mouth filled with bile and her guts clenched unhappily.

She couldn't move; she could only stand and stare at the girl. She'd been longing to see Robert again, to tell him what had happened to her and have him comfort her, as he had said he would. He'd seemed to her a haven; his place somewhere she could stay and rest. But now that wouldn't happen. Her thoughts ran in a futile, paranoid circle. Robert was no longer concerned about her; no doubt he'd written her off after he'd found out what she'd been doing, in spite of what he'd told her. He'd claimed to care for her, but he'd lied. She clearly disgusted him. She'd been a fool not to go to Newcastle with him when he'd come to see her. When he'd said he'd look after her, before the disgust had got too much for him and he'd started to look elsewhere. The disgust she imagined that Robert felt for her she began to feel for herself, so that soon self-loathing filled her, choking her.

She let out a cry, then brought her hand to her mouth, but that didn't stifle the cry properly, and the girl heard it. She reached across the table and put her other hand on Robert's arm. When Hannah saw that, the shock finally made her move. She spun round and fled the room. She heard Robert's voice call out her name, but she couldn't turn to him or even think of him; only of the girl who sat opposite him and who had caressed his arm. She came to the door of the building, then without hesitation she ran out into the streets.

She imagined Robert following her as she ran, her footsteps making a hollow sound on the flagstones. She increased her speed, running past teenagers lounging in Eldon Square, through crowds of shoppers milling around Grey's Monument, and down Grey Street. As she ran, the rain intensified, running down her forehead and making her eyes swim. Finally, she paused, leaning against a car, chest pounding, breath escaping in short, unhappy bursts. A single car whooshed past her at speed, flinging up spray, twin headlamps shining through the driving rain. All around her water drummed on pavements, sending people to cover in doorways, clutching their battered umbrellas. She was sure she could make out Robert's voice through the falling rain, calling her over and over. Perhaps she was making it up. She looked behind her. She couldn't see him, but she couldn't afford to rest; not now. Robert might be better at most things than she, but with running, Hannah had the advantage. He might run fast, but she was faster. When it came to the chase, Hannah was driven by fear.

When she could run no more, when she came to a wall bordering the river, there at last she stopped. Over her head loomed the vast arches of High Level Bridge. To her right, buildings belched plumes of smoke into the sky. There was no sound behind her now: no footsteps; nothing.

With Sal gone, Hannah knew there was only one place she could run to now; only one place where she would at least be welcome. For a moment she hesitated, eyes fixed on the river's curves below her; on the filthy water, churned by wind and rain, seething around the old bricks of the bridge. Then she turned and carried on moving at speed, towards the station.

PART 4
ROBERT

Chapter 48
London

In her dream Hannah was moving through water so blue, it was as if it were aiming to match the wild, brilliant blue of the sky overhead, and then water and sky would join in some ecstatic union. Sunlight played on the surface of the water, but she wasn't dazzled by the light; she merely fixed her sight on the place that she must reach. Her strokes were straight and confident, her body moving gloriously, with no doubt, no fear. On the shore opposite she could make out a figure waving at her. She increased the strength of her strokes, her arms stretching out even further into the water. As she came to the other side, she felt joy, the like of which she had seldom known, rise through her like sap.

It was just at that moment that she realised that the shore was empty.

She woke to a lunge of disappointment, like the thrust of a knife, and brought her knees up to her chest. Her limbs ached. On the inner side of her upper arm, where the skin was lily white, two bruises had risen, like blue-and-yellow flowers. They were the only spots of colour on her white body, save for her eyes, which, green and luminous, stared fixedly ahead.

The room was familiar to her: she could make out the

faint outline of the vast mahogany wardrobe in which she'd hidden as a child; the stain on the wallpaper by the window; the circular lampshade hovering over her, pale as a ghost. Above the brass bed frame hung a small figure of Christ on the cross that had belonged once to her mother's family, and that used to frighten her so as a child because of the pallor of his skin. The air was stale – it smelled of dust and sweat and something else; something indefinable that had, as its essence, her home. Hannah pulled a blanket over herself, letting the darkness hug her.

Suddenly she heard floorboards creak, as if in protest, and her mother entered the room. Her face was pale as moonlight, and sadness clung to her like her shadow. Hannah removed the blanket, reached for her cigarettes, and lit up. With the hit of nicotine, her blood surged. As the smoke flowed blue through the room, she watched a single ray of sunlight penetrate a gap in the curtains. In it, dust motes danced.

"You shouldn't be smoking, love," her mother protested.

"How's Jake?"

"The consultant's given him something for the pain." Her mother handed her a cup. "Here, take this."

The hand that held the cup shook slightly, as it had when Hannah was a child, when she'd sat up, hot with fever, reaching for the cup of sweet milk her mother had made for her. Something stirred in Hannah with the memory; something green and living, a little like tenderness. She put out her cigarette.

Her mother reached out a hand and touched her daughter's face. "Sleep well?"

Hannah flinched. "No."

A sudden knocking at the door startled them both.

Hannah paled, reached for her mother's arm. "Don't answer it, Mum!"

"Why not? Do you know who it is?"

A cry came from the next room, and her mother was suddenly alert, all senses poised.

"Maybe," Hannah whispered.

"Well, I'd best go to your father first." Her mother's face was fixed and her tread light and decisive as she left the room.

Hannah turned to the wall. Her eyes followed a crack that moved over the wallpaper from the skirting board to the ceiling, where it spread and multiplied, covering the plaster with fine lines, like tiny veins. A fly banged repeatedly against the windowpane. From a neighbouring house came low, somnolent music filled with static.

When she heard steps on the stairs and the front door close, Hannah stood and moved to the bathroom mirror. Her reflection stared back at her: eyes ringed by dark circles; lips that had a mere suggestion of fullness, now blue and bloodless in the overhead light. She made a feeble attempt to arrange her hair and then moved towards the stairs.

She could see Robert through the banister rails, as though through prison bars. He stood tall and straight and so still, as if he were made of stone. His golden hair seemed at odds with his drab surroundings. Hannah caught her breath. And then, as she looked down, he looked up, and their eyes met. He called her name and started moving up the stairs.

The blood pounded painfully in Hannah's head. Her throat constricted. There was no going back now; nowhere to run. She had to face him.

Chapter 49

Robert's footsteps on the stairs seemed almost defiant, as though he cared not at all about violating Hannah's space, or that she wanted to hide from him, but was determined to confront her. Hannah returned to her room and pulled the blanket over herself again, moving so close against the wall that she breathed in nothing but the dead, dry smell of plaster. She winced as she heard the door open and steps coming towards her. But the touch on the blanket that covered her was gentle; the voice that spoke her name tender, hesitant.

"Hannah."

Slowly Robert removed the blanket. Hannah turned to face him, but his eyes slid from hers.

"That's right," she whispered. "Still don't like what you see? Why did you follow me here, then?" Her voice was low and resonant, moving through the room, filling the empty space between them.

"You came to me first, remember?" Robert sat down on her bed. He leaned forward and took hold of her arm; gently, avoiding the bruising upon it. The other hand he placed behind her head as he brought her face nearer to his. His eyes stared into hers, drawn to the faint light that still glowed inside them. And he spoke, so softly she could barely hear him. "Hannah, listen—"

She shook her head. His touch was so sure that her

whole instinct was to rebel against it. "Let go of me." Her arm strained against his.

He dropped his voice. "Maya's just a friend. You do believe me, don't you?"

Hannah moved far from him so that her head rested against the bars of the bed frame. "She looked like more than a friend."

"Maybe she wants to be, but I… I think only of you, Hannah."

"I don't believe you."

"You *must*. I had been worrying about you since I saw you at the club; hoping you'd come to see me. I *willed* you to leave Charlie's. I couldn't make you do it, but I knew you'd be brave enough to do so in the end. Just like when you left Karl. And when you came to see me, I was so glad." His eyes shone. "But then you ran away again."

Hannah shut her eyes. "I disgust you."

"That's not true."

She sighed. When she spoke again, it was as if something had caught in her throat. "I disgust myself. I'm twenty and I'm back at home again, right back at the beginning of my life. You can't help me. I've no job; nothing. And nothing has changed. Everything is still the same. And nothing will ever change, not ever," she sobbed.

"That's not right. Things *will* change, Hannah. If you let them." He cradled her face in both his hands and brought it towards his own. Then, holding the back of her head, with one finger he traced the outline of her face, as if it were some infinitely precious thing that he'd loved and lost and now, at last, had found again. "I love you, Hannah." His voice was steadier now, and stronger. "I love all of you; everything about you. *Everything.* I've loved you for as long as I can remember."

Gently he pulled her towards him. She felt his lips touch hers; his body move in towards hers. Feebly, she tried to twist away from him, but he moved closer until his arms surrounded her; until all she could smell was him and all she could hear was the beat of blood in her ears, and whether that blood was his or hers or both of theirs, she couldn't tell. Finally she leaned into him and kissed him back, and desire moved through her body like a bright stream. She reached for him as she felt her body start to take over. She stopped thinking – she wouldn't let herself think. She shut her eyes.

"Open your eyes," he whispered.

But she couldn't. She only put her arms around him, and he kissed her again.

Suddenly, Hannah heard her mother's voice calling her. "You'd better go," she murmured. "My father is ill. I need to spend some time with him… I need some time to think."

"I'm scared to let you think. If you think, you'll think yourself out of this. I know you."

Her eyes slid away from his face.

"Hannah, look at me. You know you can trust me, right? You *do* know that, don't you?"

She nodded. For a while, neither of them spoke. Then he put his arms around her again and drew her back to him, and they lay down on her bed in each other's arms, their heads close together.

When Hannah heard her mother call again, she whispered, "Go now."

Robert stood, and she watched him move towards the door. But just before he got there, he flung open the curtains. Sunlight streamed unhindered into the room, and the objects within shrank back from the light.

Chapter 50

Hannah listened to Robert's footsteps going down the stairs until she heard the front door close. After a while, all was quiet.

Eventually, she heard a tentative step at the threshold of her room. Her mother came in, sat on her bed, and picked up one of her hands. "Has he gone?"

Hannah nodded. Her cheeks were flushed; her eyes bright. She relaxed with the pressure of her mother's hand, its reassuring warmth.

"How was he?"

Hannah lit a cigarette, but the smoke made her choke. She put it out almost immediately. "He... he said he loves me," she whispered. "I... I had no idea. I thought he hated me. *I* hate me."

"Why, love?"

"Because of Karl. It was all my fault. And afterwards – Carla; the club. Robert saw me – I couldn't bear that he saw me... *there*."

Hannah felt her mother press down on her hand, and she took a deep breath and then released it, and the words came tumbling out with it as she told her mother about Carla, and Charlie's club, and finally about Karl; each incident that she had merely buried, that she could never forget.

After Hannah had finished speaking, her mother

turned her daughter's face to hers. "Hannah, listen to me. It wasn't your fault, what happened to you. None of it was your fault. It was Karl's. Whatever he did to you, it was all *his* fault. And Carla, Charlie. They *used* you. You *must* understand that."

Hannah blinked back tears. "But it all still *hurts*. And Robert... the way he feels... it frightens me; makes me feel hemmed in. Like there's no room to breathe. I can't love him. I *can't...*" she sobbed.

"You *can*. You *will*. Give it time." Her mother hushed her as though she were calming a baby, wiping the tears from Hannah's cheeks with one hand.

This time, Hannah didn't flinch from her mother's touch; the tenderness broke out over her and made her cry even harder. Her throat was blocked with tears. It was hard to get the words out. "I... saw Robert at his college. But there was a girl with him. How can he love me, how can I trust him, when there's another girl?"

"Did you see him with the girl?"

"They were sitting together."

"Did you ask him about it?"

This questioning was quite unlike her mother: she was usually far more passive, content to let things – everything – go. Hannah wondered what had brought about the change in her.

"He denies it. And I... I don't know for sure... I guess." Hannah faltered. "I don't know." I feel so angry with him... and so disgusted with myself and what

I've done. I've failed at everything. I've been a fool; a stupid, fucked-up fool. I thought... I thought with Carla I'd found something bigger and better. But it wasn't – it was awful."

Her mother passed one hand over Hannah's forehead and down her cheeks, which were damp with tears because now that Hannah had started crying, she couldn't stop.

"What should I do?" she asked her mother. Someone must have the answers, she thought, and that person must be her mother, who seemed in that moment so calm and comforting.

"You must stay here and rest for a while."

"But—"

"Hannah, you must rest. Then you can decide what to do."

Hannah lay back against the pillows and closed her eyes. Her mother continued to hold her hand for a while, and then Hannah heard her light a cigarette. The smell of her mother's cigarette smoke was somehow soothing. The anxiety that had been circling her head faded and the aching emptiness inside her subsided. Finally, fear removed its sticky fingers from her throat, and she could breathe once again. She sighed – not with contentment, but with something a little like resignation. Tomorrow she would see her father, because she'd been too tired and overwrought to see him up till now, and she really needed to make herself do so. And the following day, she would try to speak again to Robert about that strange girl with hair the colour of Hannah's own. But for today – and only for today – she would do as her mother had told her to do, and rest.

Chapter 51

The curtains in Jake's room were drawn and the air was close. The room was lit by a lamp on the right-hand side of the bed, which cast an ochre-coloured light over the meagre figure lying against the pillows, and a single candle to Jake's left that his wife kept lit and that flickered and spat. The shadow made by Jake's body on the wall to his left was far larger than he and dominated the room. At his feet lay a black-and-white dog. The dog's name was Angus. Jake had insisted on getting him from a shelter when he'd first found out that he was ill. Hannah's mother had said that he'd taken quite a shine to the dog. Now that Jake was bedridden, Angus barely left his side.

Jake's cheeks were hollow, his face had shrunk, and he had lost most of his thick dark hair. The cancer must have spread quickly from the pancreas, Hannah thought, for her mother had told her that he had been diagnosed only a few months before. It must have been lurking in his depths for months; a small ball of poison in his guts, slowly spreading through his insides. Hannah shivered at the thought. She wondered how long her father had fought the pain, just like he fought everything and everyone, before finally giving in. Her mother had said that he had insisted on spending his last days at home. Hannah remembered her fear of her father when he was healthy. Now fear came to her once again, but this time it was a different kind – deeper and more shocking – for it was fear not of Jake's life, but of his death. But she hid this from him too, so that she could approach him calmly and with confidence. She drew up a chair beside the lamp and waited.

The noise of the chair moving across the floor disturbed Jake. He opened one eye, saw who was with him, and then closed it again. Hannah couldn't tell if he was pleased to see her or not, for his eyes were no longer quick and bright; pain had drawn all life and colour from them.

"So you're back again?" He spoke with difficulty, his voice harsh and rasping.

"Yes."

"You were stripping, your mother said." Jake's breathing was shallow and short, as if it hurt him to speak.

Hannah held her breath, waiting for the abuse, but it never came. "How are you feeling?" she asked.

Jake just shook his head slightly. His arms lay by his sides, his hands thin as paper. They trembled as if a breeze were stirring them, but there was no breeze in the room. The skin of his hand was translucent; the blue veins running beneath it swollen and raised. And now Jake drew the fingers of one hand together and tried to make a fist. His whole mind and body focused on this, willing the fingers to curl over. Finally, he gave up, and the hand collapsed onto the bedclothes.

Seeing this, Hannah took his hand in her own, very carefully, and held it. "Dad," she whispered. "Dad—"

Jake breathed in suddenly, his frail body racked with gasping coughs. He turned away from her towards the candle, and with his coughing the flame flickered and went out.

Hannah reached for a plastic child's drinking cup by the side of the bed and leaned over, offering it to her father. "I'll get Mum."

Jake gripped her hand with a sudden strength. "No! Don't call her."

Determinedly, he stopped coughing, but his hand in Hannah's felt limp and weak. For the first time in her life, she watched fear come to his face, freezing up his features, and it was as if it had risen from somewhere deep inside him. Seeing that, her own fear surged afresh, and again she hid it, though not for herself this time, but for him. She squeezed his hand, just as her mother had squeezed hers.

"It'll be okay," she told him.

Jake looked at her and smiled, and it seemed as if he were seeing her for the very first time. "How are you doing, Hannah?"

"Me?"

Without waiting for her to say any more, Jake went on. "You took a bit of a wrong turn, didn't you? You went off, wouldn't let us look after you. And your sister, she went too." He took another deep breath. "And your mother wanted to get her back when things got bad here. And we wanted to find you and tell you…"

Hannah hung her head. A part of her felt bad for ever leaving home in the first place.

Jake went on, slowly, "And Michael, God knows where he is. Getting into big trouble, no doubt." Another deep breath. "So now there'll be no one to look out for you when I'm gone." He raised himself up in the bed. "I worry about you girls… I've always worried about you." He paused and took another couple of breaths. "Sal," he said finally. "Sal will be okay. She can look after herself." He chuckled, but it obviously hurt him to do so, and Hannah winced. "Hannah. You're okay too."

"Why?" she asked. She didn't feel okay; not at all.

"You're okay," he said finally. "Because… well… Robert's a good man. He will look after you."

"I can look after myself, Dad."

"'Course you can. We all can. But if he's offering… well, then." Again, a strained chuckle.

"I… he had… I saw… he has another girl," Hannah said. She couldn't believe she had said such a thing to her father.

"Another girl? Jesus, Hannah, you don't have to worry about that. He's crazy about you…"

But here the effort of speaking became too much for Jake, and the coughing started again. This time it was worse – far worse, so that even Angus became agitated, panting, his tail thumping the mattress with a sound like a giant heartbeat. This time, when Hannah said that she would get her mother, her father didn't protest. But her mother was at the bedroom door already, her face white.

Quickly Hannah let her mother take her place by the bed. But she lingered for a while at the threshold of the room, watching her mother nurse her father, marvelling at the infinite patience and care with which she attended to him. And then, at last, she withdrew, leaving her mother by her father's side; he leaning against her and she circling him with one arm while laying her free hand over both of his and holding them very gently in her own.

Chapter 52

At two minutes past three the following morning, Hannah woke from a deep sleep. It was still dark, and she could barely see the outline of the old wardrobe and the bars at the foot of the brass bed. She was conscious of a stillness in the house, and of a similar stillness inside her head. To her, this was as strange and as sinister as a sudden calm at sea. She lay awake for a while, listening. Finally, she fell asleep again, but her sleep was broken and fitful and gave her no rest.

The following day, Hannah found out that her father had died at two minutes past three in the morning. She made tea in the kitchen to the sound of her mother's crying. As she was about to take it to her, Hannah heard a knock at the front door. Her first thought was that Robert was paying her another visit. When she opened the door and saw Sal's sunburned face, she was conscious of a guilty kind of disappointment.

"Sorry to see me?"

"No. I… You…" And then Hannah was angry that Sal had selfishly missed it all. "Where've you been?" she demanded.

"Who, me?" Sal asked innocently. She beamed, her cheeks brightening. Her face was, for once, devoid of make-up, and she looked remarkably healthy, as if she'd been picking apples in the country for days on end. Her grin widened. She undid the straps of her backpack and let it fall to the ground. "I've been everywhere. And you? Still stripping? Good for you. Bet you make more cash than I'll make in a decade."

"I gave it up."

Sal rolled her eyes. "What did you go and do that for? Did you get some stupid guilt complex or something? Listen to some outdated feminist bullshit? Well, more fool you. Now you'll be broke, just like the rest of us." She shrugged her shoulders and yawned. "God, I'm exhausted. Flight from Thailand took an age."

"Why didn't you come back sooner?"

"Yeah – Mum said Dad wasn't very well. But I thought she was being dramatic, you know. And I was delaying the return flight..." Sal's voice trailed off when she saw Hannah's face, and she turned a shade paler beneath her sunburn. "Why, what's wrong? He isn't...?"

Hannah nodded. She felt a tingling behind her eyes.

Sal blinked and passed one hand over her forehead. "Shit," she said. She blinked again, harder this time. "When?"

"Last night."

Sal sniffed; then she sniffed more loudly still.

Hannah couldn't bear to see Sal cry. She rarely cried. If she did, then something was very seriously wrong. "Sal, don't," she said. And she took hold of her sister and hugged her very tightly, and Sal didn't tell her to get lost or protest that she was okay, because they both knew that she wasn't.

After a while Sal drew back from Hannah and the two girls stared at each other. Neither of them said a word. They both knew then that everything had been turned upside down, had changed irreparably and forever, and there was nothing either of them could do about it. As they stood, struck dumb by this realisation, through the silence there came the sound of crying.

It was as if the sound woke Sal up. "Mum?" she asked.

Hannah nodded.

Sal caught her breath and held it, and then she reached out and gripped one of Hannah's hands. "Let's go to her," she said. And, very gently, she turned her sister towards the crying.

Chapter 53

The day of Jake's funeral dawned fair and clear. The air was mild, the breeze gentle. Pale sunshine warmed the purple and yellow crocuses flowering in the gardens of the estates nearby and made the grass shoots that had appeared between cracks in the paving stones glow a fresh, vibrant green.

Following Jake's death, their mother had arranged everything swiftly, effectively and with little fuss. She'd emerged from her grief more active and animated than she had been in years; as if, for her, a new life had begun with her husband's death. Sal said that she couldn't understand it, and that their mother was hard and horrible. Hannah understood it very well but kept quiet because she knew that Sal would think her heartless too.

A short service had been arranged at a neighbouring church at eleven. Earlier that morning, flowers had arrived: white lilies with waxy petals. Attached to these was a note which read, 'Love always, Cheryl'. The flowers filled the space with a sickly, cloying scent.

Later, Hannah opened the door to Michael, his face stony; a woman with bleached hair standing beside him, holding a bawling baby.

The family set off for the church some time before the service – a sombre group, somehow incomplete, a dark spot amid the sunshine on the street. Outside the church, another group had gathered, smoke from their cigarettes rising into the air. Two figures stood apart: both women, blonde, and expensively dressed. Hannah searched for Robert, but he was nowhere to be seen. She'd rung him to tell him about her dad and the funeral, but he hadn't picked up. She'd left a message and told herself that she'd see him at the church. Disappointed, and with the sense that something was missing, she looked away and scraped at the ground with her feet.

One of the smart figures came towards them.

"It's Dolly-Features," Sal said to Hannah.

"Who? Diana?"

"Yeah, your posh friend."

Sal and the others moved on, but Hannah stood there waiting for her old friend, the breeze lifting her hair from her head. As Diana came towards her, the sunlight made the diamonds in her ears flash and her hair shine. She came up to Hannah and stood in front of her. Her face still had the pristine prettiness that Hannah had once craved, but now no longer cared for.

Hannah continued scraping the gravel with her feet. "I like your earrings," she said finally.

"They're my mother's," Diana said.

"Right. Thought I'd seen them before."

Diana pointed to a woman behind her. "She's over there," she said.

Hannah peered at the blonde woman. She was

wearing an expensive coat with a fur collar. For an instant some of the old resentment took hold of Hannah, and then, just as suddenly, it disappeared, like a spent breath.

"She wanted to come. I couldn't stop her," Diana said hurriedly. She took a breath. "Hannah, I… I'm sorry about your dad. And I… I…" She seemed for a moment to have lost her usual cool. She was struggling. "I'm sorry about… you know… everything."

There was a pause. In front of her, Hannah could see a few people beginning to move into the church. Behind its steeple, white clouds scudded through the sky. Tears filled her eyes. "That's okay," she said.

Diana reached into her pocket and brought out a handkerchief; white with a lace trim. "Here. Take this."

Hannah turned the handkerchief over and smiled. "Do you remember that day I hurt my knee?"

Diana nodded. "Those awful girls, Lise and… what was the other one's name?"

"Kate."

"Right."

They laughed.

"How's it going?" Hannah asked.

"I… I had a miscarriage. We've been trying again but… you know… it's taking longer than I thought. Than I had hoped…"

"Oh, I'm sorry." Quickly, Hannah passed the handkerchief back to her friend. "How's John?"

"He's okay. He had to work. He… I…" Diana looked over her shoulder and then leaned towards Hannah.

"I almost left him, you know," she whispered. "There was… someone else for a while. But it… it didn't work out…" She stopped speaking. There was a sadness in her face that Hannah had never seen there before.

"I'm sorry," Hannah said again.

They stood in silence for a bit, until they heard the slow tolling of a single bell.

"Shall we go in?" Diana asked.

Hannah hesitated. "You go. I'll follow."

She waited, scanning the quiet street. Just as she turned to follow Diana, she heard footsteps come up behind her.

Robert's breathing was uneven, his cheeks flushed. "I'm sorry. I was on my way here, and then I had to get something for my mother, so that made me late. She wanted to be here too, but she couldn't. She says hello, and that she's sorry about your dad." He gestured to the church. "Shall we go in?"

Hannah put one hand on his arm. "I wanted… to tell you something first."

"What is it?" he asked softly.

"That girl you were with… in Newcastle…"

"I told you—"

"I know. She wasn't really the problem. It was *me*. Something… in me. Something I couldn't quite face. Maybe fear or… or something else. That's why. I needed to explain…"

"You don't have to."

"Why not?"

"I understand what's going on with you."

Her eyes filled with tears. "I'm sorry I pushed you away. I couldn't help myself. It was a… a bad impulse or something." She shook her head.

Robert smiled. "I want to help you. I *can* help you."

Hannah brightened. "You can?"

"If you let me." He drew her towards him then, and kissed her and held her close. "Let's go," he said.

She took hold of his hand, and together they walked towards the church.

Chapter 54
London, 2018

Hannah was running through the streets in her dream, the sky above her head swarming with stars. Ahead of her she could hear footsteps ringing on the pavement. "Ella!" she called. "Ella!" It was cold and Hannah shivered; wrapped her coat tighter about her. "*Ella!*"

Suddenly the footsteps stopped, and the street was silent; the empty, dark cars listening to her. Then the footsteps started again, this time moving towards her. Hannah stopped; waited. A fox darted across the pavement in front of her. But it was a man who appeared out of the darkness – tall, lean, his mouth twisted with scar tissue, starlight reflecting off his metal-trimmed belt...

Hannah cried out; sat upright in bed. The room was in darkness. Fragments of a Schubert piano sonata drifted over the crumpled sheets. She lay back and closed her eyes. She reached for her pillow; felt it damp with sweat. Ella had been missing for over seventeen hours now. Robert had last seen her board a bus near Clapton Station, heading towards Walthamstow. It had been the longest seventeen hours of Hannah's life.

When she was younger, and Ella was still a small, raven-haired, somewhat turbulent child, when Hannah should have been stable, responsible, at times the pressure of the home she had manufactured became as bad as that of the home she was born into, and she *had* to go. Then she would find herself running away, just as she used to do – pounding the dirty streets, running like the wind, against the wind, always running.

Often she'd only go to Sal's (her sister lived near Victoria Park), and she'd text Robert from there, to let him know she was safe. Usually it was Sal who persuaded her to return; called her a fool and worse for running off in the first place. But even if Sal hadn't interfered, Hannah knew that she would have gone home anyway, in time. She missed Robert and Ella too much. And the guilt soon became unbearable.

Then there came the time when Robert had opened the door to find Hannah standing on the doorstep – contrite, unhappy. The house smelled of spaghetti bolognese and Ella was crying in the background.

"I'm sorry," Hannah told him.

"I know you are."

"I won't go off again, I promise."

"Even if I chose to believe you, Ella might not."

"I'll always come back. You know that."

"No, I don't. The older I get, the less certain I am about everything. All I know now is that I know nothing."

Hannah had nodded, eyes filling with tears. She worried that even if she always returned to him, one day he might not forgive her for going. She would have pushed him too hard. She couldn't risk that.

Robert held out his arms. "I won't give up on you, Hannah."

"I'm not worth the fight."

"I think you are."

"I'll try harder."

"I know you will."

After that, Hannah had been forced to concede that it was easier to submit to her need to belong to a family, and she had stopped trying to escape. It had been hard, like giving up smoking, but she had managed it. She hadn't slipped again.

This, their daughter's first disappearance, meant that Robert was being put through that pain again. And this time, Hannah too was suffering; the more so because her daughter's return was out of her control. She prayed that Ella would come home unharmed, just like the household cat when he went on an occasional walkabout. Perhaps she'd merely gone to a friend's, or a neighbour's, though they'd checked with everyone they knew. Ella was a teenager, after all. London was a dangerous, desperate, dirty city, and it had been seventeen hours.

A sudden knocking at the door jolted Hannah out of bed. She moved along the hallway, meeting her husband just as he was leaving his study. Behind him she could see glimpses of the reams of tatty paperbacks that lined the shelves there.

Robert grasped her hand. The warmth travelling

from his hand to hers made Hannah's chest contract. "Don't get your hopes up," he told her. "Don't…"

But there, on the doorstep, just as they had hoped, was their errant daughter, standing as Hannah herself had done many years ago, looking a little dishevelled and equally contrite. Hannah felt herself surge with fury, but what right did she have?

Ella moved towards her mother, and Hannah took her into her arms. As she did so she felt her husband's arms circling them both. Her daughter sobbed, her back heaving.

"Where did you go?" Hannah whispered.

Ella sighed, relaxing into her mother's hold. "Only to a friend's. To Emily's. You don't know her because we're not at the same school. Her mother wasn't at home, and I made Emily promise not to call you."

"*Why?*"

"I only wanted to go a short time. School's been horrible. These girls – I couldn't bear to tell you before, but they've been so mean…"

Hannah bent her head into her daughter's hair and tightened her embrace. "You will be okay," she whispered fiercely. "You'll see. You'll be more than okay. I'll just run you a bath now, your dad will get some food on, and then you can tell us everything."

THE END

EPILOGUE
Greece, June 2024

It was that time in the day when the light was at its strongest; when it made the heaps of houses in the town shine a brilliant white so that they looked like piles of sugar cubes; when it exposed each crack and crevice in the rocks that lined the coast, penetrating every part of the land. Soon shadows would spread over the mountains and the light would turn a shallow, soft pink, but for now it was hard and white and blinding.

Ella lay on a warm rock, wearing only a swimming costume, her eyes fixed on the play of light on the sea, watching it shine as if a million jewels rested on it. Her skin had turned a light golden brown with the summer, making the intense green of her eyes even more startling. Her body was still; only her eyes moved, following the dance of the light. Overhead, the sky was infinite – a deep, dark blue – but it paled as her eyes moved down, fading ever further until it became a misty white at the distant horizon. In front of her, Ella could see the frenzied activity around the harbour, and the painted boats by the shore, their white sails billowing. But she was detached from it all – up above the houses, at the top of one of the hills circling the shore, where the air was fresh and clear, and pine trees sent their hazy, resinous scent into the sky. She stretched, her arms reaching out; her body flowing down towards her feet. And then the stretch reached her toes, and she curled them in and then out again. She yawned; her mouth, red and cavernous, opening to the air.

At last, with a sudden, decisive movement, she stood up. She was still for a moment, her eyes resting on the sea, and then she started to make her way downhill towards the shore. As she walked, she disturbed crickets from bunches of wild thyme that lined the path. She neared the sea and the hypnotic hum of the cicadas faded and she could hear the slap of water on rock, the cry of a seagull circling overhead. Instead of going down to the harbour, she took a sharp left through a belt of olives and continued walking over a path of white stone until she emerged from the trees. In front of her there was a mass of rock jutting out to sea. A narrow path led out to it, and it was this path that she took.

At the end of the path she stopped. Some ten feet below her the water curled; almost black where the rock cast its shadow upon it, and a luminous green where the sunlight filtered through it. Opposite, a short distance away, another promontory jutted out to sea. Ella didn't hesitate. She raised her arms above her head, bent her body and dived. The water was clean and cold, and she emerged breathless and happy, shaking droplets from her hair like tiny diamonds. She started swimming towards the promontory, straight towards a flat ledge of rock at sea level. She swam swiftly, her body tingling as it cut through deeper water. Bright white foam shifted around her as she slid through the sea. She was almost there now: just three more strokes and she'd reach the other side. One... two...

Three. She'd done it. Laughing, she touched the white ledge with her hands, pulled her body from the water and lay down very gently upon the stone, to dry out in the sun.

ACKNOWLEDGMENTS

I am indebted to those who provided early support and encouragement when I was working on *Hannah* and urged me to see the story through to publication: to James Lightbourne and his late parents, John and Maureen Granger, and to my mother, Doris Urquhart. Also to Philippa Ackland for her valuable input.

Thank you to Graham Rees for his talented design work, which is consistently of such a high standard. I am grateful to those in the industry who helped me to finalise *Hannah* and to get every detail right, and in particular to my editor, Faye L. Booth, for making sure the story was credible and accurate.

Jane Lightbourne
Nevada Street Press
October 2024

ABOUT THE AUTHOR

Hannah is Jane Lightbourne's second novel for adults, following publication of her first novel, *Loss*. Jane is also the author of *Bright Dust, a* collection of poems and children's chapter books *A Tale of Three Tabbies* and *My Cat Called Red*. As well as writing fiction, Jane studied Classics and then worked as a lawyer. She lives in London with her three children.

Jane can be contacted through her website
www.janelightbourne.co.uk
Email: books@janelightbourne.co.uk
Facebook: **@NevadaStreetPress**
Instagram: **@urqujane**
Twitter: **@JaneLightbourne**
TikTok:**@janelightbournebooks**